I0729339

QUEEN OF DARKNESS

DARK SPELL SERIES BOOK 4

ISRA SRAVENHEART

Copyright © 2023 by Isra Sravenheart

All rights reserved.

No part of this book may be reproduced in any form or by any electronic or mechanical means, including information storage and retrieval systems, without written permission from the author, except for the use of brief quotations in a book review.

Cover design: Cauldron Press

Editing and interior formatting: Jody E. Freeman

Michael,

my legendary publicist that has been super helpful along this intriguing journey.

You've motivated me to get the final two books of the Dark Spell Series done. You are a credit to the fantasy and sci-fi world. Your advice has been invaluable, and I am excited to see what else unfolds.

Mr Salty,

Well, here we are again. Your presence in my life certainly doesn't go unnoticed. I hope we never see the day where you cease to exist in my life, even if I do happen to annoy you a lot. May it be forever known that YOU definitely have been a crucial part of the Dark Spell Series and even in death, that can never be forgotten. Ride high upon the winds, and maybe someone will grant you the ability to magically conjure up a cup of coffee at long last.

To the King of Awesome himself,

It would be rude not to mention you, don't you think? After all, the haters and naysayers said plenty of things that will go unnoticed. I can't help but feel you play a special part. You've been there from the start—almost right where it began, and it's been a wild ride. Eight years and over time, not much has changed except maybe your awesomeness is so much more momentous. You've grown and changed and continue to inspire me whether you believe that or not. There is no other. I just know you'll do even better and go even farther as the seasons change and winter escapes us. You're capable of far more than you know.

1

Just at the dead of midnight, Astrid watched quietly as Isra tossed Alan's decaying carcass onto the green grassy field. A murder of crows gathered around, preparing to feast on his flesh. Isra stood back in awe of her triumph from the balcony of her newly acquired castle that carried the same name as her beloved dominion. The castle sat empty for a good many years, but Damien Daughtry told Astrid that Wretchenheart was unoccupied and in need of a new queen. So henceforth, Isra was to be that ruler.

Her coronation was short yet memorable and even she felt rather tired after the massive show that was put on for the over-eager citizens that had resided in this tainted dimension. Isra couldn't help but feel an emotional attachment as she watched Alan's cold body lying in a mass of green grassland. But by the same token, she didn't want his rotting corpse causing one heck of a stench. He had to go. However, she softly caught sight of all the crows preparing themselves to snack upon his lifeless body and felt it rather symbolic.

"It's sad he won't be remembered by many. It's a shame he'll only be regarded in disdain but when you consider all the heinous things he has done, well, it is to be expected, one supposes," she muttered as she wistfully caught Astrid looking upon her. "Have you been lurking there long, dear?" Isra asked in a friendly manner.

"Sorry. I couldn't help but admire you. You've become a marvellous creature. Far beyond anything any of us could have imagined. It is remarkable to witness," Astrid gushed apologetically.

"I'm still trying to make sense of all this. I was holed in a chateau for the longest time and now I am suddenly a queen of a forlorn nation. You whisked me away so quickly, it wasn't as though I had a choice," Isra commented as she perused the idea that Astrid knew more than he'd detailed to her.

This man is truly something else. His knowledge of the realms and how life manages to work itself out is overwhelming. He's so eccentrically regal that I can't help but think he was born for the role he's about to commence. That is if he'll accept my offer of becoming my king. I don't wish to have to utilise an alternative. I seldom trust men that are placed at my disposal but he has proved his loyalty to me so I'll accept no other, Isra thought as she watched the group of crows unceremoniously sink their beaks into Alan's soon to be rotting flesh. He'd only been in Wretchenheart for less than six hours but since they'd travelled so swiftly, he'd still been pretty fresh when they arrived.

All of this was so new to Isra. She'd been trapped in the fortress that was Shambre Fell and she knew it wasn't truly her idea. There were supernatural forces behind it, ensuring she was installed there. Isra was still rather hazy on the details but Astrid assured her it was the truth. She did wonder, however, if there was a way to snatch back her memories since she wanted to know all of the excellent accomplishments she had mastered in her short yet intriguing life.

"It doesn't bear any consequence. Be proud of all you've done! Alan is a means to an end but the reason we are here in Wretchenheart is that you took his precious life. You've accumulated a mass amount of enemies," Astrid carefully explained, though he was quick in changing the narrative when he reassured her, "But you are untouchable in Wretchenheart, and that's why I brought you here."

"It's unorthodox. I shall give it that," Isra responded coolly.

"Yes, and becoming queen at such a young age is no doubt a lot for you to get your head around, but I promise it only gets better from here on out," Astrid told her profoundly.

"If you do say so. I am just thrown by the whole shenanigan. So, as you shipped me over here, you said I incurred the wrath of many. I was wondering if you might be so kind as to inform me who those may be," Isra asked sweetly. "It's no matter. I was just curious," she added, motioning a pause.

She hadn't known Astrid for very long but already Isra trusted him enough to take him up on his word. He'd whisked her to this deserted, demonic dimension the moment he realised she took her revenge scenario with Alan too far. Not only that, but Astrid held only Isra's best interests at heart when he'd made the major decision to bring her here out of the blue.

"And you had a choice in it. Of course, you did, but I knew after my conversation with Damien that you couldn't simply reside at Shambre Fell any longer. I wasn't sure if you'd simply come along if I asked so I acted on instinct," Astrid admitted in a strong stance. In any event, it will be dawn soon," Astrid reminded her. "That means Samuel will soon have full knowledge of your transgression."

My killing Alan will be seen as quite an enterprising feat. If Mr Reynaldi possesses a strong stomach, it may not be suited to his well-mannered tastes. But if Astrid proclaims him to be such a worldly leader, he will undoubtedly be prepared for such an occurrence as mine, Isra thought.

It went through her mind that Samuel's already piquing interest in her might be more than just a need to quell her existence from the realm.

"He has a lot of insight into what goes on within the realms, doesn't he?"

Isra pressed the issue gently with Astrid, knowing he was somewhat standoffish when it came to the subject of Samuel. But Astrid was more than happy to divulge his knowledge despite his bitter experiences with the light-bringer.

"That he does indeed. It's only a matter of hours before the intricate organisation 'on high' delivers the awe-inspiring blow that you've taken out a Grimsbane warlock. When you look at it in that context, it sure is a talking point," Astrid summarised.

In fact, I'll be very taken aback if he doesn't know already. Samuel is the great and powerful know-it-all of our magical lands. If he isn't abreast with it, then I don't know. Except for Damien and I, who knew this would be a possibility that Isra would indeed take things beyond her means.

Astrid resigned to thinking that perhaps Samuel was already very much aware of their occurrence since he was drawn to all things unsightly.

SAMUEL SHIFTED UNCOMFORTABLY as he lay on the white silk sheets of his bed. His body rolled back and forth nervously and he endlessly grasped onto the equally soft white linen covers. The curtains in his bedroom were black, blocking out any light from the outside world. It was a bit of an odd colour for a light-bringer to choose but he was a light sleeper and easily stirred. Being in the position he was in, Samuel often had rather disturbing dreams and terrors invade his precious sleep. Tonight was no exception, considering it was just about to strike three o'clock in the morning.

THERE SHE IS. Our femme fatale, bright as ever in her effervescent energy. Oh, but look, suddenly her shimmery golden hair doesn't quite contrast with the dark shadow in her eyes. And why is this?

Her eyes look duller. Almost as though they have been tainted. Yes, something has happened, but what is it?? Now our young enchantress has had quite the enthralling evening but I wonder if she'd be so kind to reveal just what sadness lies behind those normally glimmering green eyes.

From his dream state, Samuel came face to face with Lady Isra. She stood under the merciless blinding sun, looking flabbergasting in a serene white lacy gown ruched at the shoulders while the long sleeves were brilliantly matched with black roses embroidered on the ends. Samuel noticed that they were standing on lemon-yellow sand while calm, tranquil crystalline waves glimmered in the distance.

Samuel cleared his throat, preparing to speak with Isra in her etheric form. He knew there was something peculiar about the witch, for her stomach was bubbling ferociously. His eyes gently went upward to her heart, which was bulging out of her at the rapid rate it was vibrating inside her chest. The intensity of it caused Isra to clasp her chest hurriedly.

"Well, I guess here we are. I am not sure what you are doing in my dream?" Isra questioned. She was bewildered at seeing him here.

"I think it may be a case of you eavesdropping into mine, but it's no bother, girl. Tell me, why Nefaria Sands?" Samuel piped up. He knew his question was meaningless but still, he requested the reply as though she would thoughtfully give it.

"I guess this is where it all began," Isra mused, still grabbing her stomach. "Tell me, old man, why is it when things get rough in my life, I nearly always find you in the thick of it?" Isra probed tentatively.

"I don't know how to answer that. You mean to presume I am responsible for the unholy occurrence that has emerged in both of our subconscious?" Samuel asked in an eager tone.

"I guess, one way or the other, we are going to find out," Isra recited cryptically.

Oh, boy, is this getting irritating now. Something has gone down but our mysterious yet devilish enchantress has yet to detail to me just how delicious it is. I wonder if she somehow knows about Nefaria, otherwise, why bring me here? Samuel concurred in his thoughts. He was able to put his finger on the ideation that something had gone disastrously wrong.

"Something has happened, hasn't it, Isra? Come on now. Tell me. I might be able to help. Is it the Grimsbane chap? He let you down again, did he?"

Samuel gasped, exhilarated in Isra's presence; white illuminated sparks emitted off her as she stood erect in the dazzling mid-morning sun. The seas of Nefaria Sands had never looked so pristine as they did now in their stunning aquamarine colouring. The waves crashed against the seashore ever so violently, rushing in to keep up with the current.

Isra smiled at Samuel. She held a black rose in her dominant hand and lifted the rose to her lips, winking at Samuel as she stopped to smell its pungent scent.

"I suppose it has, but there's very little anyone can do now," Isra retorted quietly.

"What do you mean, girl? It's not too late. I know why you picked here of all locations. This is where I infamously disarmed you in front of Astrid's eyes. I know the experience must have been horrifically traumatic but believe me when I say I was doing what I believed to be right. If there's a situation unfolding with Grimsbane, just tell me. I am sure I can assist you with it. It's never too late to remedy something, even if we deem it to be impossible," Samuel implored.

His voice was so scratchy that he was almost begging her to let him know whatever it was that had happened. He *needed* to know. Samuel was a very desperate man at this moment in time but he was prepared to do anything to grasp whatever Isra had to relay unto him.

"That's just the trouble. No one can help Alan Grimsbane anymore," Isra remarked.

The jet-black rose fell to the ground at once as Isra's smile switched from sweet and friendly to a most mischievous glare whereby she remained triumphant, much to Samuel's perplexity as he couldn't comprehend her meaning.

"What do you mean, child? Of course, he can be helped, but my interest is you and only you," Samuel pressed.

Isra simply lowered her gaze before turning her back to Samuel. She looked out onto the beautiful, serene blue oceans of Nefaria Sands. "I am sure you believe wholly in your stratagem. Alas, I don't trust you, but since this is a dream, I know with absolute conviction that this was the scene whereby you stole a part of my life away from me. Since that time, I have felt completely beyond your 'help,' so don't pity me, old man. Worry about yourself."

Isra continued to have her back turned and Samuel's pleas went unheard.

Samuel uttered softly, "Please, Isra. Tell me. Tell me, girl."

Isra kept her smile firmly affixed as Samuel's urgent need to reason with her dissipated from her mind. Slowly, the image of Isra began to fade until Samuel's words were not even audible and blackness descended upon the two of them, obliterating everything into nothingness.

SAMUEL AWOKE IN A COLD SWEAT, clutching his bed covers. He felt the silk on his fingertips. Reaching over to his bedside table, he put on his half-moon spectacles and ran his hand over his slicked-back black hair. He pulled the bed covers off of him as he earnestly lifted himself upright, placing his feet onto the cold stone floor.

Tonight was not going to be a night where he'd attempt to sleep again anytime soon.

"One must busy themselves with something intellectual to stimulate the piquing interests of their mind," Samuel mused.

He proceeded to get out of his elaborate bed, taking care to put the silk bed coverings back in place as he made the bed. He stretched his tired muscles and walked quietly into his office, still wearing his jet-black silk shirt pyjamas. Samuel manoeuvred over to his well-kept bookcase, pulling a thick volume from the shelf before he strode over to his red velvet armchair, planting himself down onto the seat, and began perusing the pages of the large tome. Samuel's half-moon silver-framed spectacles kept his bewildering sky-blue eyes from wandering as he came to a distinct conclusion.

"I need to contact Damien Daughtry. If something is up with Isra, he's my best chance of finding the truth."

2

"**N**o. Just no!" Isra shrieked, waking from a deep sleep.

She hadn't meant to shout so loudly but the shock of what she experienced in her sleeping form caused her to jolt herself awake. Isra remained in her velvet bed coverings, clinging to them gingerly. She sat shaking whilst feeling the soft deep violet silk of her sheets sticking to her body.

Astrid burst through Isra's door ferociously. "Are you all right?"

He ran to her, tending to her as he tenderly placed his hand on the left side of her face, only for Isra to move his hand away. She sat bolt upright, looking at him with a worried glance.

"I was in a dream world with Samuel Reynaldi. He admitted disarming me!" she blurted out in a worried voice.

Astrid looked at Isra clutching her bed covers so eagerly in her hands. He caught sight of her white silky nightdress, beautifully cut at the bosom whilst tiny straps hung off her perfectly formed shoulders, exposing just enough flesh to tantalise him a little bit more.

Isra witnessed Astrid staring at her so she quickly thrust the bed covers against her chest; a mere act to try to conceal her body from him. She excused herself in a vain attempt to cover her immaculate

8

slender frame from him. "Sorry. You should not be seeing me like this."

"Don't get me wrong," he began explaining softly, "I am wholly tempted by you but even I know taking advantage of you in this weakened state without your memories would be against everything I stand for."

He paused and returned his attention to the situation at hand. *She's dreamed of Samuel. This is no coincidence. I need to know exactly what went down. I don't know if she completely trusts me just yet but she's worried about me seeing her in her vulnerable state. The latter may indicate she is somewhat reserved, but maybe I can coax it out of her,* Astrid pursued the notion in thought. Perhaps it was best to reassure Isra rather than mock her for being cautious.

"However, I do appreciate the sentiment. But you being worried about me seeing your plentiful bounty should be the least of your concerns. Now, why don't I bring you a nice cup of hot tea and you tell me the entirety of this mysteriously enthralling dream you had, hmm?" Astrid asked in a warm tone. "I hear apple and cinnamon make an excellent remedy for night terrors. How about we give it a try, eh?"

He made the offer invitingly and proceeded to slide himself over to her on the bed and then very slowly and gently placed his arm around Isra. She flinched, trying to pull his arm away but this only made him more determined to comfort her. He gently lowered her onto the soft white pillow, pulling the crushed velvet coverings onto her body like a shroud.

"Oh, now is not the time to get a jelly belly on me, girl. Rest. Sleep," Astrid whispered in her ear.

His mumbling those words sent a silvery, sparkly energy descending onto Isra that circled her forehead, pushing her into a deep slumber that even she could not resist.

~

SAMUEL GRUMBLED LOUDLY as James presented him with a large steaming mug of coffee. It was somewhat humorous, considering Samuel had been wide awake since three o'clock in the morning but at least he'd changed into a long, smart black dinner jacket with matching trousers and a crisp white linen shirt. For today was to be a momentous occasion. Samuel had a very interesting guest in his presence since his terrifying dream dilemma that had occurred this morning.

The sun beamed down onto the iconic Spirisity, showering its mediocre light onto the greenery of the prestigious land. Just from the window, Samuel was able to see the stunning violets swishing gently in the morning winds while the yellow crocuses shone in the warm sunshine. It was not a very sunny morning for Samuel, however, who was in a vile mood. His long-suffering assistant, James, was receiving the full brunt of his heinous temper.

"Oh, that's the stuff. I do hope this coffee is going to stimulate my senses because goodness knows I am in no fit state to entertain fuckery today," Samuel stated sardonically as he reached for the caffeinated beverage in a flurry.

"We don't know Isra has actually done anything yet. Last time I checked, dreams were not a viable source of proof. Maybe someone should go down and intervene with her. It's been done before and went well, did it not?" James asked Samuel.

He truly had a disregard for Samuel's concerns. As far as James saw it, Samuel was far too preoccupied with the goings-on of Isra.

It was fine at first. There were good reasons at hand. Isra had just had her heart broken by a mortal, that spineless Jonathan chap, and there was noteworthy evidence to suggest she would eventually turn to the dark side, as she did. But now so much has happened. Samuel wiped her memories clean of any exchange she ever had with Astrid. The danger was over. Then she had a brief dalliance with Alan Grimsbane, which didn't go terribly well either, but she did and dusted herself off. I see no genuine reason to worry over something we don't even have full coverage on. So he had a nightmare; great. Don't we all? It's not sufficient enough to prove anything beyond hearsay.

James rambled to himself in thought and realised they needed to get things moving pretty damn soon. Their guest was growing impatient. He fidgeted in his seat. Let's face it; the chairs in Samuel's office were far from comfortable.

"Yes, and maybe she has joined the flying circus!" Samuel cajoled sarcastically in response.

"We still don't know that anything remarkably important has happened to the Grimsbane lad!" James reminded Samuel coldly.

He sat in his seat next to their bewildered yet extremely well-mannered guest.

"Oh, how convenient. She just may as well have taken down one of the members of the greatest witch family we've ever known, and you think everything is fine? This is typical of you, James. You have no finesse for the matters at hand. *All* our heads are going to be on the chopping block *if* Isra manages to continue the way she's going!" Samuel exclaimed, resisting the urge to grab his old reliable whisky decanter. Yet again, he was stressed beyond comprehension.

"It's just a blip. A bump in the road!" James mentioned with a severe lack of interest.

He quite honestly felt that Samuel was overreacting. *It was Isra at the end of the day, and she calmed down after a time and all was well. And not to mention, we still have no evidence whatsoever that she did anything to Alan. Fuck's sake. Why is he so determined to unravel every last detail concerning this one witch?* James thought as he drank his coffee through pursed lips.

Yet again, Samuel was throwing a hissy fit over something so mediocre and without just cause to do so.

Sure, dreams are indeed windows to the soul as the legend suggests, but there is nothing here pertaining to Isra that even begins to highlight she's vanquished a young warlock of Grimsbane's stature. If we had credible proof that something had indeed gone down, then fine. I could understand his rapt frustration, but he's literally throwing a tantrum for NOTHING.

James continued his ramblings inside his mind. There was enough to deal with but Samuel always had to get the last word in.

"A blip you say? So having the potentiality of several high-ranking warlocks screaming at us is just a minor oversight, is it? Hmm. Where is your damn head?!" Samuel screeched, slamming his hand down on his desk and overexerting himself.

Suddenly, he felt a sharp pang across his forehead. Beads of sweat began piling up in masses and he hastily made a subtle effort to discreetly wipe his brow.

Samuel and James both failed to acknowledge the presence of their rather bemused guest, Damien Daughtry, who had been summoned at Samuel's overzealous whim to regain control over the situation. Not that he'd have much of that with a rebellious witch unleashing all manner of chaos and disorder, but he could dream, right? That's if it was indeed true, of course.

"Not to mention, her just-as-destructive father is here at my request. You could at least take this seriously. Honestly, I swear; Astrid had more resilience than you!" Samuel coldly scolded James as he eyed up Damien Daughtry cautiously; lord knows what Damien thought having to listen to this abhorrent exchange between James and Samuel that was only going to get worse.

"Yes, Astrid; your prime errand boy who went and got himself turned into a human so he could shack up with her. He really had the enthusiasm for the job at hand, didn't he?" James snapped back.

He stopped momentarily before turning to Damien with an apologetic glance. James had never met Daughtry before but he was a high-ranking warlock so James felt it was polite to at least show some shred of respect for the man, even if James didn't wholly agree with the witchcraft scene.

Sure, James had magic, but it was light magic. As far as James saw it, the energy from witches was tainted. It was unnatural. It didn't bode with divine order, but witches always had to control every damn thing to satisfy their desires. James kind of understood it to a certain extent. He never wanted the privilege of being in that rich, violent world.

James let out a huge sigh. He was increasingly growing tired of Samuel's temper tantrum. It was becoming childish... Samuel screaming at James whenever something with Isra went wrong. He was bloody sick of it. It was like a merry-go-round that never stopped. Samuel had to keep holding on because the ride replayed over and over again.

"Whatever!" Samuel hurled back. *Goodness, he is not even listening to me!* he ranted in his thoughts.

"The point is that perhaps her father can get her under control even if we can't. If you want to achieve the status of light-bringer anytime in the near distant future, you should try and learn the ways of divine order. I mean, it won't kill you," Samuel countered sarcastically.

"I hate to be rude, gentlemen, but I do need to be somewhere. Plus, there's the whole element of me being in exile, so if we could press on, well, I'd be greatly pleased," Damien interjected. Honestly, he'd rather be anywhere but here.

"Yes, quite right, Damien. I do apologise. It's just been one heck of a morning," Samuel calmly uttered, finally regaining his sense of whimsy although only for a brief moment. "Oh, my. Do I ever need a drink," he erupted in frustration. "If it ain't Astrid or some prissy mortal boy she's got herself entangled with, it's bloody warlocks. What the fuck is truly going on? It's hellish."

Damien scoffed nonchalantly. *It's more frightful listening to you whine! For goodness sakes, man, pull yourself together. If this is the idiot they've got on display that is supposedly taking care of the light realms, may I just say the dark side has no concerns whatsoever. He's crumbling at the freaking seams.*

Samuel's tirade was grating on him for sure but he'd only come to throw Samuel Reynaldi off the scent. If that meant tolerating some pathetic complaining from a so-called light-bringer, so be it.

"Can't say I've had the pleasure of Astrid's company or conversation for quite some time," Damien answered, although Samuel's question was completely rhetorical. Damien was just interrupting at the necessary convenience of giving the light-bringer what he so desperately wanted to hear.

"Ah, yes. No one has heard of him for a considerable period now. I do wonder if he managed to catch up with Isra again but of course, it would be pointless. She hasn't got a clue on who he is," Samuel chortled cheerfully.

At least now he was perking up. Samuel's mood swings were an entity that should not be bestowed onto anyone. Least not a feisty warlock that sincerely would not tolerate such lowly behaviour, especially from someone that deemed themselves so righteous and good.

"Yes, I appreciate your sentimental chatter, but how about you go on and explain why you summoned me here! I said goodbye to all of this when I signed Isra over to you just over nineteen years ago," Damien queried Samuel with a questionable glare.

I discarded the girl many moons ago, as did her mother, who, quite frankly, wanted nothing to do with her. Poor Isra. She was only a tiny, wee thing. It wasn't her fault Gwendolyn was a fear-crazed lunatic but still, we can be thankful for small mercies. She has Astrid taking her under his well-armoured wing. I can't say I am not grateful to him. But I understand, she's still my blood and it is my responsibility to assist if she's gone AWOL, which she has. But I'm not going to tell this great big buffoon that, Damien uttered cautiously in thought. He'd pondered the situation heavily ever since he got here.

Samuel cleared his throat, taking in a breath in preparation for what he was about to say. It would undoubtedly rock Damien's world and probably not in a good way.

"I invited you here to come and chat because I had a beguiling dream with Isra in the wee hours of this morning. But that's not all. She was standing there, looking incredibly forlorn over something concerning the Grimsbane boy, but alas, she would not tell me what it was that had her in such a tizzy. I understand you've long loosened your attachment to the girl but as her biological father, you may well be able to assist. I believe in some form or another Isra was trying to reach out to us. Of course, she probably doesn't know this yet; it's all in her subconscious mind. But something terrible happened and she's seeking insight from another source," Samuel told Damien with a look of concern.

Damien proceeded to think hard. He felt like Samuel was trying to formulate some kind of scenario around Isra but he was using this wacky netherworld dream as a conduit.

Hmm, he's a very desolate man. He believes Isra would seek his help now? Come on, we can do better than that, Mr Reynaldi. For sure, Isra doesn't need his help. She's got Astrid right in the thick of it, taking care of her, protecting her against any force that might serve to destroy what he's worked so hard to rebuild. No, I don't think so.

"And just how do you presume she might require your services? The girl has no memory of you. Did you not callously snatch that away from her as though it was a pacifier?" Damien questioned with a furrowed brow.

He didn't believe Samuel's intentions were genuine. It was far too orchestrated and well-thought-out to be a sudden occurrence. Damien continued on in thought, still very much sceptical of Samuel.

But I guess the dreamscapade could have well been real. However, we've got no solid proof if Isra went too far or not. Astrid has not been in touch again. Neither of us is any the wiser as to whether she's committed the wretched sin or if he managed to coax her from doing so. Mr Reynaldi is simply creating a theory based on a whim so that he can rush right in and take control again. Of course, he'll say she wants his help. No, she doesn't! She's a freaking witch. She's got her own shit handled.

"Alas, I did. But she still remembers when she slips into the astral realms via the part of her I didn't take away. I can't take her ability to tap into her ethereal self. I have no say in what goes on down there. But it begs the question if something happened to Grimsbane. We will have some severe engagements. Procedure will need to happen," Samuel warned Damien.

He was doing his utmost to be formal and go along with the ways of the light but at the same time, he was no stranger to taking down those who went against it.

"Interesting predicament, but how on Earth will we know?" Damien asked in a serious tone. He wanted to believe there was some good intent in Samuel but it all seemed a bit wishy-washy.

"I am not entirely sure, but I am certain my dream was a premonition of sorts," Samuel admonished with a cautious tone. He was, however, somewhat cheery, which made Damien question again whether Samuel would have had a hand in the creation process.

"Alas, I cannot help you there. I don't have access to the light realms or to the knowledge you possess at your fingertips. It's without certainty I'd love to help but I am unsure as to how I can be of use," Damien replied curtly.

"I quite agree, but you're here now so that's the main thing. Do you think that perhaps it is time Isra was made aware of just who her father is? It may well soften the blow that was caused by Grimsbane and the other chap, Astrid. Oh, and that Jonathan one. You see, our Isra had a widely known history of taking up with men and then... Well, she gets hurt and chaos swiftly follows," Samuel enunciated with fervour.

"I am not too sure that would go down too well with Rhiannon. She has bonded with our firstborn, Everilda, and it would surely put a stick in the mud if she learned Isra was conceived after Everilda," Damien cautiously expressed.

Samuel chose to be compassionate. He understood Damien's concern. "Ah, yes. You were in your mortal marriage at that time. Rhiannon was forced out, is that not correct?" he asked warmly.

"Yes. I was with Damaris. I buggered off when Everilda was aged two," Damien confessed.

"So Rhiannon would have nothing to be offended by. Your dynamic with her was dramatically paused. The conception of Isra is irrelevant; it happened at a time when you were lost in your own life. Therefore, Rhiannon would be in complete understanding, for she, too, had to undergo her own loss when she was sent into a dimension she couldn't escape from," Samuel explained with a smile on his face.

He hoped he and Damien were finding common ground. That this wasn't just an obligation. It wasn't just some sordid affair. Damien had been genuinely discontent in his life and thus Isra came along at a time when he wanted nothing more than to indulge his selfish desires.

"When you put it like that, it is indeed feasible, but please, allow me to discuss it with Rhiannon first. I need to ensure she understands. I don't want her getting it twisted," Damien clarified.

"I understand," Samuel concurred. "I doubt the demoness will be bothered by your transgression too much, for she at heart is just as messed up as you were at the time. You found each other in your own desolation."

That notion got Damien thinking and he mulled over the consequences of his wild, carefree past just before he got expelled and banished from Wingdom's Academy.

Perhaps he is right. Maybe Rhiannon will understand, but I didn't know Isra was truly mine until a day ago. So much happened at once but if Isra meeting me and her extended family will help throw him off the scent, perhaps I should grant him this wish that has been concocted based on his fable. However, our dear Evie will not be amused. She and Isra are mortal enemies. Literally, in her case.

Damien mulled this over sorely, considering the idea that Rhiannon would perhaps be all right with him, but his relationship with Everilda would surely suffer.

3

———————

amuel let Damien Daughtry go on his way since he didn't want to be in Spirisity, but Samuel was deeply determined to get to the bottom of things. He needed to know beyond absolute certainty if Isra had done something to Alan Grimsbane, and the only way forward was to go straight to the source: "On high."

The trouble was this organisation wasn't one you simply contacted at the drop of a hat. There were channels you had to go through, ones you couldn't simply skip in order to jump to the next hurdle. It was specifically set so that only those truly employed by the forces of the light had access to "on high." Samuel had worked for them for a considerable number of years. He was light-bringer for just over two hundred years, but it certainly made for intriguing reading to learn just how he'd managed to obtain the role in the first instance.

You see, in the original circumstances, Samuel would never have become a light-bringer. There was no reason for him to be. He'd basked in the light and had it in his heritage, yes, but it was rather perplexing how it all came about. And like most situations in Samuel's life, it was anything but ordinary.

~

<u>~200 Years Ago ~</u>

Samuel Reynaldi was aged twenty-one. He had been summoned to an awkward meeting with the "on high" folk.

Now, as far back as Samuel could remember, "on high" only wanted to speak with you if you were someone they were greatly interested in or if you had cocked up. Samuel managed to scrape by the skin of his teeth out of a secondary education and win himself a place at Lightwing Consortium, a college for those that walked in the light realms and needed to know more about their etheric craft; he was rather nervous, to say the least.

Samuel's father, Bernard Louis Reynaldi, had succumbed to a vengeful demon only a day before. It was a succubus, a feisty demonic creature with a sheer knack for attracting those who were very comfortable with expressing their sexuality. Bernard not only summoned the creature but had, in fact, welcomed it; much to Samuel's dismay.

He'd always believed his father to be a proud, unconventional man. One who didn't engage in frivolity or any nonsensical buffoonery. He'd unceremoniously invited the demon unto him, and then his body was found slain the morning after. Blood dripped from the ceiling of Bernard Louis Reynaldi's mansion, and Samuel had been promptly informed. Grief overtook him until he had a very interesting meeting; he was ushered into the "on high" meeting room at very short notice.

Samuel, who'd never been here before, could only stare at the bewildering shimmering white nothingness surrounding the interior of the grand atrium—the centre of "on high's" brilliance. You'd expect to be greeted by those in charge, the light realm's leaders and their high-ranking associates and those even higher up in the food chain. It was worth noting that the real guys in power... Well, you never caught a glimpse of them. You only dealt with their agents.

A man with long ash-grey hair and golden-hazel eyes spoke in a low voice, almost like a grumble. He mustered loudly, "It is with the greatest sadness we announce the passing of Bernard Louis Reynaldi. However, his son, Samuel Reynaldi, has been selected to become the next light-bringer. Please note that 'on high' do not make this incredulous decision lightly, and we are here today to inform Mr Reynaldi of his next steps should he wish to go forward!"

Samuel, who was very shocked to hear this, piped up momentarily. "Wait! The light-bringer position... Isn't that the leader of the light realm? But, why me? I'm not connected to any of these great light beings. I have no lineage even remotely connected to that."

The man chuckled softly. "It has nothing to do with who your family are or what you're connected to. Just know that 'on high' has observed you in action and you have been selected for the role. Of course, if you don't want it, we don't have to discuss the matter any further."

"No." Samuel raised his hand to signal for them to stop for a moment. "I am just a little thrown. You see, I barely got through my college education. I have no certification to show for my time there, and I was quite the wayward student," Samuel admitted with a guilty glance up at the man addressing him.

"Exactly," he replied. "You are the prime candidate to show these lost, wretched souls amiss of all goodness just what they need to turn back to the light side. It could change your life dramatically. You would not be allowed to remain on the earthly plane any longer but since you would already be ascended, that won't be too much of an issue." The man winked.

"Oh, my!" Samuel gasped. "I have to die," he blustered with a shocked expression on his face.

"That would be the eventuality you'd face, yes. This is why we hold this assembly today, as it is not a life choice you just slip into. It will change the face of everything you know. You may not see yourself as an almighty leader, but believe in the knowledge of the all-seeing folk at 'on high' when they say you damn well can be!"

The man finished with such finesse in his voice. Those words just rolling off his tongue had Samuel in his head.

Things will never be the same again. I won't be a man. At least not in the humanised sense, but I have to reach mortality to attain this great honour.

∾

"I GOT by in the Lightwing Consortium by the scrap of my neck and somehow, I still got selected to be light-bringer. I'll never truly understand their line of thinking but 'on high' know how the world works. They never questioned the whys or how something is; it simply *is* that way. They know that better than anyone so maybe I need to go straight to 'on high' to find out if Grimsbane is indeed vanquished," Samuel murmured as he pursued his thoughts on how he might proceed going forward.

But now there was a difficult challenge lying in wait. *How do you contact an organisation that only contacts you if they deem it necessary? I mean, how does one even begin to process the emotions at hand to undergo this task in getting to these folks?* Samuel relentlessly pondered in thought.

And then it came to him.

Perhaps it is helpful if one starts at the beginning. Yes, that is it. That's the one thing I never considered throughout this chaotic mess. I have to go back to where I very first laid my eyes on Isra.

That was easy. Samuel would have to return to the scene of the crime. The place where Isra began her journey of darkness.

And with that, Samuel clicked his index finger and thumb together, smiling as he uttered, "Well, I'd best be doing some investigating. Perhaps I can pick up on the little firecracker's energy."

∾

GLAMVEIN HADN'T CHANGED MUCH. It was the same desolate, abandoned mountain peak it always was. Isra had only activated the destructive life force within it. That very same pulsating energy lingered in the deep crevice of the eyesore of a mountain for years.

Isra just so happened to tinker so far towards the darkness that she was the one that reawakened it.

Samuel materialised right in front of it, stopping to dust himself off as he emerged before it. It was hard to imagine that Isra had awakened this monstrosity two years ago, but here it was, active as ever. Green smoke was evaporating from the top, meaning some mystical energy was still very much alive inside that dark hole. Samuel wasn't magical so he couldn't get inside the gap to see what was going on. He'd have to use his intuition.

He gingerly placed his dominant hand on the side of the majestic rock, honing in to sense what irrational calamity might be occurring there.

"Ha, our little miscreant well and truly jolted the forces of nature. Well, since I don't have her knack for unleashing darkness onto the realm, I'll just have to do this the old-fashioned way!" Samuel smugly voiced.

He was determined to get to the bottom of things. One way or the other, he was going to unravel the truth of what he experienced in his dream sequence, although he was already dead-set on the idea that what he'd witnessed was indeed true. He just had to be a little more forceful in convincing the rest of the cosmos of it.

"Now, let us see what really lies inside of you, girl!" Samuel murmured under his breath.

He placed his left hand on the side of the mountain peak. Both of his palms were affixed. A bright green shimmery energy emitted from his palms, slowly engaging with the landmark.

The irony was entertaining; Samuel was a light-bringer who should have the power to be able to saunter in and shut off whatever was causing all the havoc but he wasn't dark. Therefore, he hadn't acquired the permissions needed to do so.

"Come on now. Let's go right into it. Let us see exactly what lurks inside," Samuel whispered and closed his eyes.

He then fell into a trance-like state, not asleep or comatose, but he was very much drifting into another dimension. All at once, pictures began to emerge but they were hazy. Difficult to decipher. Samuel knew he had to be patient with the process.

The blurry images were enough to put most people off. However, something was creeping up among all the haphazard pictures floating by in Samuel's mind. Suddenly, a shimmery white-blonde head appeared.

Aha, there you are, kiddo. Didn't think you'd be able to escape me, hmm? Well, now. So, come on, what have you got to show me? Don't be afraid, girl. This is the room. We are all here to unload our troubles. Something tells me yours is a bit more challenging than the average amount of teenage angst but I am told I am a good listener.

Samuel talked to the faint visual image of Isra inside his mind and tried to maintain the connection. He couldn't see her well. He could only just about make out that bobbling little white-blonde head of hers. Nothing else came into view just yet.

All right, so he'd have to go in a little bit deeper...

Samuel took a deep breath, fully inhaling the air of the wretched wasteland of Glamvein. Nothingness overtook his senses, followed by a strong exhale, that released all that frustration of not knowing, not being taken seriously over this predicament. Then he really jumped in. That was when he began seeing the serene crystalline blue. The sparkling seas of Nefaria became his reality and there he saw in front of him Lady Isra of the Dark.

"Ah, finally. I've been waiting for this moment for quite some time. Anticipating the second when you and I were able to see each other face to face," Samuel mustered boldly.

He found himself smiling at Isra. It was worth noting that this was no standoff. There was to be no confrontation of sorts. It was a meeting of the minds. Samuel was now a mystical entity with the power to be able to travel into Isra's mind. He had only achieved such a feat by connecting with the very same ferocity that she had once unleashed within herself. That was how he was able to see her in this very intricate and ethereal manner.

"Yes. I see that. I don't understand though," Isra blundered awkwardly.

She smoothed the pleats of her dark violet dress, taking care to not let it drag on the sandy yellow floor. The long sleeves of the delicate lace gown she had on completely covered her arms but her cleavage was visible. The generous neckline cut in at the chest looked spectacular. Isra instinctively made a resolve to cover herself by crossing her arms at Samuel. She looked somewhat irritated with him, as if he was interfering in her affairs.

"You don't understand what?" Samuel asked gently.

"How are you here? In my head. My most private sanctuary of my innermost thoughts. I don't even let that Astrid fellow in here. Not yet. So please, pray tell, old one, how are you able to conduct this atrocity in the name of the light?!" Isra demanded, wanting to know how Samuel was able to manifest himself into her mind.

Samuel's sky-blue eyes lit up immediately and a sly smile crawled onto his face. "Aha, so Astrid is with you? Ah, well, isn't he a resourceful little scamp. Well, now that does make a difference, doesn't it? All this time, I thought he may listen to reason but instead, he's been off carrying on with you the entire time," Samuel rambled in a gruff tone.

He couldn't help but feel an impending sense of defeat. Astrid was always going to disobey Samuel's orders sooner or later.

"He hasn't been here for very long," Isra admonished carefully. "In fact, I barely know him. But he has proved to be a loyal ally, which is more than can be said for you. It must suck being a light-bringer that has no real power in the world. Oh, goodness, how I'd pity you if this was an encounter in reality. But alas, I'll probably let it slip from my mind tomorrow."

"So where is he then?" Samuel quizzed.

"Oh, but I am not going to tell you that. What Astrid does behind the facade is none of my business. Neither is it any of yours," Isra bluntly recited.

"So you won't tell me anything of resonance then?" Samuel probed further.

Frustration came off of him in waves. It was evident he sought some tainted information that seemed to be frozen in time, in a place he could not lay his desperate hands on.

"I won't tell you about Astrid. No. But you're not lurking in the darkest depths of my mind to figure out what Astrid is up to, are you? Oh, no! You're here for something far more precious. Oh, dear, how does one even pardon such a pitiful act?" Isra reprimanded evilly.

It's funny, but for a mirage, she's quite colourful. So the conniving bastard Astrid is with her then. Interesting that nobody managed to grasp onto this. No one had the guts to see it before it occurred, preventing any mishaps along the way? No, they didn't, did they? Arghhhh! Why must my fate be such a challenging one? Honestly, I could have delved into any career path, but somehow, I chose to swerve dark souls back onto the path of righteousness. And here she is. A damned rebellious one determined to make me sweat, knowing I want something from her.

How is it that she wields the power? She's fucking nineteen, for fuck's sake. I am a light-bringer, renowned for my adept skills at bringing down those who stray from the path of enlightenment and yet she's goading me. She knows I need her to cooperate. Oh, to hell with it!

Samuel scolded himself in vexation. *I have to attain the upper hand here. Show her that I am the one who has the high ground. But how can I do that when she mocks me at every turn?*

"All right, let us not talk about Astrid." Instead, Samuel offered a compromise. "How about we find some equal footing, hmm? You tell me whatever is on your mind. Just release whatever nasty titbit is bothering you, and then perhaps we can both move forward."

Samuel kindly elaborated as though to dissuade Isra from anything that might be considered rebellious. The light-hearted approach could prove to be more successful. After all, Isra was rigid, and when it was clear she wasn't going to be moved, a much kinder way was needed.

"How can we be equals?" Isra questioned wildly. "You took my memories. But it's in this reality that I know exactly how that came to be. You wouldn't dream of saying this to me in my conscious form, now would you? You see, Samuel Reynaldi, I know more than you dare to seek to know!"

Isra held him with an icy glare. "And while I'd like to satisfy your curiosity, I think it is quite entertaining to watch you try and figure me out. You yearn so much for power or this ideal of it that you have inside yourself, but really, you haven't got the faintest idea."

"All right. Point taken, firecracker, so now how about we just move onto the subject of Alan Grimsbane?" Samuel nudged, being ever so careful to change the subject without coming under Isra's suspicions.

"I am not wholly interested in him anymore," Isra rebuffed sharply. "However, I do hope he is at peace now," she added curtly before proceeding to turn away.

Samuel put his right hand up to stop her. *No, not yet. Don't walk away from me just now, girl. We have so much more to discuss. Let us become more pleasant in our mannerisms and perhaps we may find the conversation flows more effortlessly. Look here now, we can make a breakthrough, but that needs to happen for you to trust me. We can't achieve much if there is no balance,* Samuel thought.

Yet again, Isra was proving to be tricky, but he wasn't giving up yet.

"And just what did you do with him?" Samuel pressed on, hoping Isra would slowly allow the words to freely roll off her tongue.

"I believe the crows had him for breakfast. Other than that, I don't care. I'm in a secluded place where nobody who walks in the light dare tread. You cannot delve into my mind any more than you already have," Isra recited candidly as she softly waved her hand at Samuel.

Suddenly, the vision of Isra began to fade. There was nothing Samuel could do to stop it. *Oh, goodness, that's it now. She's going. Going. Ah, now here's the climax.*

The imagery abruptly disintegrated. Samuel's hands burned intensely, making him pull them away from the side of the rock in swift anticipation. Samuel was left reeling as the pain circulating above his forehead stung sorely. It caused him to nurse the top of his head with his dominant hand. He struggled to gain his balance. Samuel felt more than a little dizzy from all the buzzing around in Isra's mind. But at least he'd gotten what he came for.

So it seems she did vanquish him. She's in a place that light dare not tread. There aren't any locations that ring any bells or scream an alarm other than Wretchenheart. Yes, Isra is in Wretchenheart.

"I guess I got more than I bargained for. She's completely untouchable where she is but one must press on, as no doubt there will be far more to this tale than one deems possible," Samuel announced, swiftly materialising himself out of Glamvein with an abrupt wave of his hand.

Samuel emerged back in his office several hours later, realising he'd been gone most of the day. He eyed his grandfather clock wearily, noting it struck six o'clock, chiming incessantly as it did so to remind him he'd taken the entire duration of the day for this extracurricular activity into Isra's mind.

Despite the mild disappointment residing inside him, knowing Isra was indeed within very close reach of Astrid and also in Wretchenheart, a location he could not safely visit without triggering every suspicion known to man—well, regarding "on high" anyhow—Samuel felt quite jolly about his expedition. He'd learned a lot. More than he bargained for. At least now, the situation occupied a lot less space in the back of his head and he had some answers.

Now the only thing Samuel could do was let it unfold and perhaps face the music when the time came that it became public knowledge. He had to admit, he still didn't know everything about Isra just yet, but he'd already decided it didn't matter.

"It will either manifest itself to be a thorn in my side or a bloody blessing. One won't know until it commences," Samuel uttered, shaking the dust from Nefaria Sands off of his tall, black, tailored dinner jacket. He aimlessly glanced around his deserted office, taking heed of the fact that his long-suffering aide, James, was nowhere to be seen.

"One must be grateful for small mercies. Now I shall curl up with a hot toddy and a good book."

Samuel proceeded to flump himself down in his comfortable red velvet chair. "Yes, that would be quite delightful. There's nothing better than hot coffee with an Irish whiskey chaser, and—"

But as he turned around, he stopped mid-sentence, his breath catching in his throat. "Mrs Zelena Grimsbane, one would presume?" he uttered.

He'd quickly recognised the forlorn elderly woman with bright blue eyes which were questionably narrowing back at him. She only asked Samuel one question but it was enough to make the hairs on the back of his neck stand up, as it was one he knew he couldn't answer.

"*Where* is my grandson, Mr Reynaldi?"

4

Samuel was quite taken aback at this intrusion. He'd met Zelena before. Of course, he had. Being the light-bringer in charge of the warring witch families—namely Daughtry, Grimsbane, Passe, and Somersby—he'd certainly met her, but he'd never seen her this close.

"Zelena Grimsbane. Well, this is quite unorthodox, let me assure you. I have no idea where your grandson is. Unfortunately, I am more perplexed at how you managed to get into my office?" Samuel asked with a worried glance. Not only could he not sit but she had placated herself right in his territory so it would be taxing to get rid of her.

"Ah. Your spiritual fortress is not as safe as you deem it to be. Even a witch of my talents can smuggle herself in, but that's not why I am here. So stop stalling. No, I am here for a very delicate matter. Namely, my charming grandson Alan. Nobody has seen or heard from him, and since my daughter-in-law wishes to do nothing with her darling boy and my son considers Alan a failure, finding him is left to me. Well, you know the story, no doubt." Zelena pardoned herself and finally allowed Samuel to say his piece.

"Ah, yes. The histrionic notions of the Grimsbane clan; I am very much aware. But I am not sure how I'm meant to help you, Miss...?"

Samuel struggled, uncertain of Zelena's proper title. She was a widow and he wasn't entirely sure if she had relinquished her husband's name in favour of her own. The very last thing you want to do is upset a powerful witch who could perhaps rip you in half with just a fleeting glance, and so he relented.

Zelena filled in the blanks for Samuel, stifling the confusion between them. "*Mrs*, if you please."

"Thank you. Kindly. But if you please, would you elaborate on why you came to me?" Samuel asked with sincere interest.

"Everyone is very concerned for Alan's whereabouts. Then my doomed son, Nathaniel, let slip he was engaging in lengthy meetings with you. And so, I ask you again, Mr Reynaldi, where is my grandson?" Zelena probed once again.

It was worth noting that she was a determined woman when she wanted to be. Zelena only had to glare at Samuel with her eyes like brazen sapphires. Her long, glistening grey hair expertly tied up in a bun only added to her demure appearance. She was suitably dressed in a lengthy black chiffon gown, loosened at the sleeves and the collar so her long neck was exposed to all and sundry. But since Zelena was a widow, nothing else of hers would ever be on show.

Samuel's head dropped questionably as he realised she had him very much barricaded against the wall. "I see you've heard about our discussions. Yes, I chatted with Alan. Twice," he admitted.

He was trying to be careful, for one slip of his tongue and he'd be at the mercy of the matriarch of the Grimsbane family line.

"And you don't know what has become of him? I heard along the grapevine that a few days later, a very furious witch named Isra ran out of the house in Immortal Yonder after a particularly diabolical conversation with Alan," Zelena piped up.

She eyed Samuel intensely to detect whether he'd be foolish enough to deny the altercation ever being in existence.

Ah, she has got me now. I can't turn around and pretend I don't know who Isra is. Mrs Grimsbane has had more than a simple discussion with her not-so-precious son. No doubt Nathaniel spilt the beans on my random occurrence whereby Isra was also present as I happened to let her in past their elaborate family shield.

Samuel cautiously tried to decide how he was going to move this conversation forward. A better option might be bringing it to a grand divine halt if such a thing was possible.

"Ah. Yes, well, it would be silly of me to say I didn't know the girl," Samuel finally agreed.

"Good. I'd like to speak with her. Perhaps if nothing else, she can tell me what has happened to my grandson," Zelena suggested.

It felt more like a demand, though. Zelena was not one to back down when she was insistent on something.

"It's completely out of the question. I'm sorry, but Isra is in a location where none of us can touch her unless they get deeper towards their darkness than they currently are," he warned with a cautionary glare.

Zelena hissed nonchalantly and threatened him with a fierce stare. "Of course, if you'd like me to consult with the bigwigs of 'on high,' I have no problems doing so. I assume light-bringers who bestow unto witches the ability to be exactly who they are have the potential to be in a lot of hot water. So, as you can see, Mr Reynaldi, we are in quite the tight spot, aren't we? You were in charge of this Miss Isra and then she absconds, quite possibly, with my grandson in tow. What is it to be?"

Zelena narrowed her eyes at Samuel, scrutinising every inch of him and letting him know she meant business.

Samuel groaned. "All right. She's in Wretchenheart. But neither you nor I have any means possible of reaching her so I am afraid that is the end of that," he pointed out sternly.

"I still want to meet her!" Zelena demanded.

Her eyes moved so close together that if Samuel didn't believe otherwise he thought he may have been looking into the eyes of a serpent. The way they merged so delicately, blending in the stunning azure hues with the blackness that resided within her eye sockets was almost spellbinding. Naturally, Grimsbanes were known to be adept shapeshifters, but he'd never seen any evidence of it until now.

"It's not possible, as I already stated. She resides in Wretchenheart. I don't know much else at this juncture. However, I will be conversing with 'on high' soon enough! I am sure they will have a far more detailed bulletin than I can give you!" Samuel mumbled awkwardly.

He stood aimlessly in his office, knowing it was going to be near impossible to negotiate with this woman. She was sitting in his damn armchair for a start and now he felt as though he was at the bottom of the pile. Samuel detested being undermined in any sort of way but he had a plan. It wasn't a very good one but it might buy him some time at the very least.

Listen up here, old chap, she wants revenge and who out of all of them wouldn't? She's a Grimsbane. Not just any one of them but a major player in that ghastly family. She's going to aim for a resolution whether I give her credence or not. The best I can do is stall her for a while. Although one suspects it won't give me very long to come up with a decent defence. I have got to speak with 'on high.' If Isra has indeed killed Alan Grimsbane, they will undoubtedly know. Either way, I'll discover my fate, Samuel surmised dramatically.

It was silly really. He had gone into this knowing Isra would end up committing some irrational act but with Zelena Grimsbane breathing down his neck, well, he knew his time was sorely running out.

"I see. It may be of use to also contact 'on high.' Perhaps they can give me some know-how on our new shrinking violet, Isra," Zelena proclaimed with a grim smile between pursed lips.

She was determined to do this either way, much to Samuel's displeasure, as he'd have to somehow coax her that he had this situation handled. He was supposed to be running things between the warring witches, keeping things civil, but it was becoming more and more challenging.

"Please do me the service of allowing me to seek out more information. If Isra has done anything pertaining to your grandson, we will formulate a plan. However, it needs to be orchestrated. Dark witches that fall to austerity are very difficult to manage but we will come to a solution," Samuel advised her sincerely.

"That you will, Mr Reynaldi," Zelena agreed. "Or it will be the very end of you. Well, I must be going. I do have to discuss this matter with my son, Nathaniel, who seems none the wiser. But you contact your people and I'll deploy mine, and perhaps we can come to some likeable arrangement."

Samuel's stare was vacant as he struggled to find the words for his response. He was left bemused at how far Zelena would get answers but needless to say, it was in her nature to be protective towards her family, even if they were less than desirable citizens.

He acknowledged her with extreme caution, knowing his time was limited from here on out. "I hope we can find a solution that will be to your preference, Zelena Grimsbane."

"Perhaps we can. Then again, it may not suffice for what you are looking for. In any event, good day to you, sir!"

Zelena evaporated out of his office in a split second, leaving him rather relieved but also frantic that she was finally gone.

"I've got to discover for sure if Isra has indeed inherited her title. If she has, we can move forward with some sort of stratagem. If she hasn't and this is all a big farce, then nothing has been lost. We move with the times. The energies around us are so fickle that one cannot truly know when one has been beaten but I must know," Samuel implored with enthusiasm.

Samuel was forlorn and still overly concerned with the details surrounding Isra's mysterious transition to the infamous Wretchenheart. It was true; he'd heard it from her very lips, although she'd been cryptic...

Samuel still managed to figure out for himself that Wretchenheart was where she was now based, but he needed to know for sure, and that meant communicating with "on high," which wasn't going to be an easy feat. He was heading for trouble. Isra had been his charge. It was his job from the outset to get a handle on her and keep her from enacting anything that might raise eyebrows.

Samuel was indeed nervous about making the first move with "on high," but as history goes, the Grimsbanes had a notorious lineage. Alan was the son of ill-fated Beatrice, who married Nathaniel at the tender age of sixteen much to the grimace of her father, Leonard Passe, who disapproved of the marriage from the start. However, Nathaniel had been very much attracted to Beatrice, which only further sent him cascading into chaos. Shortly after Alan's birth, Beatrice revealed she was a loyal follower of Damien Daughtry.

Now you can imagine how much frustration this invoked between Leonard Passe and Marie Daughtry. They were also once lovers, only adding to the long vengeful rivalry between the two main families. If you added in the Grimsbanes and Somersbys, you had a real recipe for disaster, much to Samuel's disgust, as it was ultimately him that would get the brunt of it when shit started flying. Thankfully, he'd only been light-bringer for two hundred years, and he wasn't entirely sure who had come before him.

As already stated, Samuel's father, Bernard, was never in the running for light-bringer—never mind being bestowed with the honour––and so Samuel wasn't entirely clear on what occurred before, but Zelena Grimsbane was around five hundred years old, so Samuel had known of her for a very long time indeed.

Samuel perused to his favourite red armchair, sitting back comfortably. He took his mind back to a time where Beatrice Grimsbane had indeed sealed her fate with the troublesome family he came to loathe.

~Nineteen Years Ago~

Beatrice stood nervously, looking back at her reflection in the mirror. Donning the crisp white gown presented to her, she was astounded as she gazed upon her slender figure with a rather prominent bump on her middle.

She showcased her pregnancy with pride. Despite her bulging

belly, the low-cut shimmery gown looked beautiful on young Beatrice, who was only just sixteen years of age. She held up her dark brown hair onto her head so she could envision what she'd look like when her hair was pinned into a bun. The minute sparkling diamonds embedded on the soft luscious silk fabric made her only more in love with the prosperity she was soon to have, knowing her marriage was one deemed by love and not an arranged marriage. Her father, Leonard Passe, wanted her to marry someone more eccentric.

He might have been more drawn to Damien Daughtry, but at twenty years old, he was already regarded as a troublesome soul. He'd been kicked out of Wingdom's Academy and married a mortal, so that option was quickly ruled out.

Beatrice's sister, Gwendolyn, was secretly courting Damien, which would have caused uproar if anyone discovered the sordid affair between them. Leonard Passe was getting very old and bitter as time went on. He'd been fighting with the Daughtry line for over a century with his ex-lover being the lovely Evanora Passe of whom he'd been happily wed to for many years. She managed to upset Marie Daughtry and Zelena Grimsbane to boot, so Leonard tried to stay out of the limelight, but of course, with his daughter marrying Nathaniel Grimsbane, that was going to prove tricky.

So, yes, Beatrice's options in finding a husband were limited indeed. She came to know Nathaniel Grimsbane by being at Wingdom's Academy. However, she deeply admired Damien Daughtry, Nathaniel's best friend. And so this situation was becoming complicated. Nevertheless, Beatrice was with child now and so their wedding was going ahead whether she had doubts regarding it or her future.

Beatrice admired herself one more time before a knock on the door came. Since she was standing in a tiny dressing room in the Grimsbane mansion, she had an inkling of who might be coming by to visit her.

"Oh, dear! Don't you look lovely," Zelena marvelled with pride. "Oh, come now, let me look at you. Stand up straight," the old matriarch commanded the shy young Beatrice. "Well, you'll make a fine bride for my Nathaniel."

Zelena gushed, which only made Beatrice blush. Her impending nerves were getting the better of her.

"Oh, Zelena, but what if I am making a mistake? I know this wedding has been hurried along so greatly. I am to soon be a mother, but I have no idea if I have what it takes," Beatrice wailed imperviously.

"It's no time to whine, dear. You are with child. Nathaniel may not make a great father but I do at least hope he will be a good one," Zelena solemnly reminded Beatrice. "Anyway, no more worrisome thoughts from you. On you go, dear."

Beatrice haphazardly stumbled into the church, unaware someone had his very warring eyes on her. Damien Daughtry stood eloquently beside his best friend, Nathaniel, who was soon to be wedded to the charming Beatrice. However, Damien and Beatrice had a very interesting friendship. Beatrice was invested in Damien's damning ways that had recently led to him being kicked out of Wingdom's Academy but she neglected to tell Nathaniel, who would not be best pleased. He didn't see the fuss over the whole dark magic thing.

Nathaniel looked on as Beatrice strolled down the aisle, glaring down at her prominent bump whereby he'd soon be a father and perhaps finally get the recognition he desired from his mother, Zelena. Nathaniel didn't catch Damien's twinkling eye subtly winking at Beatrice, and if he had, he might have been rather enraged.

"My, don't you look wonderful!" Nathaniel exclaimed. "I'm so pleased to announce you'll be coming to live with me in Immortal Yonder. We shall raise our child there. It's not the eccentric family mansion I've been accustomed to but it will do them good to have values and the importance of family," Nathaniel explained curtly.

"Thank you," Beatrice uttered as Nathaniel lifted her hand to kiss it. He gently pressed his lips onto his bride-to-be's hand before turning to the congregation ahead of them.

Beatrice looked absent-mindedly at Damien. It was only for a split second, but when the brunette girl caught handsome Damien's warm yellowish eyes, her fate was sealed when he responded with a fond look back in her direction.

Damien was not with anyone as of yet. His mother, Marie, was trying to placate him in some sordid mortal marriage, perhaps an attempt to keep him out of trouble after all that kerfuffle with Rhiannon, but Beatrice was deeply moved by Damien, something she didn't reciprocate for Nathaniel.

Of course, she was in love with Nathaniel. Nobody could deny it... but Damien was dark, passionate, and dangerous. He was the one that set her soul on fire. She daren't admit it in such a public forum, but she could only wonder if perhaps she'd chosen the wrong man to breed with. After all, the Daughtry lineage was one whereby warlocks were the typical forte and sorceresses followed swiftly behind them. The men in that family ruled the roost!

One only dares quell the illicit fantasies in one's mind when she is drawn to someone of the opposite sex that doesn't inspire love but the seldom quality that is enough to excite even this bride's enthusiasm.

Beatrice warbled on in thought as she was seconds away from being Nathaniel's wife. She couldn't back out now. It was far too late. Who knows what consequences that would bring? She would have to go through with it.

Beatrice turned away from Damien, doing her utmost to ignore him, and returned her attentions to her soon-to-be-wedded husband, leaving him completely dumbstruck; he'd had no idea she yearned for his best friend.

~

~Three Months After Nathaniel and Beatrice's Wedding ~

Nathaniel turned to Beatrice wistfully. His arm pressed up against the wall for support. They were exiting yet another dreadful argument. He stared at her so intensely he felt as though his eye sockets might implode. He loved this woman more than anything else in the world.

He resisted the urge to go and pour himself another bourbon. He'd consumed far too many already but it was a distressing time for Nathaniel. Here he was, a man who hadn't possessed the skill of the dark arts like so many Grimsbanes before him, and he'd instead chosen love and stability, believing with all his might it was the best path for him. It wasn't mutual, though.

Beatrice had just told Nathaniel in no uncertain terms that she was leaving him. Their son, Alan Grimsbane, was less than two months old, putting Nathaniel in a very difficult position. He wasn't doing well in the stature of fatherhood. Nathaniel couldn't help but look at Beatrice with a bewildering stare, having no inclination of what else he could say to change the young brunette's mind.

"So that's it then? Three months of marriage and you're off?" Nathaniel questioned once more.

He couldn't believe her audacity. She was so vague with him as to why she was departing. He didn't even know if he was the reason she was going to abscond someplace else.

"I didn't want this to be a dire situation. I fell out of love with you. I don't want you to be ridiculed or disgraced. Now please, just let me go," Beatrice pleaded. Her eyes brimmed with tears as Nathaniel wedged himself between her and the door.

"You didn't want it to be dire? Then maybe you should have thought of that before you married me!"

Nathaniel scoffed so loudly he disturbed the baby, who quickly began crying and disrupting the atmosphere within the household considerably more.

"I told Zelena I had doubts. She told me to go through with it and stop whining!" Beatrice whimpered. "Just let me go. I have a place among others like me. I have tried to be like you, Nathaniel. I have done my utmost to be satisfied with this suburban life of happiness and whimsical hilarity. But the truth is it's not what sets my heart alight," Beatrice admonished softly. "I'm only sixteen. Approaching seventeen. This is no life for me!"

"What about Alan? He needs you!!" Nathaniel shrieked, his voice colliding across the room as baby Alan continued wailing among the two of them arguing.

"It's never easy, but he'll be fine. I'm not cut out to be a mother!" Beatrice yelled as she desperately tried to push past Nathaniel's firm hold of the door. Grabbing his hands and abruptly flinging them back, Beatrice managed to wedge the door open and run out.

Nathaniel came after her in an impervious rage. "You get back here, girl, or you'll wish you'd have never met me!" he cursed.

He caught up to her within moments of his pursuit, throwing her against the charming white farmhouse. She begged and pleaded for him to let her leave.

"Please, Nathaniel. Don't do this. I may not be good enough but the baby needs you. Just let me go. Please!"

She went on and on; Nathaniel stared at Beatrice once more, unable to control his emotions.

He whispered, "We are a family. I cannot let you go. Don't you understand?"

Leaving Beatrice petrified, Nathaniel looked deep into her eyes. His bourbon breath lingered inside her nostrils. He was inches away from her. All she could do was reel in terror as Nathaniel made his advance upon her.

BEATRICE WAS NEVER SEEN after that. But it was revealed two years later that she'd joined the eccentric following of Damien Daughtry, leading to a very awkward conversation between the two men. However, Damien quickly dispelled rumours of something going on between him and Beatrice when he chided, "She's just a lovestruck fan. I'm afraid my interests lie elsewhere."

Of course, at the time, Damien was having a sordid affair with her sister, Gwendolyn, and so he couldn't fully admit the details. Gwendolyn had become with child and much to his disgrace, as that was the last thing he needed becoming public knowledge.

"Oh, and that worked out well, didn't it?" Samuel muttered crossly.

He turned the pages of his book, clearly not enjoying it. He slammed the large tome on his desk, eagerly eyeing up the decanter of Irish whiskey.

"If Isra has indeed become Lady Isra of the Dark, it spells trouble for all among us. But just like Beatrice, she has her role to play in the story. She doesn't know it. Just like Beatrice didn't know. They are all pawns. Isra is just a lot less hopeless than her maternal aunt, Beatrice. Goodness, these Passe women are beyond exasperating," Samuel blundered callously.

"It doesn't bode well for any of us if she has," Samuel then muttered, knowing the time was drawing near. It was just approaching midnight, which meant he'd be best discarding this matter for now in favour of something that often escaped him. Sleep.

5

"Oh, my!"

Isra gasped and jolted herself awake from her brief tenure of sleep.

That was refreshing. At least there was no awkward dream disturbance this time but what the heck? He's still here, Isra murmured as she wriggled around on the bedsheets, still half-comatose from her deep slumber.

She was just adjusting to waking in the dimly lit bedroom in Wretchenheart Castle. It was only her, that soft plush purple velvet bed with deep violet silk sheets and bed covering, or so she thought. Astrid was pressed up against the cushioned white pillow next to her. Evidently, he'd not slept whereas she'd dozed off for a couple of hours. Those night terrors she had where Samuel Reynaldi had a prime starring role caused her difficulty in falling back to sleep but Astrid made her drink a warm apple and cinnamon tea before working his own magic on the anxiety-stricken witch. Much to her surprise, Astrid was still right beside her.

Isra's piercing lime-green eyes fell upon Astrid's dark hazel spheres with glowing yellow resounding back at her. He stared intensely, watching her as she looked at him awkwardly.

"Oh. I didn't expect you to be here," Isra apologetically recited.

She felt somewhat bad for Astrid. Clearly, he'd not slept a wink. At least she had managed to grasp a good two hours of it before waking again. Astrid continued staring into Isra's eyes. His back rested comfortably against the soft white pillow adjacent to the one Isra's head was laid upon.

"Of course. I am still here. You had one hell of a nightmare," Astrid answered without hesitation. "Did you dream again? Did something happen?" he prodded.

He seemed concerned for her; very much so since he happened to have his chambers in the castle but he chose to spend the entire night and remainder of the day with Isra.

She may well be having premonitions of what's to come but she won't understand what it's all about without her memories. Damn you, Samuel! Astrid cursed sullenly in his thoughts and kept his attentions fully focused on Isra.

"Not that I can recall," Isra responded in a low voice.

She paused for a second, considering the idea that maybe Astrid had another agenda pertaining to her, one she wasn't entirely sure he was being transparent with her about.

"I'm just a little thrown. You barely know me and yet you're at my side. Why?" Isra probed with a wide-eyed stare. Her eyes glinted at him in rapt curiosity as she awaited him to give her the truth.

The thing is I've been with you since the very beginning. From the very same moment that your heart was ripped in two. You still don't know this, and it cuts me up inside. I have this bright, vivid memory of you and you have yet to remember the time we had together. If only I could reach inside your head and pluck those memories back into your being. I'd do it if I could. Alas, it's not my spell; it was Samuel's so I figure he's the only one who can undo this tragic ailment he's bestowed upon you. Of course, I am by your side. Why on Earth would I be anywhere else?

Astrid reminded himself sorely of the reason he was here. He wasn't going anywhere, much to the chagrin of anyone who disliked him or Isra being near each other, but he didn't care. He was staying put.

"Why wouldn't I be?" Astrid quipped at her back. "Look, I've been pretty forthcoming about everything. We were friends. Very close companions. I've been waiting a long time to get close to you again. You don't know about any of that because Samuel wiped your memories. Can't you trust that? Do you trust me?" Astrid nudged her pleadingly.

"I do. That's just the thing. I'm just trying to wrap my head around this. I'm only nineteen and there's so much happening around me. I'm having difficulty finding my footing," Isra admitted as she whipped the silk bed covering off of her.

Only nineteen years old and she's done it all. Lost love, swiftly turning herself over to the dark side. Watched as her enemies fell. Vanquished a young warlock, still unaware of the implications it holds. And now she's a queen. Not to mention my rough revelation of me and her being companions and she doesn't bloody recall it ever being in existence, courtesy of Samuel, Astrid mulled over softly in thought. *She's disorientated. She hasn't had time to adjust. It's partly my fault.*

"I get you. More than you know," Astrid acknowledged her. "You're restless, and it's understandable with everything you've been through. I sometimes wonder if I made the right decision in bringing you to Wretchenheart, but there was no other choice. Samuel could have done whatever he deemed necessary to take you down if I didn't whisk you over here in a flash! I didn't know what else could be done in such quick timing!" Astrid clarified.

If we stayed in Shambre Fell, there's no telling how quickly Samuel would have come crashing in, throwing his weight around while dishing out orders on what needed to commence. Isra would have been in a lot of hot water and realistically, she still is. At least in a demonic dimension, the light cannot touch her and that is why we are here. For the time being, this is home.

Astrid mulled over the conundrum of keeping Isra out of harm's way. He'd done the right thing. He didn't regret it but he did feel incredibly guilty regarding Isra's nervous disposition.

"I'm more than restless. I'm baffled, somewhat freaking out, which is bizarre considering my existing condition. I just don't know how to make sense of any of this," Isra confessed.

For a newly made queen, she wasn't doing well with the concept of having to rule her kingdom.

"All right," Astrid relented. "Get up. Adorn yourself in one of those long flowing dresses you own and put a cloak on to keep the heat in. You'll need something on your feet," he instructed, which was even more confusing to Isra as she had no idea what he was up to.

"Trust me. You're restless. We're going to do something to take your mind off it. Even if only for a time. Get dressed, and wait for me here," Astrid commanded with a slight grin upon his face.

"Where are we going?" Isra asked as she rummaged through an antique oak wardrobe, pulling on a thick, luxurious blood-red velvet gown with long sleeves that had black ruched lace details at the ends. While she was foraying about, searching for a cloak, she swiftly put two identical jet-black court shoes on her feet. But still, she was awaiting Astrid to answer her.

"Don't you worry about that for now. Just do as you're told. I promise, this will be breathtaking," he said with a mysterious glint in his eye.

I often wonder why I am so drawn to this enigmatic man, someone who deems to please me no matter what, but yet there's something so mesmerising about him and yet he insists on me doing as he states, and I have no reservations about it. It's befuddling to me. Normally, if a man bossed me around, I'd yearn to castrate him by now. But this one... oh, he's so different. I can't fathom him. It drives me crazy!

Isra sounded puzzled in her thoughts. She considered the idea of why she allowed Astrid to lead her in this manner. It wasn't control. He wasn't forceful at all. She just noted a sense of familiarity with him that made her think twice about any derogatory remarks she'd save for less fortunate men, for he made them all look like timid little boys.

Isra spun to face him. She now had adorned herself in a black velvet cloak with the hood pulled down so that it looked casual. After all, she had no inclination of where they would be going or even what Astrid had in mind. He was such a dark horse in this capacity, and she couldn't help but question just where he was going to lead her next. He had such an elusive mannerism about him that really did make her yearn to know more but yet she was also slightly wary, for she still knew so little about Astrid.

"All right, dear heart. I'm done. Now what?" Isra replied to him.

"Come with me. We're going to tour the dungeons," Astrid marvelled at her with a lick of his lips.

He was enthused by this little extracurricular activity they were embarking on. However, Isra was somewhat reluctant.

"In the dead of night? Isn't that a little unorthodox?" Isra asked with a fleeting expression placed upon her face.

She trusted Astrid, she really did. He wasn't going to lead her in the wrong direction. That was absolute. However, he had a lot of personality traits she was still unravelling in her journey to know him better.

"It's not. Think about it. You are restless. You cannot sleep, and I'm craving a tasty pile of earthworms. It will be productive for both of us..."

Astrid trailed off as he remembered they weren't just here to hide out from Samuel. Wretchenheart had a lot of delectable sights to offer, and most of them were situated in their domain. A demonic dimension wasn't just home to demons, but widely known as a place where the most magically inclined souls can expand upon their horizons, learning more about themselves than they dare envision.

Astrid hoped that Isra would take the initiative and dive deeper into this than just being a queen of a forlorn nation. There would be greater aspects at hand this time than simply a matter of the light versus dark debacle. She was now the centrefold of the dark realm, at the core hub where it all originated. She wasn't only enveloped in darkness anymore. Now Isra truly would *be* the darkness if she chose to attain it.

She has so much ahead of her. If only she knew just how it's going to shape the rest of her immortal life. Jeez, she's only nineteen, man. And she's accomplished so much already but she's only beginning. If Isra thinks shit is rough now, wait until we get to the big finish. The true eternal battle between light and dark is where we're going to find out just who she is. Will Isra step up to the plate? Will she overcome her darkness as well as the souls that masquerade as goody-two-shoe beings of wondrousness and wholesome vitality? We will find out. That is for sure.

Astrid had gone over this a few times in his head but now the time was drawing nearer.

Isra grimaced as she turned to face Astrid. She was standing right in front of him, awaiting his instructions. "Worms? How lovely."

"Well, you know I used to be a raven! Anyway, come on. Let's go." Astrid extended his right hand to Isra, signifying her to take it. "Where we are going is pretty dank and dark, so stay close to me. Your very immortal life may well depend on it."

Astrid sniggered nonchalantly. His sense of humour had not wavered what with all the chaos emerging before him.

"That has to be some snide mockery, right?" Isra asked; she didn't get the joke.

"Yip. But hey, you never know, girl! Best be keeping your wits about you. You might be a queen, but you're of great importance to the world and... Well, me."

Astrid chuckled and proceeded to lead Isra out of her bedroom.

It wasn't long before he was leading her down the long, winding hallway that seemed to go on forever before they arrived at a marbled grey set of steps that led down to yet another passageway. This one was darker and danker than the first but lit torches were hanging idly from iron holders. Astrid didn't hesitate to grab one whilst he still had Isra's hand clasped in his other hand. And then he took her down another flight of stairs, only these were more intricate and narrow.

He whispered, "Take care now. Some of these aren't the same size, so keep looking in that direction."

Astrid pointed downward, as now they had appeared to be in yet another hallway; this one much longer and went on for what seemed like miles.

Astrid said nothing as he continued to take Isra down towards the dungeons. The irony was this had been his idea to cheer her up and to distract her from the mind fuckery that was Samuel Reynaldi's twisted game. He figured something macabre would be the perfect excuse to shift her mind elsewhere, if only for a moment.

"Are we even close to it yet? I feel so weary wandering these halls. Are you certain you know where these dungeons are? After all, I presume you've never been here until now."

Isra questioned Astrid's expertise as they padded down the dingy steps that would lead them to Wretchenheart Castle dungeons. It wasn't much further now. They'd already gone down the darkest dankest passageways of this castle but Isra couldn't help but wonder if Astrid knew what he was doing or just maintaining that he did.

Of course, he was giving her the tour. Not that she needed it. She could quite happily go by herself but Astrid rather enjoyed taking her down this hidden corridor and all the wondrously dark corners Wretchenheart had to offer.

"We're just going down these steps and then we'll be right by the entrance," Astrid swiftly answered, not even looking at her as he kept on going.

"So, you ended up working for the light-bringer? I've never really had you down as the goody-two-shoes type," Isra mocked cheekily.

Astrid ignored her attitude. He flashed around his flaming torch as they edged closer to the solid oak door that would lead them into Wretchenheart's worst-ever place for anyone to find themselves in. *Oh boy, she's doing the goody-two-shoes commentary. Ha, I remember when she said that one last time. Oh, if only she remembered the banter we had. Still, she manages to push my buttons. It's entertaining if nothing else,* Astrid thought coyly. He had to look away from Isra so she wouldn't see the massive grin plastered across his face.

"I've worked for Samuel for just over a century, yes, before I decided enough was enough. Times had changed, and not for the better. Alas, I made my decision shortly after he changed the directive on who would be keeping an eye on you," he retorted abruptly as if to halt Isra's intrigue but it only plagued Isra with yet more questions.

"You worked for him for over a hundred years and yet you appear ravishingly handsome! How interesting!" Isra responded with a side-eyed glance.

"Hmm, some of us have the ability to be around for aeons and not even age!" Astrid came back at her with a glint in his eye.

He knew she was deliberately pressing his buttons. Heck, he enjoyed it but her questioning was beginning to grate on him. Astrid had come here to see the marvellously dark, dingy row of oubliettes that had been here for hundreds of years. Sadly, they had been rather neglected for quite some time judging by the amount of muddy brown dust accumulated on the grey stone floor. Nevertheless, Astrid persisted with his endeavour, for he was of fine architecture and histrionic artifices.

"You are a real silver fox then. Interesting," Isra toyed with him.

Astrid resisted the self-conscious urge to push back his silvery grey hair. It often bothered him but then again, he was just over two hundred years old. It was hardly anything new.

"I am indeed. But look at where we are, Isra. Back in the day, witches, warlocks, mortals, and many individuals were tortured, hung, and sacrificed here," he commented as he drew Isra's attention to the final lock-up they came to at the end of the narrow, murky corridor whereby a set of black iron chains hung carelessly from the wall below to where a wooden seat was placated. Astrid presumed the victim would have been forcefully affixed to the wall and seated on the wooden plank until someone deemed them worthy to be free.

"I don't have much interest in all this. But do tell me, did you enjoy your time in the light? I just find it so revealing that someone like you felt at home there when your natural form is a raven?" Isra asked with a piercing glance.

"Hmm, you're right. Ravens are mystical messengers at heart. We deliver the fateful to the unfaithful, and as to how I ended up being Samuel's lapdog in the despicable manner he had me be..." Astrid stopped mid-sentence. He wasn't entirely sure on what the truth was but went on with his reply, emitting, "I shall never know, but let's press on, shall we?"

He shut her down coolly and continued showing off the dingy, dank hole. There was an awkward pause between them, but Astrid broke the silence by saying, "You know, curiosity was known for killing the witch back in these monstrous times."

This caused Isra to be most bemused. She couldn't understand why he said it. However, he winked in her direction as if to signal her endless barrel of questions were beginning to grate on him somewhat. Although he did enjoy the cheeky banter between them, he wasn't sure if Isra would get the hint.

"Well, I must say, Sir Astrid, you are standoffish around this subject matter," Isra recited with a harsh glare, looking him right in his yellow sheen eyes.

Astrid continued with his piquing interest and stared passionately at the black iron-clad chains. "I am so intrigued to learn if these iron chains work as beautifully as they did many moons ago." He then remarked cryptically at Isra with a coy wink, "I always loved the intricate workings of whips and chains. Oh goodness, now I am showing my age!"

Isra stared at him in amazement. "But, Astrid, you would not do that to your queen, surely?"

She was shocked he'd even suggest such a thing. Her hand was still gripped in Astrid's but his dark, eccentric, flirtatious nature had her wondering if he was leading her down yet another path—in the metaphorical sense, for he seemed greatly interested to see how she'd react with every strength in which he pushed the narrative between them further ahead.

"I might if she doesn't stop back-chatting me," Astrid whispered into Isra's ear in a husky voice, flashing a cheeky grin back at her.

She did indeed react profoundly to his admission. Her lime-green eyes beamed with vast curiosity and she felt a tingle in her lower regions. "Well, Sir Astrid, aren't you quite an enthralling creature? Tell me, you wise mystic. Anarchist to the light. And now consort with your newly made queen. Is there nothing you won't attempt to entangle yourself with?"

Isra eagerly awaited his response with a wide-eyed stare. There was no denying Astrid was attractive but she seldom felt the vibratory sensation she felt underneath her thick gown until she had become closely acquainted with Astrid. It was almost bewildering to her, as she'd practically never felt anything remotely close to sensual for any man. But Astrid was the one who set her on fire. He knew how to awaken her fanciful energies in just the right locality.

"I deflowered a witch once. She was icy and demure in all the right places but still a virgin. However, she doesn't recall the event but the light folk spies got more than they bargained for when they saw me up close and personal with this eccentric villainess," Astrid hinted.

He hoped she'd understand that the witch he was referring to was her, but, of course, there was that significant distance between them now that her memories of their spectacular time together had ceased to exist.

"Well, I am not sure what you are referring to by deflower? I hope you didn't prune the girl. I am afraid I am not much for gardening," Isra explained casually, only for Astrid to truly fill in the blanks in a nonchalant way in which Isra wasn't shocked as his confidence, his manly presence, came shining through.

"I took this young, tempestuous thing under my wing. We became close and alas, one thing led to another right here in Wretchenheart. Coincidentally," Astrid admitted with another wink. "It may not have been the best circumstances but I never planned on taking her innocence. She had never been with a man before and so it was a new experience that I was more than happy to teach her about."

"I see, and has there been anyone else with whom you've been attracted to in this manner since her?" Isra asked with an intriguing look. She wondered if there was more to Astrid's words than he was letting on but perhaps she wasn't looking close enough.

"There has never been any other. She's with me always, even if it's just us frozen in time," Astrid candidly remarked.

"Intriguing as that is, I must say, I am a little jealous," Isra cajoled. Of course, she'd totally missed the mark on where Astrid was heading with this conversation.

He'd dropped all the hints he could possibly muster and still she didn't have a single inclination he was referencing her. He had to appreciate the irony; he had been so blatant, it was almost poetic. Yet deeply painful for him to express. Astrid had done everything he could to be transparent with Isra and who she used to be, but she was yet to grasp the concept.

Oh, my. She hasn't got a clue. Not even the mere fragments that have been forming every single self-explanatory notion that I've been hurling her way since we embarked on this journey. Well, Astrid, it's time to get serious. The clock is ticking. It is now or never, old son! If she won't realise I am the one that wants her so badly, I'll just have to give it to our weary enchantress straight. I am not sure if she's going to be receptive but damn, I'll try my hardest, Astrid conferred with himself, knowing if he was ever going to get a shot with Isra, it was now.

"I've never had anyone that has ever stuck their neck out for me as much as you have. I still don't wholly comprehend who you are and what it is that you do, however, I am curious," Isra softly remarked as she took a step back from the dank oubliettes that were in her line of vision.

Surely their tour was well and truly done by now. He'd taken her down here on a whim, a bizarre methodology to cure her impending anxiety over what was to come, but yet she couldn't help but feel complacent; for being here with Astrid in this dark, hellish place made her more nervous than she dared admit. Here, she was her most vulnerable. Isra being alone with Astrid made this situation even more intimate, and she would soon be forced to confess that she yearned for a lot more than just ridiculing his enlightened being.

"You need not be jealous, Isra," Astrid started with a serious, forlorn glance, staring right into her lime-green eyes. "You know, with everything that has happened recently, I have been thinking, and while I hate that it drives me crazy to even insinuate such things, I can't help how I feel. You've been through so much in such little time, and honestly? It hasn't changed anything. If anything, it makes me realise what I want so much more. So, to get right to the point, I was wondering if I might stop by your chambers this evening... but not for the same reason I've been there all along? What do you think, kiddo, does that strike you as something you might find some enthusiasm for?" Astrid asked warmly. His voice was so delicate, almost like silk, as he eloquently divulged exactly what he wanted from her.

"I think I could be appeased by such a thing. Yes, but just what might we be doing?" Isra probed with a questionable glance.

"I'll leave that to your imagination," he huskily whispered. "One thing is for certain. Our queen may well not be the same after," Astrid hinted with a grin, which brought up Isra's nervous disposition once again. She suddenly found herself with a whole new dilemma.

Bent over at the knees and me pleasing her in every way possible. Oh yes, she may not be present to the service of her subjects for quite some time if I manage to get my wicked way. I've been awaiting this far too long. The time is now. I can't help but find myself nostalgic of times gone by, for if things go sour here, we may never have this chance to be united again... Astrid stopped himself mid-thought.

While he yearned to have his hands explore every inch of Isra's body, he knew she had to give him the green light first. The glimmering invitation would beckon her towards him in a way he hoped only he would know her by.

"I know we are here under strange circumstances. Ones that I cannot truly fathom. However, there is an underlying proposition I'd like to bestow unto you. As queen, I have to say, I cannot entertain the idea of another man being my consort, or anything else, for that matter, but it's so undeniably clear to me. My king is right in my sights and with that in mind, I can think of no other that is more worthy of the role than the man who deems to reign by my side. So, you see, Sir Astrid, it is not just you that has desires for more than what we've already accumulated."

Isra finished with a low brow. Relief surged all over her body as she vastly expressed her deepest wish for him to fulfil.

"I think I can meet your expectations. I hope I prove to be satisfactory," Astrid eagerly responded. He narrowed his eyes at Isra as he realised that more than he could ever deem possible had landed right in his lap.

6

Isra was still staring back at him when she gently emitted, "I think I could see us being strong for an eternity. Goodness only knows I hate not knowing all the ins and outs of what we are. I cannot even begin to penetrate the notion of who you are, not properly anyhow, but yet I have an overwhelming trust with you. And for me, that is enough to propose that you shall be my king. After all, this isn't just some coincidental arrangement. Oh, no! We are so much more than this entails."

Isra glinted at Astrid. Her lime-green eyes glowed a little more prominently than usual as she flashed him a sweet half-smile.

"As for your memories," Astrid voiced empathetically, "I'd give anything to return them to you. So that you know me. Know yourself. I'd do whatever it took to give you that surreal technicolour world that has been thrust upon us whereby what is deemed to be the good guy is actually the enemy. Trust me, you have it on good authority, I'll do whatever is necessary to make this right."

He had such confidence. A man with magnified strength. Someone of whom you could not only take into battle but know he'd also lead the charge and get you out of harm's way. He was a man that could be relied on until the very untimely end.

"Hmm. Don't worry. After all, you did say it was Samuel Reynaldi who enacted the enchantment and so therefore it may well turn out to be that only he can undo it. It's all right; I'm a patient woman," Isra mustered with an amused smile. And then she whispered in Astrid's ear, "I guess all good things come to those who rightfully deserve them."

"That they do," Astrid agreed without hesitation.

He suddenly found himself reminiscing on what Damien said right before he dragged Isra here to be the new queen. Damien had been very clear, but it was the truth he relayed to Astrid.

ASTRID AND DAMIEN nervously glanced around the vicinity, no doubt checking for any wandering eyes that might be lurking. Damien had made the sincere suggestion that they cloak the area. All right, so Wretchenheart was out of bounds as far as the light bringer community was concerned, but Astrid was none too privy to Samuel's many arrays of tricks. He'd managed to get a spy in here before so now they were undertaking the highest of precautions.

It was needless to say that the next few hours would soon turn into days, hopefully weeks after, would be challenging at best, but Astrid was ready. He'd step up to the plate. He wasn't sure he could wholly dominate Isra in the way he knew he had to, but by golly, he was going to give it his all.

"Isra will be their new queen. Damnation knows Wretchenheart hasn't had one for aeons but it won't matter. They won't bat an eyelid. All they will see is a full-blooded witch taking the throne. They won't care too much for the latter or how young Isra is. The citizens of Wretchenheart have been through this many times out of number. They know how it rolls down here," Damien carefully enunciated to Astrid with a wide-eyed glare.

Astrid didn't completely understand Damien's words but he stood ready and awaiting every syllable. He needed to be prepared. There was a good chance that when he returned to Shambre Fell, he'd find

Isra had really run amok with her behaviour and so he would have to rein her in. To keep a young enchantress under duress would not be easy but Astrid was more than ready to go ahead and do it.

"Now, it's imperative you listen to me, boy. I know you're preparing to haul her off out of harm's way, but she still won't have her memories. Please understand that Samuel Reynaldi will do all in his heavenly powers to keep it that way! The last thing that man wants is a woman that is not only queen to a demonic lineage but also remembers what someone from the light bestowed upon her. You might think you're skedaddling out of the fire, but believe me, Isra will be more at threat than ever. Not to mention the long-running vendetta that has dominated my family and the other three families for centuries," Damien explained yet again, making his position absolute; just because Isra was swanning off to Wretchenheart didn't mean her toils would be over.

Astrid's eyes were affixed upon Damien. He wondered if perhaps there would be a way... After all, he'd be doing all the legwork. Damien would sit on the sidelines, out of the limelight. It was not worth questioning why Damien voluntarily put himself in exile but it spoke volumes to Astrid, who had always known there was far more to someone's tale than the words that came floating out of their mouth. In times of danger and uncertainty, a being would say anything to get themselves out of the shit. If Damien deemed Astrid and Isra warring against Samuel to be a liability to him, there was no way in hell he'd casually admit it.

If we could retrieve her memories, perhaps all of this would be so much easier. If she's killed Alan, we're coming to Wretchenheart. If she hasn't, I doubt she'll be safe from prying light-bringer eyes with Samuel already having conversed with her. Either way, our young witch is about to get the biggest awakening of her life whether she likes it or not.

Astrid contemplated quietly to himself, knowing he had quite the task ahead as he'd be bringing Isra here no matter what happened now. There was simply no other alternative.

Damien had not said otherwise, but Astrid knew it was for the best if things were to improve for the better regarding Isra.

"If we manage to get her memories back, this would be so much easier. Believe me, as her father, I feel darned responsible for the girl. But alas, she's got no idea who I am," Damien expressed, completely knocking Astrid out of his train of thought.

"I agree. It's near impossible, though, the way I hear it," Astrid coolly told Damien.

"It is, but then again, there *are* always ways if one looks hard enough," Damien hinted with a wink in Astrid's direction.

THOSE PARTING words from Damien stuck in Astrid's mind. The fleeting notion that there may indeed be some way in which Astrid could successfully attain the memories of Isra knowing him that Samuel had stolen was a great comfort. Astrid was a man plagued with deep anguish, knowing he couldn't do anything to stop Samuel from conducting that vile act at the time it was committed. His only peace would be snatching those discarded memories back and returning them into Isra's head without a care. And he'd take immense pleasure in allowing the news to reach Samuel because let's face it, Astrid loved to gloat.

"I know this sounds ominous, but I'll do whatever I can to get you to recall what we had. I'll muster all my strength in finding the cure for retrieving what was so cruelly taken from you," Astrid implored to Isra.

His determination was relentless. Something in him was so hell bent on making things right. If he wasn't by Isra's side, she might have felt intimidated by him; instead, she found this quality he possessed rather attractive.

"I trust you'll do exactly that, dear heart. Well, you'd best take me back to my chambers so I can prepare myself for your charming visit in the wee hours."

Isra motioned towards him. She stood so close to Astrid that her nose was almost touching his. It was magical the way their eyes glinted back at one another in such a dynamic glance. Isra's entire body felt intense heat as Astrid's dark brown golden sheen eyes stared right into her being. Never again had she felt this way about anyone, and she doubted she'd feel like this with another soul. There was just something so remarkable about Astrid. It wasn't just his handsome silvery hair that sparkled ever so gracefully in the slightest amount of light or his magnetic personality beaming full of confidence.

"You'll have to wait until the morning," Astrid whispered in her ear. He hated having to delay the inevitable but now he needed some alone time to think through his next move.

"That's a shame, for I was looking forward to you coming by," Isra muttered solemnly.

"It's three o'clock in the morning. I'll be along," Astrid uttered softly before adding in cryptically, "but I'll have to take you back now. I'll even escort you to your door. The last thing we want is for you to get lost in this macabre vicinity."

7

Astrid had only just returned from taking Isra away from the dungeons and back to her bedroom again. After all, he'd been the one who so graciously gave her the grand tour so it only made sense he walk her along the dimly lit corridors and up the creaky steps they'd walked down to get to Wretchenheart's loathsome and morbid cavernous lock-up.

Astrid had been kind enough to make her a cup of honey and lemon tea before he departed. He hoped it would make Isra sleep as she'd had those night terrors recently. It wouldn't do any harm to simply postpone their impending relationship just for tonight. He had to admit though; he had a plush bed of jet-black silkened sheets and a dramatic blood-red crushed velvet bed covering contrasting the eccentric maroon four posters also draped in matching silk, and he still didn't feel like he could sleep.

Astrid sat in his wooden chair with soft red velvet cushioning on the rear as he idly seated himself at the oak desk situated by the iron window frame. It was dark in Astrid's bedroom but the tiny candlelight that also rested on the far end of the desk provided some illumination. Since it was very late, creeping beyond three o'clock in the morning, Astrid decided he'd read through an enormous tome pertaining to folklore. However, it was worth nothing that although some of it touched on old traditions related to magic, it mainly depicted ancient lineages and cultures that Astrid barely had an understanding of but had to if he was going to succeed in his task.

"Ancient regality always encompasses the olde ways of which many know today to essentially be witchcraft," Astrid murmured as he turned the page, tutting in disgust.

Magic had become so glorified in recent years. Especially around the last century. It had all been about hexing your lover, cursing your peers, and being downright dangerous to the entire cosmos by being an unholy bad ass. Of course, Astrid knew better than anyone that there was more to magic than the commercialised version people had been sold.

"Whatever happened to good old traditional herbs and flora and fauna to create a vile yet effective potion that actually achieves something productive? Nobody has got any standards these days!" Astrid candidly remarked to himself.

He found the irony amusing, for he intended to court Isra, who was very much enveloped in darkness, but she was passionate towards the old ways. It was something Astrid found even more endearing about her.

"It's kind of old. Well, at least to the majority of souls," a voice uttered behind him.

Astrid was taken aback as he sat awkwardly in his hard wooden chair. As far as he knew, it was just him in this room, but he clearly heard that voice so something was amiss. Astrid spun around only to find himself looking dead on at a baby-faced angelic being with deep blue eyes and fluffy light ash hair framing his face. However, Astrid noticed this being's gigantic feathery white wings. They spanned around five feet either side, completely dominating what little space his room had as they had expanded around this angelic entity's back and shoulders.

The mystical being whose name was Oresis had a comical expression etched on his face as he kindly acknowledged Astrid in a formal tone, "Oh, don't trouble yourself. I'm here. You're awake!"

Astrid pinched the sides of his left wrist as he didn't believe for one moment that this could be real. *No fucking way! An angel? In my room? Huh, you have got to be kidding me. This is some funny arse delusion I've cooked up in my brain due to incessant sleep deprivation over the last forty-eight hours. There's no blooming way this is actually happening...*

Astrid discussed the concept thoroughly in his mind, for it was undoubtedly known he didn't grasp the concept of angels, In fact, he barely even believed in that airy-fairy bullshit other than them some fictional beings that walked around on airs and pranced with golden harps while shaking their feathery wings. However, Oresis was a sight to behold! He was larger than life; at least in Astrid's imagined perception of how an angel should appear to be.

"It's happening, Astrid. I am here. I can also read minds exceptionally well," Oresis replied in response to having known exactly what Astrid was thinking.

"Uh-huh. So I gathered," Astrid blundered.

He was somewhat confused as to what was happening but obviously it was real because the last time Astrid checked, haphazard delusions didn't respond to your crazy manic thoughts whereby you deemed it to be some falsehood. If he was dreaming this up in his subconscious, there was no way the entity would answer him back if he was experiencing a neurotic rampage he'd conjured up.

"You'll have to excuse my bewildered attitude, but I am rather perplexed here. Who the heck are you?" Astrid asked with a wide-eyed stare.

Astrid wasn't buying his presence as happenstance. Not for a second. There was something fishy about this angelic chap and Astrid was determined to decipher just exactly what he might be doing in Wretchenheart. Let's face it; wasn't it a place angels dare not tread?

Why on Earth would he come here of all places? Surely that goes against their fancy ass code? I'm not one to belittle traditions but it smells to me that something isn't quite right. Besides, I've never even dreamed that angels could possibly be real. Okay, so there's that angelic agent James, but he's never had freaking enormous shimmery wings, so what the heck? Astrid conferred himself in a great panic of sorts.

He was deeply perturbed. Something deep inside him was screaming that all was not well. However, Oresis was not here to bring Astrid anxiety of any kind. No, sir. But if Astrid just simmered down, it would soon become clear that Oresis was here for a much greater matter at hand.

Oresis noticed Astrid's deep mistrust and pursued on, for he had discovered this entity in many souls before. It wasn't uncommon to come to someone who didn't believe wholeheartedly in the cause, or at all, as it was in Astrid's case. This was not a time to judge people; even Oresis knew that those possessing great lack in conjuring something in their minds always had the potential to believe again. However, Oresis noted that Astrid was a proud man for a shapeshifter, predominantly in a raven form. Nevertheless, Oresis was to proceed with great caution and treat Astrid as though he was as highly esteemed as himself, for equality was fundamental.

"I understand your frustrations, Astrid. I do," Oresis began as he flicked back a loose straggler of hair from the side of his forehead. "I don't come here to bring you misfortune. I fully comprehend your difficult situation. Moving a witch rooted in darkness away from those prying eyes that you deem to be of the enemy... the light is not your battlefield, Astrid. I am one of the angelic messengers from above, true, but it's not like how you've been foretold."

With a sincere look of concern, he continued. "We wanted to personally thank you for your intrigue in Lady Isra of the Dark. It has brought our attention to a great folly committed by one of our most noteworthy light-bringers to date: Mr Samuel Reynaldi. We believe him to be a renegade who woos the opposition silently but yet continues to proclaim he is a force of the light," Oresis implored earnestly.

It didn't go amiss to Astrid's perception that perhaps Oresis wasn't what or even how he perceived most angelic beings. There was a remarkable quality about him, something quite unique, almost tantalising, in the way he spoke with such deep passion towards the ethereal pathway he had adopted. A real sense of caring could be depicted in Oresis's voice. It clearly wasn't his first rodeo, attempting to convince someone like Astrid that the light souls were actually good and kind beings simply out to help others.

"Oh, he's a rebel all right," Astrid pronounced with caution in a low voice. "So, pray tell, why would 'on high' send you to speak with me? Someone who used to reign supreme as Samuel's right-hand man, or right wing to be accurate," Astrid asked with profound curiosity.

"Because you took the initiative, Astrid. You not only turned away from Samuel Reynaldi but you crushed his ghastly plot pertaining to Lady Isra of the Dark. You revealed his greatest secret and his worst folly. For that alone, we see you as someone who is a most noble ally. It won't be easy, I can tell you that. Samuel Reynaldi... Well, it could take aeons, maybe even another century to remove him from office but if you give me your trust, I can assure you that one day, it will be inevitable," Oresis affirmed.

He had a wistful, friendly look about him as though he could be a great entrusted friend and also a strong warrior to have at your side, which, of course, was a quality Astrid also shared with him. Both were mighty men with deep hearts confounded to always do what they deemed to be right.

"Hmm. I'll drink to that." Astrid chuckled before taking a breath, looking upward at Oresis. "Meanwhile, here we are, in a demon dimension. Bit of a weird set up for you, I imagine," Astrid presumed.

"Oh, I'm not afraid of these places. You see, I'm not from the same dimension Samuel believes himself to be dealing with," Oresis blurted out without warning, causing Astrid to look taken aback. He was sure it was "on high" they had been dealing with all this time.

"Oh? How so? I mean, aren't you part of the mystical messengers that basically call the shots from upstairs? On high? I believe that is the fond term of phrasing that Samuel uses," Astrid continued on briskly.

"Yes and no," Oresis began before coming to a pause. "Why don't we have ourselves some refreshment? I feel like I'm going to deliver a rather cruel blow in your domain. I'd rather we didn't start on bad footing."

"All right, but I warn you, all we have in the pantry here in Wretchenheart is some weathered old-aged whiskey, and while I am quite tempted by it, it really makes my insides tingle," Astrid nervously admonished.

Oresis ignored Astrid for a second, and he began concentrating. Gently, he closed his eyes, mumbling something under his breath. It was probably an ancient language since Astrid couldn't make heads or tails of the dialect but no matter; Oresis pushed on and within a second, a silver platter appeared on Astrid's well-kept table followed by two tall clear shot glasses. Next, Oresis muttered another word and a large fern-green bottle presented itself next to the crystalline shot glasses.

"Oh, now that is much better than what I had in mind to offer," Astrid gushed in response to Oresis's marvellous creation.

"Yes, well. I rather like the apple taste. I always found it to go down rather nicely. I have an eccentric palate, you see. I don't agree with things that aren't of the finest excellence. This is ninety-per cent proof, mind you, so you might want to pace yourself a bit. Although as far as liqueurs go, it's one of my favourites. Here, try some!" Oresis offered by swiftly pouring the dark green liquid into a glass before also filling up one for himself.

Astrid held the glass of sweet apple liqueur to his lips, becoming deeply aware of the rich, robust scent wafting up his nostrils. A faint hint of spicy cinnamon could be detected just as Astrid tipped the glass backwards to gulp down the entire concoction.

Oresis was bemused at Astrid's action. He knew that it was a rather potent beverage. However, Astrid knocked it back, not even batting an eyelid as it slid down his throat, gradually moving into his intestines without even the slightest hint of nervousness.

"Wow, you really enjoyed that, huh? Okay, maybe you should sit down for a moment or two," Oresis suggested, but then he realised Astrid was already seated upon the wooden chair. "Ah, never mind, then. I'll just plant myself on this cold stone floor. It's no trouble."

Astrid then lifted himself from his seat to retrieve a silky black velvet pillow from his bed, handing it to Oresis before seating himself on the end of his comfortable bed before they proceeded on with their discussion.

"Thank you. You're too kind." Oresis motioned towards Astrid as he carefully eyeballed him with wild intrigue, wondering why he was so level-headed after swigging that diabolical beverage. However, Astrid wasn't affected in the slightest, which was bewildering to Oresis to say the least.

"No problem. Anyhow, you were saying how things with the 'on high' are not what I have been told, so do you mind elaborating on that?" Astrid quizzed.

He now found himself buzzing with intrigue at the notion that perhaps Samuel had yet again not completely been transparent with him. *It seems we're saying that he's never been a completely one-sided guy. Makes sense. He embraces many types of truth. The trouble is I wonder if he knows which ones are real and which are false in his mind because many I suspect he's created. If it turns out there is no higher realm, then what?*

Astrid carefully mulled over the conundrum in his thoughts. Although Oresis had good and just intentions, perhaps he wasn't being wholly honest with Astrid either.

"'On high' doesn't strictly exist. At least not in the way you've been led to believe," Oresis began, to which Astrid's ears immediately pricked up upon hearing.

"What do you mean?" Astrid quipped. "Surely 'on high' is the foundation of those who have ascended? Without it, there would be no angelic souls. No light-bringer. No celestial realm. Or have I thought way too much into this?" Astrid pressed the question to Oresis, as none of this made any sense.

"It exists. It's just not 'on high.' So in the beginning, there was the creation. The stratosphere, which eventually expanded to other planes of being. There are the lower planes of consciousness, the dense areas whereby demons, vampires, and the like occupy. Then there are the slightly higher terrains, but they are still very much attached to lower consciousness. So while lesser demons can be found there, it is not quite celestial realms at this stature. Finally, we have the ascended realms. Spirisity is one of many that happen to exist all over the dominion. Don't think for one second that there is simply just that one locale whereby celestial beings interact with one another. After that is the heavenly plane, so when someone's soul lingers after passing, they go to this world. Then there are those who choose to stay on after dying; they don't ascend or descend. They stay right where they are. This is referred to as limbo by one's own admission, meaning they make the choice to not be an ascended being. They decline the fortitude of angelhood and from here on out, they can choose how the rest of their story plays out. The seventh realm is the ascended ones, so these are the people who have already been human and have thus died and now become something their human species cannot comprehend. This is what Samuel Reynaldi deems to be 'on high,' when in reality, he's colliding alongside the fifth and sixth stages of cosmic infiltration," Oresis earnestly admitted before looking over at Astrid to see how he was reacting.

Astrid looked back at Oresis, gobsmacked. His eyes narrowed in a scrutinising manner as though he didn't quite comprehend what he had heard but yet some part of him also soaked it in.

"What you are saying is that Samuel, although he is one heck of an old timer, especially for a light-bringer, is not actually—"

"Not ascended. No," Oresis finished. "The human version of Samuel Reynaldi did die, that is for certain. He is indeed immortal, but he's not reached the heights of which he proclaimed he has. Hardly anyone is aware of his treachery but those that are atop the food chain, metaphysically speaking, are very much knowledgeable on this matter."

Oresis paused and noticed Astrid's rigid expression placated on his forehead.

"Ah, so 'on high' are...?" Astrid pushed his inquiry further, although Oresis was somewhat vague on the matter. Astrid was determined to know, for it now meant a very different outcome for himself and Isra if Samuel wasn't quite as high and mighty as he originally claimed.

"The real 'on high' are the Sanctification of the Unseen. Typically speaking, they are rarely ever witnessed by anyone but those are the beings that have truly ascended. They have accomplished great feats on both the Earth worlds and then the spiritual realms before finally being promoted to the top dogs of all worthy creation. But you won't ever hear this being talked about. Quite frankly, they prefer to be invisible so that is why when Mr Reynaldi talks about 'on high,' he's talking to heaven-sent beings; however, they are not the ones who truly wield all the power," Oresis admonished.

"Samuel never actually had it then?" Astrid quizzed.

Astrid still had quite the perplexed expression etched onto his face as though he wasn't entirely sure he believed any of this but there was also far too much detail to disbelieve it. Everything was lining up perfectly, much to Astrid's distaste; that meant he had very little to dispute.

"Power? I am sorry to say, but no. He did not. Never has. We are not entirely sure how someone that diabolical even made it to light-bringer. It does make you question the whys and wherefores a little bit more now that is brought into view," Oresis sorely retorted.

"That it does indeed," Astrid replied. "I knew something was amiss. Damn it. I should have seen it," he scolded himself.

He placed his head in his hands, wearily running his fingers through his uncombed dark grey hair. The silver ends glinted slightly in the dark that was softened by the dim haze of candlelight.

"And so, you see the predicament we are in, considering Samuel Reynaldi used a Sleeping Beauty spell on Lady Isra of the Dark shortly after he'd magically disarmed her," Oresis responded in a woeful tone.

"Hmm-mmm. I was there," Astrid murmured sullenly. "Dare I say it, but what happens now?" he asked with piquing interest.

He'd listened to all Oresis had to say with deep intrigue but now it warranted the notion that there had to be some kind of universal comeback. Karma, if you will pardon the expression, would be lying in wait for Samuel.

"For the time being, the real 'on high' are investigating why Lady Isra of the Dark was allowed to kill a warlock when she was Samuel's charge. He was supposed to remove her powers at a very young age to prevent any mishaps. However, fast forward nineteen years, and here we are. It's all very mysterious, but he was supposed to raise her, encourage her, keep her away from the darkness. Alas, that has not been the way of it, but it does provoke one's mind into presuming why he didn't do what he was deemed, doesn't it?"

Oresis motioned forward but Astrid remained silent, taking all of this in. It certainly didn't bear any consequence to him. At least not yet anyway, because if Samuel was now under suspicion, that meant his dalliance with Isra, or impending romance, was very much safe from prying eyes. If the Sanctification of the Unseen were only invested in Samuel's actions and why he had done what he had, then everything else was unimportant.

"Hmm. Well, will you keep me posted? I am rather concerned, as his aide, James, a one-time comrade of mine, well, more an enemy, is very much entwined in all of this. Can you figure out if he's involved, too?" Astrid knew he was prying a little too much but inquiring minds yearned to know.

"James is an angelic soul. Very close to ascension. He chose to stay in the limbo stage and thus became a warrior, but he will have the opportunity to push forward should he choose it. As for if he is involved in this debauchery, no. The young man is completely in the dark," Oresis told Astrid with a smile.

"Good. It's probably for the better if it stays that way," Astrid muttered solemnly.

Samuel pulled the wool over all of our eyes, eh? Never, ever bloody ascended. How could someone even fake that? I mean, how the heck does somebody like that even manage to become the light-bringer that is the guardian of the spiritual realm? Not just that, but he's in charge of all the dark souls that come tumbling down from the heavens into his domain. He's the one fated to bring them back towards the light. The man not only restores their faith in the light world but also facilitates it. He has done exactly as he was told but it's all an illusion. Samuel Reynaldi is not the great worldly leader he claimed to be. Oh, he climbed his way up, that is for sure, but he committed the immortal sin of prevarication. I do wonder, if all of this is undoubtedly true, why he targeted Isra like that? Unless she was the one that could so easily expose his facade. It doesn't bear thinking about but our light-bringer is in for one hell of a surprise because if the real enlightened messengers bring him in for questioning, we might just see who he really is.

Astrid hashed out this mighty blow of a revelation quietly to himself in his most private thoughts.

8

James stirred uneasily in his sleep. Something was vastly trying in vain to capture his attention. Goodness knows why because it was the unseemly hour of three o'clock in the early morning. However, James knew better than most that those spiritually inclined rarely succumbed to sleep. He quickly straightened himself out, eagerly putting on his glasses as he sat up in bed, slightly disturbed at the vision playing out in his mind's eye.

"Gracious, what the hell?" James questioned the visionary image as he began to hone in on exactly what the strange, lucid pictograph was trying to tell him.

It was clear as day. Samuel Reynaldi was sitting in front of a large audience in an auditorium. Plain white walls dominated a large oval-shaped room. There was nothingness all around but a small formal congregation could be spotted at the back of the room. The rest of the participants were eagerly waiting to be addressed; this great meeting would soon take place. Samuel stood awkwardly in the middle of the room soberly as a man with grey hair began asking questions about his untimely reign as light-bringer, but wait! There was more. Samuel was given the opportunity to speak, which is rare at these types of gatherings; defendants are only granted one or two passes while the minister in charge at these particular setups does all the talking.

"Your name? Rank and titles please?" the man muttered sternly in Samuel's direction.

"Samuel Reynaldi. Lord, chief and light-bringer of Spirisity," Samuel responded swiftly in order so they could press on with the dire matter at hand.

"Good to know," the man sniped back. "Tenure of ruling to date please?" he asked Samuel.

"Just over two hundred years, sir," Samuel quipped.

"Hmm, it appears we have a rather sticky situation with... now who is it? Ah, a Miss Lady Isra of the Dark? A young charge that was believed to be under your guardianship," the man began.

He stopped, stuttering as he came across some disturbing information on his large pile of parchment papers, much to Samuel's grimace as he knew in that fatal moment that "on high" would potentially uncover everything he was vying so desperately to cover up.

Everything in that meeting, in that very room, became discombobulated. People's faces and all in that room became blurry as it started whizzing around at rapid speed. A strong male voice assertively gave instructions on what was to happen next.

"Yes, Isra. She's the one that got him into this mess. But alas, there will be a summons called. When the tall hand strikes seven just before dawn, Mr Reynaldi will attend without delay. And do so he must if he is to maintain his coveted position as light-bringer. You will get him here or he may well forfeit the sanctuary of us all."

The vision faded. James quickly realised he was laid up in his bed, aware he'd just experienced being at the infamous "on high" auditorium.

He'd never actually been given the chance to visit it in person, which was a good thing in James's mind. You were only granted access to it if you had been a very strong leader or if you were in deep trouble. But he'd just been there in the metaphysical sense, watching that tense meeting unfold before him. Samuel stood in the centre of it all, being observed by high-ranking men of authority while he nervously awaited their harsh decisions upon him.

"Well, it looks like I best get my ass over to Spirisity. It's the dead of night but this is urgent. Samuel won't like it, but no matter. I don't have any say of how or what 'on high' decides to relay me," James told himself.

He immediately began to fumble around for clothing, throwing on white puffy shirt and black shirt trousers without hesitation. James took his calling seriously. He was Team Peace all around. He knew there would be very little chance of being anything else other than a lackey but still James took the job incredibly to heart.

SAMUEL STIRRED RAPTUROUSLY in his sleep. As James bravely stepped into Samuel's bedroom, Samuel mumbled something James could barely make out. James knew his appearance wouldn't be welcomed so he quickly walked over to the far end of the bedroom, pulling the jet-black curtains that normally kept this room in darkness wide open. It was time for the ever-prominent light-bringer to get up.

James attentively noticed that Samuel's crisp white bed linens were crumpled as the sleeping man lay there in desolation so he gently tapped Samuel on the shoulder, nudging him as he did so.

Samuel's eyes opened immediately, glaring at James with a furrowed look of concern although it was doubtful he'd have this disposition for long as he would soon be filled with nervousness and frustration.

"James, one would ask just what you are doing here at this ungodly hour?" Samuel questioned his employee briskly. A slight hint of gruffness was detected in Samuel's voice. He was groggy from just being woken and already that mild grumpy vibe was very much present in Samuel's demeanour.

"Good morning," James interrupted Samuel's perplexity.

James manoeuvred himself by the light-bringer's bed, forcing him to sit at the foot of it so he could detail to Samuel why he was here.

Normally, James wasn't one to disturb Samuel while he was at rest but considering he'd been awoken at the eerie witching hour of three o'clock, James had made it in Samuel's best interests to head over to Spirisity without a moment's delay.

"I'm afraid I don't bring good news. I had a rather disturbing vision that I must immediately bring to your attention," James advised in a low voice.

He was doing his utmost to remain in a calm, well-mannered state at this point, for what he would have to relay wouldn't be received well but it was imperative James told Samuel what he had seen.

"A vision, eh? Come on then, boy, out with it. What was it?" Samuel quizzed somewhat harshly.

The light-bringer had sat himself up in bed, affixing his half-moon silver spectacles onto his nose. James looked up awkwardly at Samuel. Oh, hell; he didn't want to say it but he knew he had to. There was no other choice, not when the order came from "on high" so he was damned if he didn't.

"Erm, the gist of it is 'on high' wants to converse with you. Seven in the morning, just before dawn. The rest... Well, it was some jubilant scene in which you are the rebellious anarchist held down for questioning. It was rather hazy actually, but that was the long and short of it," James lied through gritted teeth.

Thankfully, Samuel's room was very much sheltered away so no light could creep in so that Samuel could clearly see James's prevaricating face.

Of course, James was lying but he'd much rather sound like some dim-witted fool than admit the truth to Samuel, which could indeed cost him far more than he deemed possible. When it came down to weighing up his choices, James figured a tiny white lie wouldn't do much harm in the long run. Let's face it, Samuel wouldn't have a hope in hell of finding out. Visions were often weary, elusive creatures that seldom gave you the chance to see them again so if you didn't pay much attention, you were screwed. There was no trying to discover what you missed. Oh no, not a chance.

"Ah, I see. So what's the commotion then? They want to see me? Hmm, interesting, I must say! Well, you'd best get the coffee on then, boy, we've got one heck of a day! Onwards now. Aha, yes, you may go."

Samuel excused James as his mind ventured over to what might be causing all the intermediate fuss pertaining to himself.

It's just a meeting. What could go wrong, eh? I can't imagine there will be anything so terrible that they can't say it at anywhere other than their grand hall. However, it does bug one that 'on high' wants an audience with me as that rarely bloody happens unless you've caught their attention for all the wrong reasons. Hmmm, Samuel thought to himself as he proceeded to get dressed and ready for the day ahead.

There would be very little time to ponder. It was only a few hours before his judgement would commence.

MORNING BROKE in the quaint terrain of Spirisity, but it was not to be a joyous one. Samuel was awaiting his impending fate. Three hours ago, his long-suffering aide, James, had revealed that "on high" wanted to converse with Samuel, and this was not good news considering Lady Isra of the Dark's most recent transgression of plundering herself even further down the dark path. Samuel was deftly sure she'd fulfilled the prophecy that foretold she would be Lady Isra of the Dark now, so with less than an hour to spare, to say he was nervous was an understatement. But at least his coffee was steaming hot. That was the one thing keeping the light-bringer sane for the time being. Having a caffeinated beverage that was so hot your mouth was almost bleeding satisfied his worrisome mind but still, it hadn't done much to stifle his already foul mood.

"Get to it, boy. I've gotta toddle on very soon! I can't sit here dawdling all fucking day, and while you're at it, whip me up another cup of coffee," Samuel ordered James as he slurped down the last drip of his first mug. Ironically, he'd guzzled it in a matter of minutes but then again, as a mystical being, Samuel wouldn't feel the effects too much.

"All right, keep your hair on! I'll get on it for you," James wailed back.

James was also incredibly nervous because he'd blatantly lied to Samuel. He told Samuel about the vision he'd had regarding the grand "on high" meeting that was to happen this morning, however, James left out several details regarding it because James knew if Samuel had known... well, his temper was unpredictable on a good day but now?

Knowing "on high" wanted to formally interrogate Samuel for his involvement in Lady Isra's transition to darkness didn't exactly signal good things ahead for the treacherous light-bringer.

Now, let's be honest, James didn't know all of the details pertaining to Samuel's debauchery but he bloody knew enough to know when to keep his damn trap shut. And so that was why he'd been smart in pretending he didn't recall his vision terribly well. As far as psychic phenomena went, it was believable as visions, dreams, none of it was clear-cut. In this world, you either understood that shit the first time or it masqueraded around you so you failed to get it and had to dance around it a few times before it became clear.

Samuel accepted James's explanation and that was that, but it didn't reassure James that he was out of the woods yet, for Samuel's temper was frantically rising by the second.

"Oh, just get on with it. What the hell am I doing here if I can't even get a decent cup of coffee? Jeez, it's one thing being in charge of a magical realm. Having all this prestige and power. But not one scrap of that forceful agility allows me to magically conjure up my coffee! I'm telling you, it's not right! It's really not."

Samuel scolded James once again as he disappeared swiftly out of Samuel's office, presumably to get on and make that damn coffee Samuel so desperately wanted.

Just what other calamities are we going to have today? It doesn't even bear thinking about, does it? Hmm! Samuel huffed impatiently as he waited to see just what this encounter with "on high" would bring.

9

Finally, here he was, standing outside the grand "on high" centrepiece he hadn't seen in aeons.

In fact, Samuel had only had the privilege to see "on high's" glory just once. That was when he'd first been bestowed with the offer to become light-bringer. Even then, he didn't really understand what he was getting into. Now he was just befuddled because all of the shit was about to come out in the wash. It wouldn't be easy but Samuel was just going to have to wade through it and hope he came out unscathed.

It was the same round, white dome it had always been with the ornate golden bells that Samuel could hear ringing gently in the summer winds. He imagined the interior would be very much the same but Samuel's memory neglected to recall the exact details. He did remember that "on high" was only accessed by a secret portal and THEY told you where to go and exactly what to do so you didn't have a hope of hell of getting in unless you were damn well invited.

Samuel had been preparing for this for just under four hours. It was all very short notice since James had come over to Spirisity as soon as he relayed the message for Samuel to get his butt over pronto.

Finally, he was granted access to the prestigious "on high" after several years of never setting foot in the place. He had to admit, it was the same as he remembered it—an enormous white oval-shaped roof covering a most intriguing building where on the outside it seemed normal. To the naked eye, it might be your average domicile with a bit of spin on the outside decorum. But inside, lavish deep purple walls saturated the corridors leading to the grand atrium, best known as the Sanctuary of the Light. This was the gigantic meeting room where those deemed worthy enough by "on high" were granted full permission to say their piece or they were here for a very different reason, which could be relevant in Samuel's case.

A small bronze bell hung on the mahogany door whereby whoever was about to enter could pull down on it and let the members of "on high" know they were about to come in. Of course, Samuel hadn't been here for aeons. He barely cared for the procedure but it was all very official, especially since you only really got to speak to "on high" unless you were a tremendous leader or if you were in deep shit.

Samuel summarised the latter as he walked in quietly, not drawing any attention to himself. Waiting to be called up, a man grimaced at him from the centre of "on high's" majestic stratosphere. This man looked very forlorn and more so around the eyes as he sighed nonchalantly in Samuel's direction, knowing this was going to be strenuous.

"Your name? Rank and titles please?" the man muttered.

Samuel knew this was a waste of his time. They had all they needed to know. It was just more of "on high's" elaborate theatre. They asked a bunch of questions they already knew the answers to but it was all designed to test the reactions of whoever happened to be put on display.

"Samuel Reynaldi. Lord, chief and light-bringer of Spirisity," Samuel responded swiftly.

"Good to know," the man sniped back. "Tenure of ruling to date please?" he asked.

"Just over two hundred years, sir," Samuel quipped. *It's not going to be any more or less than that but again, they know all this. It's pathetic, you know, but they'll go on and on like a dragon that continuously needs to breathe fire to live. Except these morons aren't doing it out of a necessity. It's all designed to piss whoever falls prey to their demands at any given time.*

Samuel ranted nervously, fearing just when the subject of Isra might arise. Of course, she was going to come into the festivities sooner or later. He'd been charged with her upbringing from the very start.

"Hmm. It appears we have a rather sticky situation with... who is it? Ah, a Miss Lady Isra of the Dark? A young charge that was believed to be under your guardianship," the man began.

He then stopped, stuttering as he came across some disturbing information on his large pile of parchment papers, much to Samuel's nerves, as "on high" would pretty much uncover everything from Isra's strange parentage to her being given up and her finding herself under Samuel's care; even the whole sodden mess with that Jonathan chap. Yes, they would bring it all up.

"Yes. I was made her legal guardian from the moment she was a baby and handed into my care by her parents, Damien Daughtry and Gwendolyn Passe. Of course, you know of him. Famously got himself expelled by teaming up with the demoness Rhiannon when he was young. As for her mother, well, Passe was a mortal so that was out of the question to Daughtry, and he had to get rid of this illegitimate child sharpish," Samuel explained curtly.

"We don't need the unnecessary details, Mr Reynaldi. However, the young witch was placated in YOUR care, so please tell me why the hell her powers were not extracted when you already agreed to do so? I'm reading the file. It sure does make for very perturbing reading. Treaded the dark path, aged just seventeen because of a mortal dalliance that went ghastly wrong, then she teamed up with one of your most trusted employees. Astrid, I believe his name is? Is that right? And then tried to destroy the unholy cosmos we deem to dwell in? So, the real question, Mr Reynaldi, if you beg my intrusion, is why in damnation was she allowed to suddenly be in the presence of one of our youngest warlocks that was also deemed just as dangerous as she? Hmm?" the man asked Samuel candidly.

"Well, sir, let me begin by saying our Isra is a bloody abomination. It's true. I didn't remove her powers since I am her legal guardian, well, because I hoped perhaps she'd mellow over the years. And did I forget to mention she's crafty, too? The first conversation I had with her, she'd just summoned a monstrous dragon. Of all creatures, we know they are not only hideous beasts but way too flighty. Something our young little miscreant happens to share with it," Samuel retorted, recalling the time he told Isra to get rid of her scaled pal, Franco, so that he could talk to her personally.

"Be that as it may, Mr Reynaldi, you are still in charge of this girl. Now she's gone and vanquished a warlock from the Grimsbane family. This leads to serious consequences and 'on high' is extremely concerning. Your involvement is problematic at best. As you know, these families have been warring with each other for centuries, and for one of them to vilely dispose of another without just cause adds fuel to the fire."

"I can only apologise, sir. I've done all I must as light-bringer, but Isra just doesn't listen to reason. Wait... what do you mean I am STILL in charge of her? She's the queen of a freaking demon dimension, for goodness sakes!" Samuel spluttered, not knowing how to proceed.

Isra was still his problem, and if she was reining chaos and bloodshed, he was in the shit for it even if he couldn't get within an inch's distance of her. *Bloody rules and regulations and their loopholes. Yes, Isra is out of reach to me physically, but according to the legislation I am still responsible for every damn thing the bloody witch enacts. So even if I cannot get to her; the moment she does something frowned upon, my ass is getting thrown right back into the fire.* Samuel hissed impatiently.

Oh, how Isra being a thorn in his side was becoming more and more apparent by the day. It didn't matter what interactions he had with her or how fatherly he tried to be, she wouldn't listen. Sure, it was partly his fault that Alan Grimsbane had perished because he'd tried encouraging the romance, but Grimsbane himself couldn't handle her so that put paid to that.

"She is *your* responsibility. It has been from the very start. The least you could do is show some restraint. Had this been finalised years ago as it should have been, perhaps we wouldn't be all sat here with vacant expressions as we are now!" The man huffed with disdain in Samuel's direction.

"May I interrupt?" a female voice piped up from the congregation.

Upon looking over, they saw the familiar hair tied neatly into a bun was visible from the back of the room where she had promptly seated herself before this hearing began. Looking deeper, it was very clear that it was indeed Zelena Grimsbane. You could tell just by looking into those shiny bright sapphire eyes of hers.

"Of course. Mrs Grimsbane. Go ahead."

The grey-haired clerk spoke to her in a kindly voice. Evidently, she wasn't going to be on the receiving end of the same hostility Samuel was getting, much to the annoyance of Samuel.

"As a result of a brief courtship with Lady Isra of the Dark; of whom Mr Reynaldi was deemed to be in charge of, my dear grandson, Alan, perished. So I hope you gentlemen come up with a resolution that will satisfy an old woman because it appears she's been allowed to run riot. And that sort of thing doesn't bode well. We've not had one second of peace at all in the entire lineage, at least in my lifetime, and so Isra doing this is not welcomed by us Grimsbanes. My son isn't dealing with the grief so well and prefers to bury his head in the sand but I knew from the moment I spoke with Mr Reynaldi that he was hiding something," Zelena explained, but she didn't need to say much to get the auditorium on her side.

Light-bringer versus one of the most high-ranking witch matriarchs? Yeah, don't bet your life on that one. Of course, they were going to be more swayed towards her side. Grimsbanes wielded a lot of power, and the last thing that "on high" needed was an all-out blood bath.

"I understand, Mrs Grimsbane, but we're trying to fathom as to why such a union was encouraged when Miss Isra was indeed a flighty soul in matters of the heart," the clerk continued in a warm tone. He was being incredulously polite with Zelena.

"Damaged? I would presume," Zelena interrupted without hesitation.

"Yes, perhaps," the clerk answered without looking up.

"Yes, well, none of that matters," Samuel interjected. "Isra was in my care. I do accept that, but I cannot control her reactions when something doesn't quite go the way she wanted."

He was about to protest further when he suddenly spotted a black raven on the arm of Zelena Grimsbane. He looked several years older than Astrid, possibly about ten if he was to hazard a guess, but this raven also had Astrid's yellow sheen eyes despite the fact he was somewhat larger, which was interesting to Samuel since he was certain Astrid was with Isra in Wretchenheart.

It did pose a question, though. Who the hell was this raven if he looked practically symmetrical to Astrid?

"What exactly am I expected to do?" Samuel requested. He knew there was very little purpose in asking because he already knew this answer.

"She ran off with Astrid, your employee? Did she not? So perhaps a little finesse is required," the man instructed in a formal tone.

"Oh, I have finesse. I have it practically coming out from my rear end, but how in the name of chaos are we meant to tackle someone who currently resides in a demonic realm with a notably just as dark figure along with her? I raise my hand. I fucked up, but honestly, I don't know what the way forward is. I've exhausted all my resources with Isra and more. Besides, just what can one do in these dire times?" Samuel pressed diligently before moving forward with the inevitable comeback, "How are we going to disarm a woman we can't even touch? She resides in the fierce rupture in the earth's crevice, better known as Wretchenheart to your more uncivilised man."

"The circumstances aren't important to us. She's raising hell and not in the literal sense, bringing a lot of attention into places we'd rather keep sacred. Mr Reynaldi, you'll damn well find a way or you could well be saying goodbye to Spirisity."

The man threatened Samuel with a fierce glare. A look that signalled "on high" meant business. This was it. It was now or never.

"Oh, is that so? Well, then, good sirs! I'll do my utmost to find a loophole as the expression goes. We also need to apprehend Astrid. He's just as cunning as her. Perhaps more so. But he's been with me for years. It will be difficult to convince him without a strong, insurmountable amount of force," Samuel commented, knowing how much of a rebel to the cause Astrid truly had become in the last couple of years.

The moment he'd laid eyes on Isra, he had a soft spot for the witch and to the cause that was dangerous. *It could have been you that was responsible for dragging her back down to earth, not encouraging her to rise even higher. Nobody has any principles anymore. Back in the day, we did things differently with somebody like Isra. It never went like this with her grandmother but never mind, another time for that one. I'm tired,* Samuel thought.

He noticed this meeting was dragging on. But at least they got to the purpose of it so now Samuel knew what he was up against.

"He's somewhat of an anarchist. Doesn't care for rules and regulations. Bloody well makes up his own!" Samuel ranted needlessly.

He was trying to be formal and polite but it's a very enduring task when one is placed in front of the highest organisation ever known and then being interrogated by them. It was nerve-wracking at best, not to mention humiliating because being the light-bringer and Lord and Chief, you'd never expect yourself to be centre stage here. But circumstances are funny little things. Stranger things have happened.

"Then I suggest you find a suitable resolution to deal with Lady Isra of the Dark," the man muttered in an annoyed tone. "Anyway, that shall be all. Good day, Mr Reynaldi!"

And before Samuel could protest, he found himself standing outside "on high's" grand artifice. The entire congregation vanished in a flash. Well, they'd sent him hurtling out of their premises instantly and without warning, but still, it caused Samuel to feel some mild nausea as it was so fast.

"I have to find a way to get to Isra. By any means necessary. But the question is how?" Samuel asked himself in a frustrated tone. "She can't be reasoned with. She just won't listen. Just like her father, she's a stubborn character but even those that are the most rigid can be moved. I just need to find a way to break down her walls."

Samuel proceeded to wave his hand above his head, dissipating out of there before any more chaos could commence.

~

"I APPRECIATE it didn't go your way today, madam, but he is my brother." A jet-black raven with dark grey circles under his weary golden-orange eyes and long tail feathers that had faded significantly to an almost ombre black in recent years perched on the shoulder of his mistress Zelena Grimsbane piped up in a low voice. "It's true that Astrid and I share remarkably different paths but I will not do anything that remotely puts my brother in harm's way."

"Oh, I don't doubt you, Silas. You have been a most loyal servant. I am just rather dismayed at how this has all unfolded. That ghastly Reynaldi buffoon still has us all on high alert and here we sit, in that wretched auditorium, and your brother's name is sounded out," Zelena countered in a sombre tone.

She was vexed at having to deal with the venomous Samuel Reynaldi earlier today. Just watching him standing there cordially agreeing with all he was accused of was gut-wrenching, especially as it was formally confirmed that Lady Isra of the Dark had indeed vanquished the late Alan Grimsbane, Zelena's grandson.

It was duly noted by Zelena that Alan had not been progressing well in his witchcraft; he had been majorly slacking on all of his metaphysical studies. He seldom took any witchcraft in his inherited tradition of becoming a warlock but because Nathaniel grievously failed in that department, Zelena wanted one of her boys to succeed. Sadly, that was not going to be the case for Alan.

"I have to admit, I was disappointed when I heard Astrid's name but more so when I heard he was with a witch responsible for murdering Alan. I have to say, I don't know much about Lady Isra but for Astrid to give himself up to a witch, to go beyond the cause and touch that boundary line... well, it is devastating for me," Silas remarked quietly. "I don't quite understand his reasoning for it, but ravens are meant to be familiars to witches and nothing else. He's not only gone past this line that has been around longer than he, but he's pushed past the point of no return by harbouring a witch that very much needs a lot of help," Silas ventured eagerly. "It's not like he hasn't done this before."

Silas was instantly reminded of Evanora and all that went down over her.

"Perhaps you should go and have a little intimate chat with your sibling on this delicate issue," Zelena suggested with a warm glance. "At least so that we may gain a clearer picture on why he embarked on this path of sorts while I may understand the woman who killed my grandson so cruelly."

"I could indeed go and chat with him but I am told they both reside in Wretchenheart and that's somewhere the light cannot tread," Silas replied. He felt like he was repeating what "on high" had already said but it was true.

"Which is why Mr Reynaldi believes she is untouchable. But nonetheless, she's Damien Daughtry's illegitimate daughter, something that poses further problems down the line with all of us warring families. I've been fighting this for almost three hundred years, Silas, and believe me when I say I am tired of it," Zelena mustered quietly.

She'd been entangled in this mess longer than she cared to know. It had originally started with the Passe and Daughtry clans but over time it managed to interlink with both Somersbys and Grimsbanes, which now added fuel onto the already existing fire between Grimsbanes, Passes, and Daughtrys. Zelena detested the idea that this whole debacle would be reborn, and it was the last thing she wanted.

When her husband, Lethaniel, was alive, it thankfully ceased a great deal; however, it was far from over, even back then, and that was almost forty years ago. Now Isra was only a young witch and as far as

Zelena saw it, incredibly naïve, misunderstood, and likely misrepresented. But then again, they all were at that age.

"How can someone as powerful as she is, and immortal nonetheless, be so impulsive as to court a warlock while she was grieving a previous loss? Why wasn't action taken to prevent this happening again? The last one was a poor mortal or so I have been told. But Alan was a warlock, not exactly smart, I will grant him that, but still, something should have been undertaken."

Zelena griped endlessly to Silas, who could do very little to comfort the old woman's grief.

"I will do my best to ascertain all of this if that is what you need from me," Silas motioned.

"I would appreciate that, Silas. Thank goodness Lethaniel isn't around to see this. The last thing he'd want is to bear witness to such a loss. It would have broken the man," Zelena muttered in exasperation as she flumped down into her comfortable royal blue velvet armchair, still feeling incredibly frustrated with how today went down.

10

Silas flew for what seemed like many miles, travelling from Immortal Yonder to Wretchenheart. He hadn't much time to prepare for what he'd say when he arrived but he knew the message he delivered would likely not be welcomed. After all, he worked for Zelena Grimsbane, the head of the Grimsbane clan, and Isra had just recently murdered Alan Grimsbane in cold blood. If he added in his brother, Astrid, to the very awkward scenario that presented itself, it was a recipe for disaster.

Silas was firmly rooted in tradition and upheld his beliefs that it was wrong to become too involved with the cause that one embarked upon when it came to dealing with witches—in this case, being assigned to a witch that had tragically befallen to darkness.

Astrid's task, from Silas's viewpoint, was that it may have been more professional for Astrid to pull her back from the brink, not fall in love with her as it seemed he had done. But what did Silas know? He hadn't heard a single thing from his brother in five years, and that was a long time not to know someone. The brother he had known had seemingly changed.

Still, at least the scenery he found himself greeted by Wretchenheart's historic castle was something to gush over. It was an enormous eccentric château with black iron gates merged with shimmering gold along the railings while a cerulean-blue moat fiercely surrounded it. The drawbridge was, of course, closed, but Silas was a raven.

He most certainly would not be going that way, for he was seeking the first open window he could find and letting himself in. It was typically frowned upon but since this eccentric monastery was home to Astrid, Silas figured exceptions could indeed be made. The pale ochre desert just beyond Wretchenheart's biggest attraction only signified that this was very much a place the light dared not tread. Luckily for Silas, that criteria didn't apply to him, for he was one drawn to the dark worlds, always had been, but then again, ravens were primarily dark messengers, so it fit.

Silas eagerly braced himself as he surveyed the area around Wretchenheart Castle. He wasn't entirely sure which would be the most efficient way for him to enter but then he saw a neighbouring window that had been left ajar three stories up. He figured this was the best way he was going to gain entry. Without hesitating, Silas proceeded to squish his body through the tiny gap, enough for him to push past, and he found himself face to face with a young woman with lime-green eyes and lucid soft, white, fair hair as she sat upon the edge of her bed.

"Who are you?" Isra asked Silas with a glare.

She wasn't used to having to deal with intruders and this was not going to be an exception. However, Silas knew how it went when it came down to negotiating with someone and so he began diffusing the situation by addressing her calmly.

"Oh, please do beg my pardon. My name is Silas. I am looking for my brother, Astrid. I apologise if I got the wrong window. Sadly, I haven't seen him for a long time and I wasn't certain where I'd locate him," Silas gently explained. His bright orange eyes glowed like fiery embers.

Isra found herself satisfied enough to drop her guard and so she loosened her stiffness. "Oh. Astrid is due to be here at any given moment but I must inform you that he is late," she cordially replied.

"I had no idea he had a brother. Mind you, I am not completely familiar with him, you understand? Still, you may wait until he decides to show himself. Whenever that will be."

Isra was coy, much to Silas's relief, for she was far more forgivable than he imagined her to be.

"Thank you very much. Again, I do apologise for the intrusion. I'm here because of Zelena Grimsbane," Silas articulated in a low voice. He was quiet as to not cause a ruckus but he was trying to be tactful since Isra's eyes once again flared upon him in a scrupulous manner.

"Grimsbane? That name I know, yes. I do not know Zelena, though," Isra surmised amicably.

The penny hadn't dropped that Zelena was a relation to Alan so unfortunately it looked as though Silas would have to delegate with Isra and also spill the beans that she was in hot water with both Zelena and the light.

"Yes, she's the paternal grandmother of Alan... the young chap of whom you recently disposed of," Silas disclosed.

He did so with as much compassion as he could muster because Isra had become antsy within seconds of him saying it. Her face dropped instantly but her eyes continued narrowing on Silas, much to his discomfort.

"Oh. I had no understanding of his family. I'm afraid I am a little perturbed. You say you are a relation of Astrid's, namely his brother, but yet you're also here because of Zelena Grimsbane. I presume she's aware of what happened to her grandson?" Isra asked with a fierce glare.

"That she does. It's not going to be pleasant but you're in no immediate danger. Zelena wants to know what happened to Alan and because you're the person right in the middle of this, you are the best one to tell the story," Silas went on further, which somewhat reassured Isra. She felt less awkward now, although it was still bewildering; her being asked to recall her tale to a stranger.

"What happened with Alan, eh? How long do you have?" Isra

teased apologetically although there was some seriousness in her voice.

"I am not short on time. Believe me, there's nothing you can say that will shock me," Silas softly affirmed. "It is what it is. These situations happen. There's no point dwelling on it. One best get on with it and hope to find a way in which to remedy it or at least find a probable cause to have closure... neither of which sound as though they are possible," Silas advised Isra with a look of caution.

At that moment, Isra's bedroom door burst open. Astrid was carrying two steaming mugs of coffee in his right hand while his left carefully wedged the door open. He stood there aimlessly staring at Silas.

"Oh, brother, I was wondering when you'd get here." Silas chuckled.

"Yes..."

Astrid paused momentarily. He set both mugs of coffee upon the table while keeping eye contact with Silas, who he noted was sitting rigidly on the edge of her bed. He proceeded to situate himself next to her just so that he could be close by for whatever discussion was being held in his wake.

"Oh, don't be alarmed. I'm just here to have a little chat with your ladyship is all. There's nothing to be overly concerned about at this juncture," Silas added, making sure Astrid knew there was to be no animosity between them.

"A *chat*?" Astrid asked Silas with a forewarning glare.

He wasn't entirely sure that he liked the sound of that. It felt ominous and vague. Silas hadn't exactly been crystal clear with his meaning but Astrid didn't like that he'd just shown up in Isra's bedroom of all places with this rather bizarre interest in his witch.

"Yes. A lot has commenced in the years since we haven't had the chance to converse but I am sure you are aware, I've always been loyal to the Grimsbane family as a familiar, and, well, Zelena Grimsbane wants a personal account from Isra on what happened to her beloved grandson, Alan," Silas explained in a low voice.

"Well, what happened to her dear old grandson isn't something we are willing to share," Astrid firmly asserted.

His shoulders were tense. His jaw was rigid. He was almost forming his hands into fists as he resisted the urge to punch something into oblivion.

So the Grimsbanes want revenge, huh? Well, she doesn't want information on what happened to her dearly departed grandchild for the sake of it. She wants to know Isra's part in it. Not only that, she wants the blow for blow account of what went down. Well, let's break it down, shall we? Alan courted Isra. Isra wasn't too receptive at first, but Alan convinced her otherwise. Alan then ditched Isra after she discovered his betrayal with none other than her nemesis, Everilda Daughtry. Isra was furious and killed the bastard. There you go, love, that's your in-depth personal account of what commenced between the two of them. Sorry, but it won't be what you want to hear.

Astrid cussed callously in his thoughts, already done with this little discussion of sorts. As far as he was concerned, it was over. There wasn't going to be any more elaboration on it. He felt incredibly protective of Isra, and now even more so since he sensed there was a potential threat to her safety.

"I understand you're vexed, Astrid, but Zelena simply wants to learn the truth."

Silas tried in vain to diffuse the situation. He knew his brother was short-tempered and often jumped to conclusions without having the complete picture of what was going on. However, Astrid was also very guarded. Especially if it pertained to something he hated to lose.

"Does she now? Do you have any idea of what that pathetic joke of a man did to Isra?" Astrid beseeched angrily as he defensively pointed his finger at Isra.

"I can speak for myself, love," Isra pointed out.

She flashed a nonchalant glare at Astrid. Her eyes flickered at him in an annoyed manner before she returned her attention to Silas, who presumably was waiting for her to start talking.

"It wasn't a pleasant experience but like you say, it is what it is. Sometimes life delivers us experiences we cannot handle as well as we think. Alan was the first person I laid eyes on in a very long time. Shortly before I turned nineteen, I had a bizarre experience whereby I cannot recall just over a year of my life; just after I switched to the dark side. All I remember is holding my battered heart up to the dark skies. The rest is somewhat of a blur," Isra told Silas candidly as she recalled her experience.

"Alan was the person that listened to me. I didn't feel like I was ridiculous or stupid at not being able to remember things. Alan dropped numerous cryptic hints over my transgression, indicating perhaps he knew what happened to me, but he wasn't very forthcoming either. However, he was charming and invited me over to his quaint little farmhouse in Immortal Yonder. We began courting. Albeit I was reluctant in him pursuing me at first, but eventually, I adjusted to the idea and then I discovered he had a relationship with my former best friend and hid it from me. He denied it despite Everilda practically screaming it herself... I saw all of the warning signs but then Alan became distant. He was odd in his demeanour. He was suddenly brash as well as conceited and then he discarded our union as nothing more than a sexual encounter. Suffice to say, I wasn't best pleased. Would you be upon receiving that news? Sorry, that wasn't a rhetorical question." Isra excused herself as she witnessed Silas's perplexed stare.

Silas motioned to Isra. "No, I understand. Please, do continue."

"I tried my utmost to be patient with the man. I didn't comprehend what had happened at first. I thought it was just some juvenile breakdown of communication because that type of thing does occur, you know? But he was so rigid after, even swearing blind that Everilda threatened him. But she has no powers. Wingdom's Academy saw to that, so I don't see what all the fuss was. My heart was torn, but I was comforted by Astrid... in his raven guise," Isra quickly added, although a picture was beginning to form in this elaborate story.

Astrid had somehow inserted himself in Isra's life as a raven just miraculously as this was all going down?

No, something doesn't smell right. Why would he be in the perfect place at the right time when Isra needed somebody most? There has to be some history between the two of them because Astrid felt the need to ditch his feathers in favour of a more desirable human form. He's not telling her everything, and one thing is for sure, she doesn't know the full story of how he manifested himself into her life. More importantly, it makes no sense whatsoever as to why a raven would indeed find himself romantically drawn to a witch. One wonders how that all came about but it's doubtful he will ever tell me. Astrid is a tricky soul when it comes to matters of the heart. He's very tight-lipped on that kind of thing. He's never been open about it before so I don't suspect he will start now, Silas thought as he considered the idea that perhaps Isra was a crush that had been acted upon. Truly, she didn't seem to be aware of it.

"And after that; no, well, sometime after..." Isra paused as she remembered the way Alan came to her door in that erratic fashion.

The poor man wasn't in control of his emotions. He'd truly let himself go. The simpering soul was wailing, creating all manner of chaos, shouting and screaming his undying love for me through the rooftops, but the irony was when I didn't give him the satisfaction, he decided to repay me with a deluge of insults. I wasn't going to take that lying down, was I? Isra surmised carefully in thought.

She didn't think she'd done anything terrible. Alan deserved what he got because he had been a real arse.

"Alan came back to me. He was a mess, really. I don't understand what got into him but he was weeping and begging for my forgiveness. When I wasn't receptive to his advances, he launched into a tirade of insults. Astrid tried to get me to cool off. But when Alan and I were left alone... Well, let's just say he wasn't on his best behaviour. One thing inevitably led to another," Isra coolly informed Silas.

"I hope that is enough for your employer to understand my role in this. I don't regret what happened, only the audacity of it all. Alan sadly did bring this upon himself," Isra finished curtly yet still was cordial and polite.

Astrid, on the other hand, was far from it. He couldn't hold in the venomous frustration any longer. "He got what he deserved. Trust me, he was a piece of work and he got it right in the ass. I won't miss the cocky bugger. That's for sure," he retorted in such a sardonic voice that Silas strongly held back from rolling his eyes.

"I think it will suffice," Silas kindly affirmed. "Well, kids, I have to get on. Things to do, you know? But I will be back if there is an update." He then spoke to Isra with fondness as he arched his wings in preparation for departing back over to good olde Immortal Yonder. "It was very nice to meet you, Isra. I hope my next visit won't be met by such an unfortunate circumstance."

"It was lovely to meet your acquaintance, Silas," Isra returned sweetly. *He seems such a nice fellow but more level-headed than his wingless counterpart. It's interesting as to why a man would want to give up his freedom in such a way to be condemned to spending eternity in a meat suit. But then again, I've never understood why humans so desperately want the things they cannot have. Anyhow, he's a nice chap. He'll report back to Zelena Grimsbane and perhaps we'll know how much trouble I'm really in. I don't regret my actions, as extreme as they were, but we'll see if I've got a fight on my hands,* Isra thought diligently to herself.

Of course, it totally slipped her mind that Astrid had come over to supposedly plunder her into indulging in lavish fancies. But at least Silas provided a very eye-opening view of what Astrid's humble beginning might have looked like. For Isra knew very little of the man she was allowing to court her.

Before Isra could allow her thoughts to wander any further, Astrid turned to her thoughtfully. He'd just watched his brother leave through Isra's open bedroom window and had a grim look planted across his face as though he was very much troubled over something. Isra didn't like this about Astrid. She detested the idea of him being sad but nonetheless, there was something preoccupying his mind.

"I must go..." he announced in a sombre tone. "I'll be back. I just need to fathom out something that's grating on me. It's nothing to be overly concerned about. Don't forget we have a rendezvous here, and I'm not one to go back on my word."

Astrid winked at her as he reached over to place his arm around her waist before swiftly making an exit.

Isra said nothing as she watched Astrid leave. His moody disposition was concerning but she knew he'd be back once he dealt with what he needed to.

~

ASTRID RAN INTO HIS BEDROOM, slamming the oak door behind him. He thudded his fists on his desk in fury and flung himself into his wooden chair in frustration. This latest instalment with Silas coming over to speak with Isra on behalf of Zelena Grimsbane was too much for Astrid to bear. He was absolutely seething. Beads of sweat dripped down his forehead as he reached for the Irish whiskey in a pander.

"Oresis!" Astrid called out angrily. "Get yourself over here, you son of a bitch! I want words with you."

Astrid eagerly poured himself a large glass of whiskey, not even stopping to catch a breath as he upturned the tumbler to his mouth, gulping down the lot without a care.

He heard a fluttering sound behind him along with a slightly modest yet impatient groan. Astrid turned his head to see Oresis sitting on the edge of his four-poster bed.

"I'd appreciate a little less of the name calling but I understand why you are angry with me, Astrid," Oresis started. His voice sounded apologetic as he awkwardly tried to reach Astrid in the most amicable way.

"It's not just the light that is after her now! The Grimsbane matriarch wants to know what happened with Alan. Then I discover this so-called 'on high' folk have held the meeting with Samuel, like you stated they would, but what isn't clear to me is whether they intend to punish Isra for her crime in murdering Alan Grimsbane."

Astrid moaned impetuously as he placed the tumbler back on the table. He'd been so focused on his anger he'd forgotten it was still clasped in his hand.

"Calm yourself. The light doesn't want Isra; at least not yet. They are asking a lot of questions as to why her powers weren't removed when she was a baby. Although that is no fault of her own. But they are very interested in what Samuel will do in an attempt to redeem himself," Oresis told Astrid in a formal manner.

He'd slowed his speech just enough so that Astrid could comprehend every single word he said.

Astrid suddenly glanced up. Something Oresis said caught his attention. His ears were on high alert. His mind was abuzz with the possibility that Samuel was actually being held responsible for this and not Isra. However, the light were not very well known for backing down when it came to giving somebody second and even third chances to rectify a situation whereby they'd make a real pig's ear of it.

"Yes, I am aware she was supposed to be made mortal when she was young but Samuel must have taken it upon himself not to do that to her. He was her legal guardian after all," Astrid rambled on, feeling the need to fetch himself another glass of that sweet, sticky alcoholic beverage that was sliding so well down his throat. But then again, he needed to be somewhat sober for his little engagement with Isra, so Astrid thought better of it.

"And will he want to do that?" Astrid pressed Oresis for the answer.

"The light has a funny way of handling these types of scenarios. She's a witch rooted in darkness. Daughter of the notorious warlock Damien Daughtry. I mean, am I wrong? They may suggest that Isra agree to a compromise of sorts, but Samuel will be given the chance to put it right because he wants to remain in power. If he doesn't act, and I can guarantee that he's been ordered in no uncertain terms to take action regarding this, he's in a whole world of chaos. It's the last thing he and the light wants. So yes, in some respects, Isra may have to face the music," Oresis advised with a look of caution as he stared right into Astrid's golden sheen eyes.

Oresis quickly changed his stance when he saw how worried Astrid immediately became. All of the colour evaporated from his face. Astrid was almost white as he shifted uncomfortably in his chair.

"I've done so much to keep her out of harm's way. I understand what she did was wrong, but if it all comes apart now... I've got nothing to even begin salvaging this," Astrid admitted with a low brow.

"Please be aware, we don't know everything yet. Your brother has to report back to his employer. After that, if there's going to be any follow-up, you'll soon be informed of it. As for Samuel, he's still a light-bringer, and you and Isra are both still dwelling here in Wretchenheart, where it is nigh impossible for him to reach her. It will take him a very long time to even piece together a strategy of how to proceed and even then, he may not be able to wrangle getting himself over here without some dire consequence to himself," Oresis warned, but still, he was doing all he could to explain what the potential outcome would be without adding to Astrid's already immense anxiety.

"Anyway, I am sorry for all this, but I must go," Oresis calmly asserted to Astrid. "Get back to Isra. Enjoy any happiness you two can share. I'll be around."

Before Astrid could react or even dispute Oresis abandoning him in this dire time of need, he vanished.

"Well, that is that then," Astrid muttered away to himself as he stood aimlessly in the empty bedroom.

11

Astrid knocked on Isra's bedroom door by rapping on it loudly. He'd only been gone for around ten minutes, but it felt longer. Heck, he didn't even have to knock. He could just simply let himself in but he wasn't at that stage with her yet, she'd have to let him into her life and her heart.

"Come in," Isra uttered sweetly.

Surprisingly, she was still sitting on the end of the bed, awaiting Astrid's return. The two coffees he'd placed on the table were still there in the exact way he'd left them. Astrid walked in and immediately eyeballed the two caffeinated beverages. He touched both mugs and found they were still hot, much to his intrigue. He expected them to have gone cold by now. He grabbed Isra's and presented it to her while also fetching his own as he sat on the bed next to her.

"So, there's a lot going on here. I understand completely if you don't want anything to do with me," Astrid started with a chuckle as he looked at her warmly. "I know a lot of this is confusing, and if I happen to be a reminder of all the chaotic crazy, perhaps you may not want to see me in your life in this manner," he continued, much to Isra's dismay as she could care less about his admission.

"It's nothing new to me. I've always known life to be like this in one way or another. It doesn't really matter. If it wasn't you, it would be some other drama right at the heart of me that threatens to yank everything away at the seams. I barely know you, Astrid, and yet some part of me knows you more than I dare to remember," Isra told him as she reached over to clasp her hand over his own.

"But that's not just all, is it?" Astrid probed. "You have both the light and possibly the Grimsbane clan wanting to see you fall. That's not just something you can wiggle your way out of. Sure, you're safe here for now but we don't know how long all of that will hold. You've been through more in your short nineteen years than I've known anyone to withstand and yet somehow through it all, you've been this powerful, magnetic force that takes it in stride other than the weeping that commenced after Alan," Astrid softly continued.

"Ha, Alan. I don't give him much thought," Isra confirmed in a low voice. "I imagine he's off somewhere in the netherworld, licking his wounds, but frankly, his consequence is his own. I don't have to justify it."

Isra motioned forward and Astrid seemed pleased she felt that way, so much so that he took her coffee cup out of her hand and placed it on the floor while also doing the same with his own. He figured they wouldn't be doing much drinking of anything with the pent-up urge that was racing through his body. His mind was abuzz with the notion of just reaching over slightly and placing his hand across her waist, hoping that she'd do the same in turn.

I don't think I can resist much longer. I want so badly to kiss her. For my lips to smack against hers ever so gently as I wrap her up in my passionate embrace. Our bodies sliding together as we meld in a perfect blend of magic. Plus, she's over Alan. Finally, I am so pleased it sunk in. She was so much better than the treatment he exacted upon her, Astrid thought as he pursued what he wanted to do next pertaining to him and Isra.

"You're over Alan? I am thrilled. That's excellent news," Astrid whispered in her ear as his two manly arms weaved themselves around Isra's waist and he ever so slowly leaned in so that his nose was almost touching hers and his lips were about an inch away from kissing her.

"I am dying to know what this feels like again," he said softly as he went in for the kill.

He felt the softness of her lips on his own as he delicately pulled Isra down onto the bed and she gently reciprocated his affection. He circled his tongue around hers. The kiss grew stronger and more intense as Astrid held her down onto the soft velvet purple covering. He ran his fingers through her soft, golden-white hair, gently pulling at her gown as Isra reached for his shirt, tugging at the collar in a bid to get it loose. However, Astrid was way ahead of her as he peeled her long velvet gown off her body, leaving Isra in her undergarments, much to his delight as he'd yearned to see this for so long.

"It feels so much different than what I imagined," Isra voiced huskily.

Her heart beat rapidly and she struggled to get out her words, but it didn't matter. Astrid reached over and yanked his black trousers off before drawing the curtain around Isra's four poster bed, pulling it all the way shut.

Silas saw the opened window left for him and proceeded to launch himself through the gap landing on Zelena's settee by the fireplace somewhat haphazardly.

"Oh, sorry about that. Long flight," Silas apologised.

Zelena barely looked up. She was reading a large deep violet tome but she acknowledged Silas's presence by grinning slightly as she chuckled.

"Oh, it's all right, Silas. Don't worry yourself. How was your trip?" she asked as she put down the large tome and removed her red-framed spectacles.

She only wore them for reading so they weren't needed for any other purpose. Despite being nearly four hundred years old, Zelena's eyesight was in remarkable stature.

"It was interesting," Silas began as he settled himself down, perching by the fireplace although he wasn't particularly cold but the cool summer breeze had hit him swiftly on his journey home. "Isra is quite the character. I'm afraid you may not like what I have to tell you, Zelena, but it appears young Alan was indeed courting Isra and hadn't exactly been transparent about a dalliance with her former best friend."

Silas was sure revenge was the focus for Zelena right now and knew what he had to say would be hard for her to hear.

"Please start from the beginning, Silas," Zelena instructed.

The old woman was sitting on her dark brown leather settee with a warm cup of tea in her hand that had gone a little cold due to being left idle while she read, but Silas could still smell the punchy raspberry flavour emitting from the shallow cup.

"Isra met Alan mysteriously in Immortal Yonder. It appears Isra went through quite the transgression. You see, she has no memory of the past twelve months, and Alan kindly answered some of her pressing queries although it wasn't enough to get her lost memories back. Alan became interested in Isra and thus they began courting," Silas slowly explained, recalling what Isra told him.

"But Alan failed to disclose he had a rather failed dalliance with Isra's former best friend, and that friend also threatened Alan, promising to disclose all to Isra if he didn't immediately stop delighting in fancies with her. Alan refused to cooperate with the witch's demands, but the witch went to Isra anyway and she discovered Alan's cruel betrayal."

Zelena threw him a disapproving look. "Unfortunately, I happen to know of this failed relationship. It was Everilda Daughtry, and you know how much trouble that family is to us. Well, at least Damien Daughtry anyway, but she's his daughter and I hear she somehow lost her powers. Of course, I don't follow these things, but being made mortal after making a mistake isn't something that should be taken lightly. But it turns out Alan courted Isra? All right, please do tell me more, Silas," Zelena said warmly as she went to take a sip of her lukewarm tea.

"It should have ended there with Alan admitting the truth, but alas, he did not. In fact, he broke the relationship off with Isra, suggesting it was nothing more than an infatuation. Astrid, my brother, told me how heartbroken Isra was. Apparently, she's a fragile soul despite her complicated resume but Alan made the stupendous mistake of returning to Isra's home in Shambre Fell to try and win her over. She wasn't receptive to him since she was done with the matter but he persisted and because she wasn't taking it the way he wanted, he resorted to tearing her down... or shall we say attempting to?"

Zelena let out a pent-up sigh. "Oh, goodness. I can see where this is headed." The old woman let out another drawn-out sigh. "Alan was always a hit with the noble women but unfortunately, he lacked the finesse to treat them with respect. I can very much predict how this went down, much to my shame," Zelena remarked dryly.

"Isra tolerated a vast deluge of insults until she had enough and then poor dear old Alan was no more," Silas confirmed soberly. "It's not the best of ends but even I can relate to why she did that. I imagine it's not much comfort to you hearing this, and I understand you may well still want revenge against her, but I must remind you that Astrid is my brother. I agree he's taken things too far with his dynamic with this Isra but I cannot become involved in something that causes great harm towards somebody my brother cares greatly for. I'm afraid it's just not in my nature."

Silas finished in a low voice. He didn't want to have to say it. It was awkward for him to have to justify Astrid's actions at the best of times, but this one was too close to home.

"No, I'm not seeking revenge. At least not now. I'm a very old lady, Silas. Revenge does little to remedy my heart. It cannot absolve someone from what they've truly lost. While I do mourn my grandson, I can't help but feel sympathy for Isra's plight. In fact, I may need you to facilitate an arrangement for Isra to come here to Immortal Yonder," Zelena expressed warmly.

She felt some mild comfort despite the abhorrent circumstances and she did feel some warped loyalty, for she knew Isra suffered significantly prior to her becoming acquainted with Alan.

"Come again?" Silas questioned with a furrowed brow.

He was shocked to say the least. He'd expected her to be vengeful but instead here she was, displaying compassion and warmth towards the woman who brutally murdered her grandson.

"I want to meet this charming young lady. Damien Daughtry's daughter or not. That's not her misgiving and neither should it be. Please, go back and arrange this for me, Silas. I shall not put you in any more uncomfortable positions after this, and if you wish, you don't have to comply. But it would be greatly appreciated if you could undertake this small task on my behalf," Zelena instructed with a smile and then softly added, "It would mean the world. I don't mean to impose on your brother's magnificent world. Muddling around in people's private lives is not my cup of tea, as you know, but this is a matter of great importance."

"I will do anything you say, Zelena, you know that. I've given you many loyal years of service but I think the best course of action to follow here is for me to fly back to Shambre Fell and speak with Astrid before we go any further," Silas advised in an assertive manner before he turned to face the window, sighing as he felt a rumble down in the pit of his stomach.

"I suppose I could stop for some worms before I set off," Silas suggested, knowing he'd be setting off again before he even had a chance to snatch himself up some lunch.

"Thank you, Silas," Zelena replied in a kind voice. "You're a good friend. It brings comfort to this old heart of mine," she said softly.

ASTRID AND ISRA'S bodies were entwined with one another when a loud rapping could be heard from the glass windowpane, much to Astrid's annoyance as he was having quite the time with her.

"Who the heck could that be?" Astrid quizzed the dazed Isra, who was nestled in between him and the bed covering. Her head lay upon his chest and she could hear his heart beating peacefully as she rested comfortably while wrapped in the silken dark purple sheets.

"I have no idea. Your brother again perhaps? I did leave the window open just in case," Isra murmured softly.

She hadn't known Astrid's brother for very long but already she was very fond of him. Silas had an endearing nature, which ultimately made Isra feel she had known him for many years despite only conversing for a few moments. That was a true bond that had to be treasured in her mind because you could only have that with so very few.

"Hmm. Yes, that is a possibility. But why would he be back so soon? Surely Zelena Grimsbane hasn't made a decision this fast?" Astrid questioned again.

The rapping continued, followed by a sarcastic drawl.

"Oh, Astrid. I can hear you in there!" Silas called out with a somewhat amused tone from where he was perched on the windowsill.

Astrid panicked. He was in quite the state of undress; only having a silk sheet to cover his modesty, and he was sure his brother didn't need to see him this way, especially since Silas wouldn't be fully used to Astrid's humanised form just yet.

"I'm not decent!" Astrid yelled out. *I hope he understands my meaning. He has feathers instead of flesh so it may totally go over his head,* Astrid muttered away to himself in an awkward fashion.

"Yes, well, you never have been. Can I come in?" Silas requested.

He neared the edge of the delicate four poster bed that Astrid and Isra were very cosy underneath those silk sheets with nothing else for cover. Silas was just inches away from pulling back that curtain to reveal the two love birds, an event Astrid was trying to avoid as he never for one moment suspected he'd be caught in the middle of sexual intercourse by anyone, let alone his brother.

"No. I'm *naked!*" Astrid screeched from his position as he lay on the bed. "And so is Isra!"

"Oh, that sounds horrific. Well, best get on. Come on! Chop, chop.

I have news," Silas pestered without paying much interest in Astrid's somewhat bemusing predicament.

"No, I mean I have no *clothes* on," Astrid uttered in exasperation; holding that sheet as close as he could to his secluded areas.

Silas had no sympathy for Astrid's plight and simply commented, "Yes, well, that's what you get for trading feathers for flesh. Throw something on, quick now!"

"All right, all right. Keep your hair on!" Astrid blundered awkwardly, reaching down and picking up Isra's gown for her to put on while he threw on his trousers and shirt. To be fair, he still looked dishevelled but it would do considering the time contingency placed upon him.

"Oh, really?!" Isra moaned. She didn't sound terribly impressed at being moved from Astrid's chest so abruptly.

"Yes," he told her sternly. *Trust me, I am not happy about it either but needs must. I fucking hate that expression.*

"Fine," Isra growled and allowed Astrid to pull her dress over her head, instantly covering her fine body underneath the heavy, thick velvet she had become so accustomed to.

"All right," Astrid muttered, pulling back the curtain of the bed as he walked out with his shirt buttons entirely undone.

"Well, it's better than before, I suppose," Silas rambled impatiently, wanting to get on with the proceedings.

"Isra," Silas turned to her thoughtfully with a warm glance, "I have good news, and what you may interpret as bad news but ultimately the choice is yours to do as you please," he informed her curtly.

"Aha, not what I had expected, so what is it?" she asked with a questionable look as her piercing lime-green eyes narrowed at Silas without meaning to.

"My employer, Zelena Grimsbane, has no intention of moving forward with any grudges towards you but..." Silas paused awkwardly, "she does want to meet you."

Astrid immediately jumped in. "Oh, hell no. No chance! That is not happening under my watch," he barked furiously.

He was still standing by the bed but now he had his arms folded across his chest in an aggressive stance. *No bleeding way is that going to happen. No! It's a one-way ticket to hell's doom and we're not having that. Well, I am not. We're not going to be seduced by the sob story of some old woman who is in bereavement. How stupid does she think Isra is? Or me for that matter?* Astrid ranted angrily in his thoughts.

"Hang on, Astrid." Isra cautioned him with a serious glare. "Let us at least see what she wants. How can there be any harm in that?"

She motioned in Silas's direction as if to ask the raven if there would be any consequences from her making such a decision but without actually asking him.

"There won't be in any way, shape, or form. Zelena assures me of that fact and has given credence to it," Silas formally affirmed in his low voice that was just about audible when he knew he needed to be serious about something but also loud enough for people to hear.

Astrid turned to Isra with a forewarning glance. "This is suicide, Isra. We know Samuel wants to latch onto you, and if you go to see this lady, he might just be able to catch you," he said gravely. His face was pale and full of foreboding.

"It's in Immortal Yonder," Silas advised softly.

"That's still dangerous," Astrid uttered solemnly. He hadn't relaxed his stance, still having his arms folded across his chest.

"Actually, it's not. Immortal Yonder is only accessible to a witch. It's a secret realm of sorts because only those who truly wield the witch or warlock power can enter," Isra retorted in lieu with Silas's admission.

"Samuel's got himself in there before," Astrid warned her. "Ultimately, it's up to you but I must advise that I also attend this meeting of sorts, just so that I can be sure there is no harm; whether indirect or otherwise intended towards you." *Oh, I am going if she is. It's going to be better that way as I can ensure for certain there are no surprises,* Astrid thought as he looked in on Silas and Isra, still having his arms folded as he didn't trust any of this at all.

12

"All right," Astrid instructed Isra in a stern tone, "we're finding that veil that goes to Immortal Yonder, and then we are finding the Grimsbane mansion. I will be with you at all times, and you best not expect anything less," he uttered as he led Isra by the hand.

They were walking through the clearing just beyond Shambre Fell. Silas accompanied them also as he flew above, staying at a very close distance much to Astrid's annoyance; he felt Silas was judging him.

They weren't headed that way since they'd come from Seclara, which was pretty freaking dangerous. Spirisity was just over the bend from here. Isra wasn't supposed to be anywhere near there, so Astrid wanted to ensure they got to their destination fast and were gone again before anyone noticed. Of course, Isra didn't fully understand the severe danger or threat, so Astrid had to take charge.

"Fine, but it's somewhere around here," Isra said.

She extended her right hand in mid-air, feeling around gently as she honed in on the energy. She closed her eyes. It had been a while since Isra was here, but she remembered it from the very first time. There had been that secluded area by the trees and then a small archway which she walked straight through while feeling some tingly sensation of something passing through her. That was the time she first stumbled upon its existence and met Alan.

Now it would be considerably different since they were heading through the veil, but they had to walk along past the farmhouse where Silas would guide them the rest of the way. That's why he was coming along—only he knew the area well enough, and despite Astrid insisting on being there to protect Isra, he didn't know where they were headed either.

Isra felt something ever so slightly touch her hand. *Oh, that's it. That's the one. Magnetic yet surreal but just enough to convince yourself that you aren't crazy.* She chuckled to herself as she proceeded to lead the way, walking in with Astrid. Silas entered also.

"Now it's here, but we've got to walk around the lake and past the farmhouse. Silas, I believe it's over to you," Isra calmly announced as they began striding past the deep midnight-blue lake.

It was as she looked overhead whilst still attached to Astrid that she caught sight of the glorious sunset glistening from above. Those deep red and warm orange tones seemed brighter as she looked around for the familiar yellow and pink she'd seen on her last visit here. However, it seemed to be somewhat lacklustre as she looked up to see mustard-yellow instead of the usually serene golden shimmer.

Strange, I wonder if that is the effect of me killing Alan? Still, I guess it isn't important but I used to love staring up at that sunset, Isra thought to herself.

Astrid halted her out of it by pulling her after him as he had noticed her dawdling. "Come on, we don't have much time. I don't want anyone to be aware of your presence here," he cautioned.

"Oh, be quiet, children! Here we are," Silas uttered.

Just beyond the farmhouse, Isra saw what looked like a larger than-life-building, only it looked as if it was miles away and they'd already done so much walking.

Isra chuckled merrily. "Why couldn't we just magic ourselves here, anyway?"

"Because magic is easily traced. Samuel's eyes and ears could be anywhere, and James is likely his top lookout now since I've retired from the role. I can't have him finding you," Astrid told her plainly.

"Keep walking, folks!" Silas called out to them from above. He soared higher to get a keen eye-view of their destination.

Eventually, after what seemed like forever, the large prominent building stood out; Isra and Astrid finally arrived. You couldn't miss the brilliant white cottage-like exterior with dark brown wood framing the windows and doors. Then just outside the front door lay miniature plant pots decorating the outside while a grey stone lion guarded the eccentric Grimsbane mansion beyond the blood-red front door.

Isra felt anxious. She edged closer to it but before she could even express this deep-seated feeling of nervousness, she noticed a grey-haired woman materialise outside the red door, which bemused Isra greatly as she hadn't expected that.

"Hello. My name is Zelena."

Zelena introduced herself warmly. She wore a very heavy, thick black cotton gown with lace edging at the sleeves. This was her usual attire since her husband, Lethaniel, had passed on.

"Isra…"

Isra breathed meekly. *Oh, golly, that's her; the woman whose grandson I just took out of this world.* Isra took a moment to gather her thoughts but she was not the only one thinking it.

Astrid caught Zelena staring at him in a bemused manner. Her watchful sapphire-blue eyes glanced up at him as she hadn't expected anyone else other than Isra and Silas.

Well, here we are, people. This is the grand duchess herself; let's see what she has to say, but I'm coming right in there with her. Isra, that is.

"Isra, it's nice to finally have made your acquaintance. Please don't be alarmed. I, too, wish this could be in better circumstances, but it is what it is. Come on in, dear," she offered as she held the door open for Isra, Astrid, and Silas to enter the premises.

"Oh, you must be Astrid!" Zelena greeted him formally.

She hadn't recognised her charming male guest at the door but proceeded with pouring hot lemon and ginger tea for her special visitors before she sat on the middle of her enormous couch after indicating that her guests were welcome to seat themselves. Of course, the fire roared happily so Zelena's living room was beautifully warm for an evening whereby they were already in August.

"Yes, I am," he cordially mouthed.

He didn't trust Zelena's intentions and felt that there was something shady lurking beneath her warm and sweet demeanour, as though it was a ploy of some sort to try and engage Isra into speaking far too much than what was necessary to give the light ammunition to strike. Mind you, Astrid was very much the sceptical type. He'd claw their eyeballs out first and ask questions later. That was just his way.

"Good to meet you, dear. Silas has always spoken of you so fondly," Zelena wistfully remarked before turning to Isra with a slight open smile. She didn't want to appear too kind but did indeed want to question Isra. However, it was only to gather the full story from Isra's perspective, not to interrogate the young witch. "So Isra, Silas has indeed told me the mere details but I want to hear from you as to what exactly happened. I hope you can appreciate that me inviting you into my home like this isn't to cause you any distress. I understand Alan was deeply problematic when it came to the ladies, so pardon any intrusion. Nevertheless, I do need to know," Zelena began openly requesting Isra to tell her story.

Isra took a breath for a second. She was taken aback by this but she gently took a sip of her hot tea, cradling the porcelain teacup in her hands before she mouthed softly, "It was so fast. I had landed in Immortal Yonder, not even realising it was this magical realm, and he was just there. He came out of nowhere, startling me with the way he just majestically materialised out of thin air. He very much knew who I was before he asked my name, as he mentioned a witch who was under a mystical stronghold that everyone over there had heard of."

"Yes, dear. I know of this tale as well. Please do continue," Zelena calmly expressed.

"Alan invited me over for some of his famous cookies that very same night. I was shocked because I'd only recently discarded a man who had betrayed me and so my heart wasn't very open. Needless to say, I came and he was very endearing and we became close. It started with a couple of visits and before I knew it, we were a couple of sorts. It wasn't the most conventional relationship, you understand, as at the time, behind my back, my ex-nemesis Everilda was blackmailing Alan about their previous history and how she was going to disclose it to me. But you see, I had no idea of any of this at the time!"

Isra paused as she recalled Alan being so emotionally numb with her that she couldn't figure out what was wrong with him... or her as she presumed at the time.

"As it turned out, Everilda was getting to Alan mentally despite being a very much desolate mortal now that she had got in his head. He practically wanted nothing to do with me overnight. Alan was restless, anxious, and all over the place in his behaviour. He became something I didn't recognise. He lost that fun, charming vibe I loved so much when we first met and then he did the inevitable and discussed that I was nothing more than a mere infatuation."

Isra stopped for a moment to contain herself. She felt a tiny pang of guilt lingering inside her heart. Although it was just for a few seconds, it was enough to send vast pain into her chest and she felt unable to continue until she regained her composure. It was so little, but just focusing on that memory made Isra realise she was more vulnerable than she had allowed herself to believe she was.

Yeah, she could actually crack at any moment. It's a good thing I am here, Astrid thought candidly as he watched Isra struggle to follow through. He'd been observing her from the moment she entered the living room. She was a ball of fiery nerves. She wasn't okay, and she seemed very off-colour from the usually bold Isra that he knew.

"Needless to say, this pushed me to the brink, and so I wept many tears," Isra added after the brief awkward two-minute silence.

Zelena was already sympathising with Isra as she elaborated bluntly, "As have many others, dear."

"Right, and so I believed that was the end of it. He'd toiled with my heart but Astrid was supporting me. Of course, I didn't know he was into this shape-shifting stuff then or know anything about him at all really, but I was slowly healing, you know? And then that fateful morning... Alan came by my place and he was erratic. He begged for my forgiveness and then when I didn't respond the way he wanted, well, he started insulting me. Accusing me of being unfeeling and harsh. Then it escalated further. He couldn't stop. I had to do something; he was sending me to crazy town with his constant yammering of how bent out of shape he was feeling this way for me, blah blah. Typical male, you get the idea. So I just flared a few lightning bolts at him and encased him in an energetic prison to keep him at bay. I wasn't intending to harm him."

Isra made that final part astutely clear. It wasn't her aim to injure or cause bodily harm to Alan at all but he literally hadn't shut up with his tirade of insults toward her.

Isra paused again as she solemnly recalled the event in which she struck him so violently before continuing. "And so eventually, my resolve broke. I don't wish to detail it explicitly, but I lost my mind for a brief moment and after, well, it was too late," she expressed honestly.

"I understand," Zelena addressed Isra softly. "Well, I appreciate that it was swift, even if he did provoke you, which I believe, as you tell it, he did. So I guess that puts paid to that, but Alan wasn't completely there. He had a very disturbing relationship with his parents. His mom abandoned him so young and then his auntie, well, she didn't exactly do herself any favours when she went off with that married warlock, Damien Daughtry."

"Daughtry?" Isra piped up. "That's Everilda's father?"

"It is, but Gwendolyn wasn't like that. She wasn't the fly-by-night type. She was such a prim and proper girl but after she ran off with Daughtry, she wasn't the same. The child that was born as a result of their calamity was handed over to Samuel Reynaldi. It's all very sad, but it deeply messed up the Passe lineage, really," Zelena drawled on.

"A baby was handed to Samuel Reynaldi?" Astrid questioned Zelena with a wide-eyed glare. He had heard this story very recently but wanted to confirm it was indeed the same one before he launched his own attack on Samuel.

"Yes, she was Alan's cousin, but we never laid eyes on her. She was removed from all of us until she properly came of age. They were deemed to remove her powers but alas, it never happened," Zelena coarsely explained. She didn't enjoy recalling the disaster of family lines to a stranger but it gave her comfort in her elder years to express her story to someone else.

"Oh, my goodness!" Astrid blurted out.

His face completely dropped. It was almost as if he'd have fallen onto the floor at any moment, as he knew very well that Isra was Damien's illegitimate offspring.

"What?" Isra suddenly latched on to his shocked expression. She had no inclination of why he was so gobsmacked, but then Zelena calmly filled in the missing piece.

"Oh my, Isra..." Zelena clasped her hand to her mouth in horror, recoiling at her previous statement.

"Exactly!" Astrid joined her shock in unison.

"*You* were the one under Samuel's charge, were you not, dear?" Zelena quizzed Isra as she awaited the answer with bated breath.

"I was. Well, I sort of still am. It's a long and bewildering story but being in Wretchenheart, Astrid assures me I am safe from his ghastly hands, even if I don't know all of the events that led to him wanting to capture me," Isra recited calmly.

"Dear girl, you *are* under Samuel Reynaldi's care, and there is only one young female witch that was handed over to that man nineteen years ago!" Zelena admitted.

"It's me, isn't it?" Isra gasped. "I've sordidly courted my cousin and never knew of it."

Astrid interrupted Isra and Zelena briefly as he confirmed what they both needed to know earnestly. "They never reached the stage where removing clothing was required."

Zelena expressed a sigh of relief. "Thank goodness."

"Yes," Isra joined her, "but can we please get back to the fact I am

Damien Daughtry's daughter and why *you* didn't tell me, Astrid?" Isra probed with a furrowed brow.

She was beginning to trust Astrid increasingly and this significant bombshell could possibly push all of that away. She was struggling to comprehend the facts that had been presented to her although it was becoming clear Zelena knew about Gwendolyn Passe. And so, for the first time, Isra could find out something about her mother as information relating to that had been extremely limited since childhood.

"I've only known for just over a week," Astrid stammered somewhat awkwardly. "I'd have told you sooner but there was the whole getting you out of Shambre Fell before Samuel could roast you and put you up on a mantle bit, and so I didn't because I was preoccupied. I'm sorry," he muttered.

"And Everilda is my sister?" Isra quizzed Zelena, although she wasn't entirely sure if she could trust this woman yet.

"Half-sister," Zelena confirmed. "Your mother is Gwendolyn Passe, and your grandmother is Evanora Passe-Somersby. Double-barrelled, as she married a witch in retirement named Denzil. Unfortunately, Samuel Reynaldi was gunning for her as well."

"He was? Like he has been me? I mean, Zelena, there are events in my life that I cannot even remember. It's like he doesn't want me to know," Isra said in a sad, weak voice. "This is not my style. I am supposed to be the strong, powerful one. Hell, I am a frigging queen! But yet there is this part of me that's so confused about who I am. It's unnerving."

"He pursued Evanora for years. She still resides with her husband, Denzil. I could perhaps discuss you with her if you'd like. I know I brought you here to question you, Isra, but I do believe this is an opportunity for you to finally get some answers on your past so that maybe you can consolidate your future. As for the light, I wouldn't worry too much. They will try all they can, but taking down witches, especially you," Zelena narrowed her eyes on Isra carefully as she spoke, "is a very difficult task indeed because you've gone past the point of no return."

Isra blushed. "I'm still embarrassed I was courting my cousin."

Zelena reached over and grabbed Isra's hand. "Then let us keep that scandalous knowledge between us. Nobody has to know."

"You know, there is another informal hearing coming up for Samuel Reynaldi regarding you and how he lost his way because he couldn't keep a grip on you. I am happy to speak up in your defence of whatever counterattack he has planned," Zelena admonished in a low voice. "We shall not discuss what has happened here today, Isra. It will not go back to anyone outside of this room. In the meantime, I will contact Evanora and try to get you two together. Perhaps we can come to your castle in Wretchenheart so that it will be safer."

Zelena looked over at Astrid with a wink as she muttered, "I am sure your man is anxious to get you back over there and us conversing is surely making him nervous. But I do give you my assurance, Isra. We may have met in bewildering circumstances, however, no malice resides in my heart."

Astrid breathed a sigh of relief. "Oh, that I am!" he mustered boldly.

"Silas will report to you if and when we have news," Zelena quipped in Isra's direction. "He's very happy to assist me and he's no stranger to the loyal service of being here, there, and everywhere."

13

Zelena Grimsbane was on a mission. She had a full discussion with Lady Isra of the Dark and while she accepted that Isra had indeed played her part, so had her ill-fated grandson, Alan Grimsbane. So, instead, Zelena offered to reunite Isra with her maternal grandmother, Evanora Passe-Somersby much to Isra's surprise. Zelena felt moved by the amount of tragedy that had occurred in young Isra's life and so she decided revenge was no longer her focus.

Zelena was now hell-bent on discovering more about how Alan and Isra had come to court in the first place. She believed Samuel Reynaldi had, in some way, manipulated Alan, as they had held two private meetings at Samuel's dwelling in Spirisity, but Samuel had been very sketchy about his involvement. This made Zelena suspicious because surely if the man had nothing to hide, then he wouldn't have asked Alan to keep their engagements quiet. Zelena was trying to fathom if anyone else knew anything that might shed light on this matter.

She was a very high-profile witch at just around three hundred years old and so she had plenty of associates in both the witchcraft realm and the love and light brigade, as Isra so fondly called it. The old woman knew if she prodded hard enough, she could get something that would place hard-nosed Reynaldi on a very slippery slope; the famous "on high" was already investigating him, much to his dismay, but Zelena strongly believed if she dug deep enough, she'd get enough insight to not only provide evidence to "on high" that went against Reynaldi but also be able to confront him, something she desperately wanted to do despite the grandmotherly endearment she had shown towards Isra.

And to do just that, she needed a little bit of assistance; enter in her long-time, loyal servant, Silas.

Silas was instructed to spy on Samuel and capture anything that looked unorthodox and to report back to Zelena. Zelena also affixed a powerful charm amulet onto Silas that he would drop securely into Samuel Reynaldi's home whereby it would conflict the light-bringer if he didn't tell the truth. Zelena was covering all bases with this one, and she wasn't going to stop until she had what she needed.

Silas set out just after eight in the evening. He figured that would be the best time to take a stroll into Spirisity. The skies had a significant amount of cloud cover so Silas was well hidden as he launched himself up in the air. After a while, he caught sight of the eccentric, grey, tall château and the mass of yellow crocuses dominating the dark green grass that was just about visible in the darkness.

He paid great attention to the distinct location of Samuel's fortress by listening to Zelena's keen instructions on exactly how to bypass all of the shortcuts to get to the neighbouring window whereby Samuel's office was to be found. Silas cleverly dropped the tiny charm just on the window ledge, out of sight in the corner where it wouldn't be seen, and he waited to see what would develop on this fine evening.

He sat on the edge of the window ledge and spotted two men in avid conversation. One of them was clearly Samuel Reynaldi. There was no doubting it as that famous slicked black hair was unmistakable. Silver-framed half-moon spectacles sat upon his nose while he glanced over at his occupant with his bright blue eyes.

The other person wasn't someone Silas recognised, so he figured it was the long-time aide, James. That mousy brown hair creeping over tiny red-framed spectacles that just about made his green eyes visible indicated it was the person Astrid had accurately described although there were some tones of resentment, but Silas hadn't expected anything less from his brother.

"Isra is out of sight, however 'on high' are intervening more," Samuel muttered with a low brow.

His favourite decanter of Irish whiskey sat idly on his wooden desk while two crystalline glass tumblers were presented next to it. It was at the dead of night so it didn't seem like a terrible time for Samuel to have himself a drink. James was reluctant to join in; of course, he took his job more seriously than Samuel. However, Samuel insisted on pouring James one so he couldn't exactly refuse.

"Down the hatch, boy!" Samuel chuckled as he poured the whiskey into the two tumblers, handing one to James and clasping the other in his dominant hand.

"Thanks, but it's a little early for me," James rebuffed.

"Nonsense, boy," came Samuel's gruff answer. "Come on now, it's been a torturous week. At least do me the favour of indulging in a little debauchery. It might ease the mood."

James stiffly took a look at his glass, taking care to sniff the contents inside before softly taking a sip of it. He found it to be not as unpleasant as he had expected as it travelled down the back of his throat and down into his intestines with a ferocious low growl.

Silas was bored with the chicanery, but at least he knew that when two men drank, it was also when they both talked. *If there is any tasty tidbit for me to know about, then tonight the masks come off. And the truth shall be unleashed,* Silas thought, having the knowledge that this was going to be a very long night.

It was after a few seconds of beseeched silence that James finally spoke. "Do you think we can latch onto Isra with all of these obstacles standing in our way?"

"A man that focuses on success in such a way that he cannot comprehend anything but not being successful will never attain his desire. We'll get her. In time. I am just not so sure how. Yet." Samuel motioned in James's direction as he reached over, fetching himself another glass of his favourite tipple.

"In the meantime, I have the battle of my eternal life unfolding at my feet. 'On high' will truly pull out all of the stops to knock me off my pedestal if they suspect for one second that I contributed in any way to the death of Alan Grimsbane," Samuel remarked candidly before he got back to the matter of importance. The reason why he was facing defeat at this incredulous moment.

"Zelena Grimsbane is a remarkable foe. She's at the top of the hierarchy and with that comes a woman who wields an immense amount of power. Far greater than Isra, and certainly more than I can muster. And to her, a light-bringer like me, despite all my years working in this space, I'm just a rat to her. I'm just a rodent. Small fry. I don't count," Samuel expressed softly. "It is what it is, boy. There's no point getting blubbery about it. That solves nothing when it comes to facing facts. And face the truth we must, for my position as a light-bringer is indeed under threat."

Silas's ears pricked up. *Aha, so Zelena was right. Moody men in desolation do talk and boy, do they talk about the right things! My goodness. Talk about dropping the apple right into the deceiver's hand,* he thought. He was shocked at what had just landed indirectly into his lap.

"And they do have their own ideas about this. I know many eyes and ears are making themselves known at this time. It won't be over until the fat lady sings," Samuel chided sarcastically. "That bitch will be stone-cold dead by the time the inevitable commences. It's just the way the cookie crumbles. Life. Death. How does any of it matter? I've already been around for two hundred years. It seems so trivial to me. So meaningless," Samuel continued wistfully.

"But you did attempt to manoeuvre a proposed union with Isra and Alan right, and 'on high' aren't aware of that? So all should be well," James implied with an earnest tone as he accepted a freshly poured glass of the golden brown liquid Samuel generously gave to him.

"Theoretically. Yes," Samuel piped up, but his expression quickly turned into a frown, which prompted James to question further.

"Why do I get the feeling this is more complicated than you are making out?" James quizzed with a scrutinising glare.

"Astrid is going to be an even bigger problem. He's been quite the thorn in our side for some time. He rebelled against everything we stood for, and it's because of him that Isra has succeeded for as long as she has," Samuel explained in a gruff voice. "To get to her, we have to vanquish Astrid."

"And that won't be easy."

He, too, had been privy to Astrid's anarchist behaviour long before they'd been able to stronghold Isra, a metaphysical prison that even she had managed to get out of, no thanks to Astrid coming along and reminding her of who she was.

"Not with them holed out in Wretchenheart, no. I know you went there to spy on them both once but it was risky and you could have been killed. I can't go there. That's for sure," Samuel remarked, sounding slightly irritated at the predicament looming in front of them.

"Plucky Isra, eh? She's taken Grimsbane out of the picture, eh? Danced with the darkness. Crushed her enemies. She's now ruling a demon dimension with Astrid? An impressive resume for a nineteen-year-old; and tell me again why you couldn't stop her? Bloody useless. All of you," he chided.

James had been responsible for notifying "on high" that Isra had indeed gone off the rails with Astrid and thus Samuel was able to disarm her but it wasn't going to be that easy this time. The situation had expanded way beyond impossible.

"Your intended plan had been that Isra would marry this Alan lad, and that was your way to keep her away from Astrid? Had it worked, he'd still be fluttering around in his raven form." James scoffed ardently. He'd come to the conclusion over why Samuel had done what he'd enacted but, of course, there would be great consequences because of it.

"Yes. And, boy, did the young chap refuse. He hesitated from the get-go. I couldn't even convince him that this union was a good idea. Still, thankfully, it was a secret only held between me, him, and now you." Samuel finally finished with a grin.

Errrr, not anymore, old son! Silas chuckled away to himself in thought. *The cat is out of the bag now. Well, unless there is more to discover, I better get right back over to Zelena. She sure knows how to get what she wants. Very respectable lady!* Silas murmured as he turned away from the window, launching himself into the cloudy midnight-blue skies.

Now it would only be a matter of time before Zelena came to confront Samuel herself. A meeting that was for sure going to change the outcome of his fated upcoming hearing with "on high," better known as the Sanctification of the Unseen, but Samuel didn't know of their true identity.

~

SAMUEL WAS STILL DRINKING MERRILY in his office. James was also still seated with him since James's presence brought a small shred of comfort to the light-bringer in his unsettling time of need. However, Silas had flown back to Zelena Grimsbane just over four hours ago, and now Samuel's sordid world was about to be blown apart.

It was just striking midnight—the witching hour, as it was collectively known. Nobody suspected for a moment that there would be any purpose to tonight's festivities other than an employee and his boss knocking back copious amounts of ye olde Irish whiskey. Samuel's favourite tipple. He seldom drank anything else as it wasn't good enough for his morally important high standards. As usual, it was part of his holier-than-thou attitude.

But no one could have prepared for the surprise that was coming. Samuel's dimly lit office was saturated in darkness already when his candles began wildly flickering. Thinking it was just a bewildering occurrence, he turned thoughtfully to James and suggested, "Oh, it must be awfully windy out there!"

However, it was a night in August, so it was highly unlikely that the cause of this was nature's elements. Now a swooshing, whirring sound echoed throughout the room, causing Samuel to screech out, "What the hell?"

He and James placed their hands upon their ears as the sound was so eerie. Could you imagine something scratching down on a wooden board and then shrieking wildly? That was exactly what this sounded like, and it was getting worse by the second! Wailing could be heard along with the whooshing. If Samuel wasn't wise beyond his years, he'd assume this was some otherworldly spirit that had got lost between the realms, but he knew better.

The darkness of his dimly lit office was overpowering the tiny amount of light as the vast swishes of wind could be heard alongside all of this commotion. Then his main candle by the window ledge miraculously came back to life as if by magic and so did all the others.

Samuel scratched his head in bemusement. He hadn't expected something so bizarre, especially when the seasons didn't call for such an occurrence. Samuel turned his attention back to his empty whisky tumbler and leaned over to fetch his decanter when he suddenly caught sight of black murky smoke lingering in the middle of the room. After a moment, Zelena Grimsbane stood triumphantly glaring back at him, which instantly put him on edge, causing him to yank the decanter of whiskey into his hand and immediately rush to pour himself one as he eyed her cautiously.

"Oh, fuck!" Samuel could be heard murmuring under his breath, but it was loud enough for James to hear.

He uttered awkwardly, "Miss Zelena Grimsbane, one would presume? I am James."

"Yes, well, I can't say I care much for that, dear."

Zelena ambushed James's introduction and manoeuvred over to where Samuel was seated in his red velvet armchair before she yelled at him, pointing her finger in his direction in an accusatory manner. "Samuel Reynaldi. You lied to me," she barked at him.

Samuel didn't know where to look. Needless to say, because Zelena was hollering at him in his domicile and not somewhere she had been, he had nowhere to run or hide. *How the hell am I going to wheedle out of this one? She's standing right by me. Shit. All right, Samuel, pull yourself together. It's not the end of the world. Well, not yet anyway. There has to be some way to stifle this chaotic fiery woman who happens to be standing before me*, he thought as he put up one heck of a defence.

"I have not lied to you," he said plainly. "And please, do enlighten me on how you seem to think otherwise. It may well assist the both of us," he muttered sardonically.

Zelena turned her nose upwards, much to James's peculiarity. He was the one closest to her. The last thing he wanted was to get caught in the crossfire between Samuel and a matriarch witch that could turn him into a horned toad. He wouldn't look good covered in warts, that was for sure.

"You attempted to encourage Alan to court Isra. Oh, and you thought you had covered this up, but oh no, Mr Reynaldi. I have many beady eyeballs dotted all over the place," Zelena asserted firmly as she folded her arms in a cross stance.

"Now this has nothing to do with me, so I'll be going," James announced in an anxious tone.

He prepared to leap out of his chair. He wanted to skedaddle out of there and leave Samuel to his mess. Let's face it, this was yet another one he had not only participated in but hadn't also created.

"Ha, you'll be doing no such thing, laddie!" Zelena waved a naughty finger in James's direction. "I want a witness to this nonsensical charade that this man has been putting on."

Okay, so I am going nowhere. Fine. Guess I'll have to tolerate listening to this idiot attempt to waddle his way out of yet another catastrophe. Great, but if I'm to be light-bringer someday, I have to do better than this. At least one would hope I'll be, James conferred to himself eagerly in thought. Despite the nuance, he seemed to have been thrust into, James appeared to be quite motivated by it.

"Oh, no. You'll sit right there until I say otherwise, and you'll shut the hell up until I give you the nod," Samuel instructed James coldly. Suffice to say, he was in no mood to deal with anyone's insolence this evening.

"Speak for yourself, Reynaldi," Zelena interrupted. "Now you had two separate meetings with Alan in which you attempted to strongly push him towards Isra. The real question is why you tried hiding it if it was as innocent as you claim to be!"

All right, so now Zelena had Samuel backed into a corner with this one. There was no way on this Earth he could deny this claim without sufficient evidence to back it up. Of which he was not in possession of. He would have no choice but to admit to this severe failing whereby he'd made a complete pig's ear of it.

"You don't understand, Zelena. May I call you Zelena? Isra is trouble with a capital 'T.' I was simply trying to keep her away from my former employee, Astrid. Notably, he worked for me for years, and he was loyal to the cause until he laid eyes on her. Naturally, the rest seemed to consolidate itself. Astrid fell head over heels for Isra, and boy, did he rebel against my authority. He blasted our entire plot pertaining to her by spilling the beans directly to her about it. That meant we had no hope in getting her to switch back towards the good and kindly ways. I had no alternative in the end."

Samuel rambled on as he told his story. This time, there were no holes in the plot, which might have reassured James, who was still present to this awkward debacle of sorts, but Samuel was very much on tenterhooks right now.

"All right, that's the man taking good care of her now. Why would you try and stop them from being in a union? He seems like a good match for the girl who has been through quite the ordeal," Zelena piped up in Isra's defence.

Samuel was not appeased to this, as he had been trying to paint Isra as the enemy.

"Because they are too dangerous to exist together as one. Now she's in Wretchenheart after having murdered your poor grandson, cooking up goodness knows what. If you're looking for someone to blame, it should be Isra. I only tried to encourage Alan to woo her. I thought it would be a stable dynamic. She could have married into one of the greatest families this realm has ever known. Sure, it wouldn't have been perfect, but she would have adapted," Samuel explained curtly.

"Flattery will get you nowhere, Samuel. I met Isra and believe me, I don't doubt for one second she would have adjusted. I have heard from the get-go they were problematic so she wouldn't have tolerated any more than she did. Not to mention half of her memories are missing, so my grandson simply filled in a gap from when there were more pleasant times," Zelena informed him with a glare. "Anyhow, I don't wish to keep this going all night. I just wanted to warn you that when your next hearing commences with 'on high,' I shall be speaking in defence of Isra."

Zelena didn't care for Samuel's needless explanations and quite frankly, she was tired of hearing it. The end of the road was looming, and Zelena was going to back Isra all the way.

"Oh, is that so? Well, one must work harder if they are to be exceptional. Still, I see you are crestfallen for Isra. It doesn't matter. Honestly, she's a manipulative so-and-so. She won't rest until she has her way. The same for Astrid, which explains why they are a match made in hell. But again, dear, it's no quandary," Samuel retorted back to Zelena.

He was trying to sound confident and truthful, but he wasn't at all sure whether it was convincing. Acting like he didn't care for her opinion was just one way of excusing the fact he'd been caught with his pants down.

He couldn't blame Isra. Not now. For Zelena had already decided where she was placing her bets and Samuel's position was growing shakier by the second as now he knew there was going to be a second hearing with "on high," which he had not been formally told. No doubt Zelena was more than happy to gloat as she told him.

14

Samuel stood nervously as he waited to be asked to speak by the grand judge questioning him today. This was a hearing that "on high," better known as the Sanctification of the Unseen, arranged super quickly but they only told the defendant, Samuel Reynaldi, less than two days ago. The way they saw it, if you were deep in hot water, you didn't need much time to prepare your testimony. This additional hearing was commencing following new evidence that had recently surfaced concerning Samuel's involvement with the late Alan Grimsbane, who briefly courted Isra until his ill-fated demise by her hand.

The powers that be wanted to question Samuel on why he had not told anyone when he was initially questioned and most importantly why he'd encouraged Alan not to tell anyone. Of course, his grandmother, Zelena Grimsbane, was fighting his corner in his absence but surprisingly, she was piping up in defence of Lady Isra of the Dark, Samuel Reynaldi's charge that he was supposed to guide and nurture throughout her transition from light to dark, which brought up another widely used argument.

Some of the bigwigs at "on high" deemed that Isra would never have switched over to the dark side if Samuel had been with her from the very start when all the trouble first emerged.

But Samuel was going to defend himself. He didn't need to enable their angry and frustrating lack of decorum. No, Samuel was going to keep his cool as "on high" asked their wasteless questions that were absolutely as useful as tits on a man. Well, that was how he had worded it.

These folks are going to dig up every last sordid detail about my involvement with Isra. Oh, is nothing sacred any longer? Hmm. Whatever happened to having the decency to cover up every scandalous act? Virgin sacrifices, for example. Oh, we had a few of those back in the day.

Samuel rambled to himself with a sly chuckle. That last part amused him. It was a small sentiment to distract him from what he'd be undergoing today.

It was just forty-five minutes past ten in the morning. The hearing was due to begin at eleven, eleven exactly. It was rather an odd time in the morning to hold a hearing but "on high" insisted, and those guys were running the show. Not our doomed light-bringer; much to his disgust at having to be here, placed on display for all to hear about his antics as the nation's do-gooder that was caught being rather naughty.

Samuel already stood in the dock so he didn't need to do anything to prepare. The large auditorium was surrounded in brilliant white; supposedly, this was to symbolise the light realms, was empty. Evidently, they had to get Samuel in place first and then one assumed all of the ministers from "on high" would make themselves known. However, Samuel knew better. The golden bell, the symbol of divine communication, was present just by the empty desk at which the judge would soon be seated at. Samuel knew the golden bell represented the angelics, and if they were going to be involved, there was no way he'd get away clean.

Finally, after what seemed like a lot longer than those fateful fifteen minutes, the lights in the room increased in luminosity so the white was more prominent, almost blinding. Samuel had to shield his eyes as he watched the enormous room fill with participants, and it was no surprise when his beady eyeballs spotted Zelena Grimsbane sitting at the very back of the hall.

Well, she wants to batter my balls. Why am I not surprised, eh? Of course, she's going to get a ringside seat for this one, Samuel thought as the grand judge also materialised.

Samuel gulped. It was soon to begin. Whether the grand jury considered him guilty or not of these chargeable crimes in the name of the light remained unknown, but he'd be soon put out of his misery.

The judge stood. Much to Samuel's shock, it was a short man who couldn't have been any more than four feet tall. He might have been a dwarf, as he stood on a stool so that he could view Samuel keenly with those dark grey eyes with the tiniest hint of orange.

I'm being questioned by a fucking midget. Oh, you have got to be kidding me? How standards have fallen. Goodness gracious, Samuel observed as the dwarf-man was seconds away from addressing him. Or so he thought.

"Good morning. I would like to welcome everyone here today. Especially those gracious souls from the angelic realms who kindly agreed to join us despite the predicament they face up above. And also Mrs Grimsbane, who is very passionate in her cause of discovering the truth. May we find her justice. Finally, I will also introduce myself. I am Grockhel Silversunder. I am the grand judge representing the heavily weighted organisation collectively known as the Sanctification of the Unseen. I speak on behalf of the bigwigs themselves, and as you know ladies and gentlemen, they are elusive buggers."

Grockhel chuckled as he finished his speech. Samuel was sure he was about to be mentioned but strangely Grockhel hadn't even paid him much attention other than a passing glance.

Grockhel then turned his eyes to the rear of the auditorium and appeared to signal Zelena Grimsbane with a sly wink. That sort of thing was usually frowned upon but when you're a mighty witch, anything goes as there is very little anyone can do or say that can top the power that one holds when in that position. He then flashed his cold, grey eyes on Samuel nonchalantly.

"Good morning," Grockhel announced in Samuel's direction as he stood in the middle of the room, carefully placed in full view of everyone. "May I have your name, rank, and tenure please?"

This was a rather pointless question, and it was guaranteed that Grockhel was already aware of this information, but it was a technique "on high" used to make defendants sweat. Asking needless inquiries over and over again until someone hopefully lost all restraint and kicked off led to an unceremonious decision made by the jury. Judged by the fact that the person in question had lost all control.

"Samuel Reynaldi. Light-bringer, lord and chief of Spirisity. Tenure is just over two hundred years, sir," Samuel answered swiftly.

There was no time for being smart. It was quick answers or face judgement for looking like you might be hesitating and therefore unsure of yourself, which in turn led people to question whether you were wholly truthful.

"Thank you," Grockhel acknowledged Samuel's response. "Now we are here today because of a concern surrounding Lady Isra of the Dark, whom I believe was your charge and a matter regarding the heinous murder of Alan Grimsbane. I shall make it astute if you wish to deny the charges, that is fine. However, we will go through everything very carefully today," Grockhel announced in a formal tone but then he became serious as he eyed Samuel with a forewarning glance. "Unfortunately, new information has come to light that you were in cahoots with Mr Grimsbane shortly before his death and that you attempted to encourage his courtship with Lady Isra of the Dark? Is that true, Mr Reynaldi?"

Grockhel made his inquiries with a wistful attitude. It was his job to be patronising towards the accused. There was no other way around it. You simply had to be a complete ass to every so-called love and light soul that was stood up in that box.

"I did converse with Alan on two separate occasions, yes. He was a very troubled young man and seemed to have found some stability courting our young Isra," Samuel piped up. It wouldn't be wise for him to lie at this stage, for he'd be in more trouble when he was found out.

"And he was in an impending courtship with Isra, is that correct, Mr Reynaldi?" Grockhel asked.

"He was indeed. Alan confided in me that he felt unstable for a long time, and I simply put forward the idea that settling down with Isra might be the best path for him to undertake," Samuel asserted in a modest tone.

"Aha. I see; Isra wasn't exactly a model citizen. You performed a Sleeping Beauty spell on her after permission for a memory lapse was granted less than two years ago. She was in an unsavoury relationship of which you stepped in to show support but it was too late as she had already turned the tide. Then the journal has the most interesting entry when this Astrid fellow showed up."

Grockhel continued in a bemused tone. Almost as if he didn't believe the story, but it had to be true as it had been written in the book of records and such things were not in there if they were false.

"Yes. Sadly, Astrid was a loyal servant, who was by my side for many years but he fell for Isra, and the rest is history," Samuel muttered with a slight tinge of resentment.

He hated how that whole thing went down. *Why did Astrid have to fall for Isra in the first place? He was breaching his boundaries, and there is no way of resolving that as the damage is done. He had also well and truly fucked our plan to get Isra back into the good graces by telling her EVERYTHING we had in mind for her. So alas, the little witch rebelled and Astrid... Well, he was her leader. Naturally, he led the revolt. Who else could it have been?* Samuel recalled in his mind, knowing the betrayal still stung.

Grockhel interrupted Samuel's train of thought. "So, let me get this clear; Isra rebelled against your cause alongside your former employee, who not only lied constantly to you about his dealings with her but told her about the grand plan to bring her back down to earth. It makes him quite the anarchist. I believe it would be beneficial if the congregation conversed with this Astrid," Grockhel proposed eagerly. "If not for you, then for us to gain an understanding of what went on."

Samuel was rather shocked by this idea. He confessed, "Well, that could be tricky as Isra resides in Wretchenheart with Astrid as we speak."

"All right, let's go back a bit, shall we? So, Isra was magically disarmed after this tragic relationship that had gone belly-up, is that accurate to say?" Grockhel pressed Samuel with a concerned look, trying to get to the bottom of the issue at hand.

"Yes. It is," Samuel promptly answered.

"Ah. Now then, she was in a vulnerable state, wouldn't you say? And to then be accosted by yourself, because as I understand it, in your words, there was no other alternative. She refused to adhere to all manner of reason, yes? And therefore, when her memory was removed, she would have not been in any fit state to undertake anything even remotely emotional. So, my concern here is why no additional support was provided to Isra? Surely, you must understand that this would be very unsettling for a woman of only eighteen to undergo," Grockhel interrogated Samuel without care.

"I see your meaning, but honestly, I saw no need for intervention as we were keeping an eye on her at the time," Samuel quipped in his defence.

"But she *wasn't* being monitored. She had entered into a dalliance with Alan Grimsbane so the real question we have to ask today is why did you stop surveillance on Lady Isra, Mr Reynaldi?" Grockhel further probed as he delved so much deeper than Samuel imagined.

"I stopped for a time. I admit that, but I didn't foresee her meeting Alan or even becoming friendly with him," Samuel admitted with a low brow.

He knew in this instance he was done for now. If he had kept a better watch on Isra, perhaps this whole mess could have been avoided. It was partly his fault. He understood that.

Yes, unfortunately, it is my fault and mine alone. I should have been more diligent with her. Perhaps even shown some small shred of care, but I was too focused on keeping her away from Astrid. Such good that did, Samuel berated himself in thought.

"But she did get friendly with him. That is the issue here, Mr Reynaldi. One you could have prevented by being more observant with the girl. For goodness sake, she'd shortly turned to the dark side and then you simply abandoned her after confiscating very dark magics, I am led to believe? According to the entry in the journal. But to wipe her memory like that and then leave her isolated only proved more harmful in the long term," Grockhel explained gravely.

He had a sour look etched upon his face, the one you see when someone enacts something that results in dire consequences but they have some kind of inkling that their actions incur that and do so anyway.

"I believed she was safe. And more importantly out of harm's way," Samuel implored quietly. He was sure there was very little he could say to disprove the court's reasoning now.

Grockhel adjusted his half-circle spectacles carefully and looked down onto Samuel with a frustrated glare. "Yes, but she *wasn't*. She was able to roam around the wilderness and shortly after this commenced, she met Alan Grimsbane. Leading to further chaos in this young woman's life and a murder that could have been prevented," Grockhel admonished as he looked on in the direction of Zelena Grimsbane.

"I think this hearing will need to adjourn to collect its findings but I hope you understand, Mr Reynaldi, Isra was in *your* care. You are registered as her guardian although it is in my findings that she is not aware of this. You are indeed her benefactor—a person invested in the girl's future whether she deems to find it necessary or not. There is no one else handpicked for this role but you. So, what we have here is a failure to perform," Grockhel advised Samuel with a forewarning look.

"I see. Well, if that is what you have concluded, I guess that is what I will have to accept," Samuel politely responded.

"This is a very young, ill-advised witch with so much trauma in her life that it's unthinkable to even suggest she'd be mentally able to withstand an emotional bond with another, let alone be comfortable by herself. Her father has been absent all her life as has her mother. Gwendolyn Passe has not been seen for almost twenty years; she has vanished off the face of the Earth. Meanwhile, Damien Daughtry has not wanted any contact with his daughter since he handed her to you, and that was in your contract; that he would never have communication with her. Some serious intervention is needed," Grockhel told Samuel carefully, as he didn't believe there was much more to say.

This was pretty much an open and shut case. Isra needed a parental figure, and Samuel was deemed to be that yet had not been there. That was the bottom line here. The point that Grockhel was doing his utmost to get across to Samuel. You see, it wasn't enough just to berate Samuel publicly for his failings; they also had to get him to comprehend that Isra needed assistance and had needed so since the start of her life.

Being abandoned as a baby is never an easy feat to conquer. Samuel should have understood that and while he did place her in Wingdom's Academy, that was not until she was seventeen. Where the fuck had he been for the remainder of her life? These were all probing questions that needed answering, but Grockhel suspected Samuel wouldn't have a very passable answer for any of it. This was a man that had been focused on his career and not much else. Of course, he'd neglected to take heed of his responsibilities but since atrocities had been conducted by the wayward Isra, further action needed to be taken against Samuel.

"I agree," Samuel joined Grockhel's enthusiasm in suggesting Isra needed some help at this time. "But just what might be useful to her now? How are we to move forward from this? I understand I've screwed up to quite a considerable extent but if you could let me know how I could fix it... Well, I'd be grateful," Samuel elaborated, almost sounding like he had a conscience for a second.

"I will certainly be asking what is to be done. I don't believe I have any more questions for the time being, Mr Reynaldi. I see no reason to strip you of your title as light-bringer for now. However, please be advised, we may choose to do so if further issues become unresolved as a result of this situation," Grockhel commented to Samuel.

He suddenly addressed the entire room in a loud, formal voice, "This hearing shall take a recess. We will reconvene here in one hour. Thank you."

And with that, Samuel was allowed to be let out of the dock, if only for a short time. The jury would soon return with their decision.

SAMUEL ANXIOUSLY ENTERED the dock again. He'd been allowed to retreat outside for a time to stretch his legs and collect his thoughts since this had been quite the gruelling day. He looked up at Grockhel, who had also materialised once again with a stern look on his face, and he addressed the main audience that was seated all around him, whether it happened to be at the rear, front, or sidelines of the large hall.

"Samuel Reynaldi. Thank you for coming back. So, I have had a chance to discuss at length what disciplinary measures we should undertake in regard to your failure to apprehend Lady Isra of the Dark when she went off the rails," Grockhel began quietly, although he still sounded very much stalwart as he spoke.

"All right," Samuel uttered in a swift motion. "A decision has been made then? Am I to face any purgatory?" he asked bravely. He was certain the outlook wasn't good if they deemed he needed to be punished.

Grockhel straightened his glance on Samuel. He showed some compassion towards the light-bringer's plight as he simply said, "No. We are going to give you the chance to capture Lady Isra of the Dark and enforce any discipline you believe she needs to receive to be rehabilitated following this experience."

"Oh, wow," Samuel gushed, feeling immense relief all over his body as the tension dissipated. But there was a grave look of concern as well. It dawned on Samuel just how impossible his task would be. His eyes almost dropped out of their socks as his mouth went unbelievably dry. Like a saltine cracker. Coarse and highly laden with salt. "She's in Wretchenheart, though. How will I successfully gain access to her?"

"That will be for you to figure out. Nobody will be allowed to assist you with this. It is your mission and yours alone, but the good news is we see no reason to remove you as light-bringer," Grockhel blurted to Samuel with keen interest.

"Right. I see," Samuel muttered, exasperated. He tucked his hands into his suit pockets nervously. "That may be difficult to undertake, but you're saying I can freely take her by my own means and do what I feel is necessary to rectify this course of action?" Samuel questioned thoughtfully, as it had caused some thought-provoking ideas of his own.

"Yes. She will be brought to justice at your hand, and I hope you provide the necessary means to show compassion towards this young girl's plight by housing her in your dominion, Spirisity," Grockhel instructed. "At least until she can stand alone."

"We do need to speak with this Astrid fellow also, but I understand that may be somewhat foolproof," Grockhel insisted to Samuel with another concerned glance.

"Yes, I feel Astrid will be my biggest obstacle. He won't let Isra be captured without one heck of a fight," Samuel confessed, feeling overwhelmed.

"Then a show of force must be made. We are not in the business of mollycoddling souls who have strayed only to further encourage their behaviour. He was your employee. We need his cooperation. Without that, this task will prove to be very taxing indeed," Grockhel surmised weakly.

"I see. Thank you," Samuel acknowledged with a formal tone.

There was nothing else to say. The decision wasn't entirely out of his favour but they provided Samuel with a lot of leeway here. More than he deserved, in fact. And Samuel had to truly recognise just how lucky he was.

"So, you'll be on your way now. Apprehend the girl. Get her into your custody and then begin her long journey towards rebuilding her life while being reprogrammed on how to conduct herself. I must warn you, Mr Reynaldi, we don't hand out things like this every day. If you fail to deliver, we may have to reconsider your standing as light-bringer, and we'd rather not do that, so please do not screw this up," Grockhel advised carefully.

It was a very important task he'd been given to complete and Grockhel wasn't entirely sure Samuel would succeed.

"Yes, I understand just how rare of a circumstance this is," Samuel answered stoically.

He proceeded to let himself out of the dock. He had a lot to prepare for when he got back home to Spirisity. There was a lot at stake now. He would remain light-bringer for the time being but that may become shaky if for any reason he wasn't able to do what they had asked of him.

In conclusion, it hadn't gone down as terribly as Samuel expected. It was fairly satisfactory. Yes, that was it. So, the good news was that Samuel was to remain in Spirisity having not been convicted of any wrongdoing, but he had been formally told off for his actions towards Isra. He hadn't exactly got away clean here.

But now the hardest task of his life awaited him. He would have to somehow ensnare one of the most powerful young sorceresses he had ever laid eyes on. Now just how would one conduct such a feat?

MIDNIGHT WAS DRAWING on in the midst of the secluded demonic wilderness, Wretchenheart. Astrid stood sullenly by the open doorway to his bedroom when he heard a rapping on his window.

Right on cue. Come on, let's see what old Samuel has to say for himself. I want to know everything that commenced, Astrid thought to himself as he impatiently waited for Silas to make himself known. It was late in the night, but it was the best time for Astrid to mull over everything.

Things were beginning to hit crisis point in Wretchenheart, and it was only a matter of time before Isra and Astrid's enemies came seeking them out since Samuel's hearing with the Sanctification of the Unseen had not gone down well for anyone involved.

Silas finally emerged, looking exhausted as he flumped down onto Astrid's bed. "Ah, much better. Thank you. Long flight, and it never gets any easier. Ah, so I suppose you want to get straight down to it," Silas guessed.

"Uh-huh. You're late."

Astrid scowled at his brother with a fierce glare. The raven-man wasn't at all impressed with Silas's tardiness and it showed as he pressed his arms against his chest.

"Yes, well. Apologies," Silas uttered. "I haven't had time for a snack, you know? It's just so busy. All right, so do you want the good news or the really terrible news?" Silas proposed, sounding friendly enough to soften the blow he was about to deliver unto his brother but also formal in a bid to convince Astrid not to do anything rash.

"Just get to it, will you? I want to know what the hell we are up against," Astrid demanded. He really should have been more polite, but he was in no mood to do that just now.

"It's not good for Isra or Samuel," Silas nervously began. His feathers were shivering and not from the chilly night winds.

"How so?" Astrid probed with a look of concern. He suddenly found himself going over a million scenarios in his head as he wondered just what was going down. *Well, what the hell does that mean? Not good for Samuel? But also not a good result for Isra? How can that be? Surely the real 'on high' have decided to pursue their investigation regarding him. Otherwise, this doesn't make sense,* Astrid rambled on, trying to distract himself. He didn't want to think too much right now.

"Here is how it's going to roll. The Sanctification of the Unseen decided that Samuel must pay for his crimes against the light. There's no question about that. However, they are giving him a shitload of leeway here, too. He's been ordered to capture Isra and rehabilitate her. He will be her guardian, but he will be required to keep her in his custodianship, and so you can see shit is going to get very real," Silas admonished before pausing. He realised he had left out one crucial detail. "They insisted Samuel do this or his position as light-bringer will be under threat."

Astrid interrupted Silas with his conclusion, "And since he got there by treacherous ways, he will do anything to keep his place in the high and mighty lands. Right, I see. So what about me and Isra being here? Surely, he can't get himself here?" Astrid questioned. He needed to know what to do next if that was going to be easily dismantled, too.

"At this moment, he's told 'on high' very clearly that he cannot get himself over here without great difficulties. And that is exactly true, but with the orders he's been given, don't think for one moment he won't send someone who can get himself over here by deceptive means. Nothing is sacred, Astrid. You know that better than anyone," Silas confessed in a modest tone. "Still, at least for now, keep Isra here. The heat will be off you both but the Sanctification of the Unseen do want to converse with you."

"You have got to be joking? No chance in hell!" Astrid angrily exclaimed. "Not with all of this going on. Do they honestly think I am going to trust them? They must be insane. No way!"

Wow, is there no low these imbeciles won't stoop? Sure, they want Samuel's head on a silver platter and that's great and all, but jeez. They also agree to allow him to somehow lure Isra into his clutches. Well, not on my watch. No way. I don't think we'll make that trip to see Evanora either at this rate. It will be the easiest way for them to set up a trap...

Astrid went on into a tirade of frustration in his thoughts. He was furious with the way things had gone down. He was expecting an equal balance, especially with what Oresis had told him, but then again, angels are always full of shit.

"I should have known." Astrid scoffed. "That bloody Oresis buffoon came to me with all this enlightened crap, suggesting they'd throw Samuel to the wolves, and now we see the tables have not only turned but that Samuel is being given the chance to be in their good graces again whereas Isra is the wicked witch of the realm in their eyes. It's just bloody typical," Astrid yelled.

He flung a glass tumbler against the wall in exasperation. The precious thing smashed into many fluttering pieces that hovered in mid-air until they landed on the cold stone floor, making a large crashing sound as they collided with it.

"Calm down, brother. There will be a solution," Silas chided him.

"Oh, yeah; you really think that? Because I'm telling you, there's nothing good here. It's only a matter of time before everything slaps us into oblivion, and I've worked so damn hard to get us where we are. At this moment. Right here, holed up in this place. I've done all of it!" Astrid exclaimed as he placed his head into his hands, just so sorely done with it all.

"It will be if you allow it. Anyway, who is Oresis?" Silas inquired with intrigue. He'd never heard the name crop up, so it sparked some bewildering curiosity in him.

The calamity of Astrid's uncontrollable rage generated something else in the process. Astrid's bedroom door burst open and in walked open a very sleepy Isra, adorned in a long deep violet silk nightdress that just about covered her tiny figure.

"What's going on? I heard a whooping crash," Isra asked with keen interest.

Her eyes also fell onto Silas, who looked just as bemused as her, and so her suspicions were instantly raised. She looked at Astrid inquisitively as he seemed to be somewhat flustered. His eyes glazed over her in impending anxiety. Something inside him looked like it might burst right open.

"Nothing," Astrid softly answered. He straightened himself out, but Isra was no fool. She knew something was awry.

"Yes, and you just happened to launch one of our finest crystalline glasses at the wall for no reason? Poor thing," Isra sympathised sardonically as she stood by Astrid, who was sitting on the edge of his bed. Now she wanted to know what was going on.

Astrid noted Isra's annoyance and urged her to sit by patting his hand on the bed. "I need to tell you something. We're not going to be able to meet Evanora with the way things are now."

Isra threw a confused sideways glance his way. "What do you mean?"

"Samuel had his hearing. He's been told to undertake a capture mission against you. He won't stop until he's got you in his custody. This means rehabilitation of the highest order, and the light has given him the green light on it. We absolutely cannot stray from Wretchenheart now," Astrid admonished to Isra with a forewarning finger. "You cannot leave my sight, not now."

"Then I won't," Isra whispered, looking right at him.

He looked deep into her enchanting lime-green eyes. Astrid gingerly climbed over to Isra. He gripped onto her waist as he tenderly breathed down her neck. He was so stressed that he was ready to lose himself in her strawberry-scented musk that lingered just below her breast.

The energy coming off of Astrid was intense. He wanted to see if she would accept him at this moment as he softly brushed past her lips with his own. Just as Isra reciprocated Astrid's advances by sweetly kissing him back, Astrid's tongue made its way into her mouth. He was so locked into this passionate embrace, it would have been touch and go whether he was going to come up for air. For a moment, he forgot the bullshit the light was playing down, and he almost neglected to remember Silas was still here, no doubt watching as an unwilling participant.

"Ahem." Silas cleared his throat. "Honestly, if you're going to engage in hanky panky, could you at least wait until I've buggered off?"

"Oh, shit." Astrid excused himself as he moved off of Isra's lap.

"Yes, well, forget that. Who is Oresis?" Silas pressed in Astrid's direction.

He was dying to know who would be visiting Astrid, claiming to be an agent of the light while implying some grand plan to castrate the fancy-pants light-bringer.

"He's an angel. Or at least he told me he was one," Astrid informed Silas with a careful glance, but he was more focused on having to detail to Isra the full entirety of what lie ahead for the both of them.

He narrowed his eyes at her carefully. A hard expression formed upon his face as he emitted soberly, "You cannot, under any circumstances, meet Evanora. I know that comes as a punch to the gut. I know you are dying to meet your family, but if you stray from these secluded metaphysical walls, you become vulnerable to Samuel's magic. We already know he's done it before. He won't hesitate again. Not now that his role as light-bringer rests on whether he can get to you. This is serious. I can't have you wandering out of the realm."

"All right, I trust you, dear heart," Isra agreed wistfully before she remembered a crucial detail surrounding all this had not yet been mentioned. "But what about Zelena?"

"Ah. Slight problem," Silas divulged to her softly. "The Sanctification of the Unseen didn't allow her to broadcast any kind of defence regarding you. All they did was demonstrate her case that you were indeed vulnerable at the time of your courtship with Alan and therefore Samuel is liable for misconduct. That's what they want to get on him. You do understand that they hope he will fail? But they can't throw the book at him without giving him the opportunity to rectify it first," Silas explained with great detail so that Isra and Astrid were aware of exactly what was occurring.

"Nothing is imminent, then," Astrid mouthed sarcastically.

"No, but they do want to convene with me, and you should allow them to," Silas urged Astrid with fervour.

Astrid's eyes fell on Silas with a serious glance. He had his hands clenched into fists as he sullenly asserted, "I am not going to anything of the sort. Samuel wants Isra, he'll do anything to get her. Even convincing the light to try and get someone like myself on board. Well, I don't think it's past his expansive array of talents, do you? No, we won't be doing that. I am not handing him Isra gift wrapped for his own pleasure."

15

Astrid stood strong in his reasoning as he elaborated further with a death stare in Silas's direction. "You have to tell them I won't be doing any of that. As far as they are concerned, Isra and I are the enemy."

Silas shook his head in disapproval. "Well, I can't say I am happy with any of this. It doesn't bode well for any of us, you know. I do have to say I'm glad that those 'on high' have taken the initiative that Samuel should be punished, but you know they have very underhanded ways of doing that. He will think he's the king of everything right now so it's not going to be long before that attitude causes him to slip up," Silas suggested pointedly.

"Anyway, I best go. It's one o'clock. I'd like to snatch myself some worms before they bugger off. Good tidings to you, Astrid. Be well," Silas said before he departed out of the nearby open window in the bedroom.

Now it was just Isra and Astrid alone again. He knew they needed to have a very serious conversation about what was ahead. Not just about the fact that Samuel was gunning for Isra and would do anything humanly possible to get his hands onto her. But solely because if he wasn't able to ensnare her into his seductive trap, he may well be looking at the prospect that he would not be the light-bringer any longer. That meant no more living in Spirisity.

He would quite possibly be banished from the realms, and that, my friends, was more embarrassing than you can fathom, especially if you've upheld the position for more than two hundred years. What's worse is Samuel used underhanded tactics in the name of the light to get himself right to the top. But nobody knew that but Astrid and Oresis at this moment in time, so it paved the way that going forward, Oresis would have to speak up also, as he had told Astrid just how Samuel had gamed the system.

Astrid walked over to the window and slammed it shut before he drew the dark black velveteen curtains. He then walked over to the door and closed that, too. Isra looked at him with great hesitation. She wondered what was going on. The raven-man's mind seemed to be somewhere else tonight. Astrid wasn't his usual uplifting self, bursting with enthusiasm for just about everything. No, something was deadly off, but Isra could not fathom just what that might be.

He's ever so mysterious. More than usual. He's often an elusive, cryptic bastard but now he's baffling me. I wonder if he will tell me just what weighs heavy on him. I know he's concerned about Samuel Reynaldi capturing me, but oh no. It's more than that, Isra pondered in her thoughts as Astrid returned before promptly seating himself on the bed again, looking at her with a serious expression.

"I wondered if we'd ever be alone. All right, so you know it's crunch time for us, don't you?" Astrid asked in a sombre tone.

"I understand things are going to be challenging for sure. But I don't quite comprehend why you are so antsy about it," Isra answered with a curious stare. Her eyes glazed over him for a second, almost diving deep into those dark brown bewildering commodities as she found herself losing focus.

"And I can't have you doing that either. No slipping. No losing the face of it all. We are knee-deep in hell's bosom here. Metaphysically speaking," Astrid explained. "You think Samuel wanting to snatch you into his realm is bad? Try the major cataclysm that is soon to be coming your way. You are Damien Daughtry's daughter—a man I worked for and have been loyal to for many years. He's helped me out a number of times, and for me to have the realisation I am with his girl, well, I can't help but be worried because I know what's at stake here."

"And just what might that be?" Isra pressed.

It's true she wasn't clued up on everything just yet. She was only just dipping her toe into the pool in a sense. She had no idea she was to be forced up against.

"First of all, you mentioned meeting Evanora Passe-Somersby... Don't," Astrid warned Isra bluntly.

He had a cold glare about him. It sent chills down Isra's spine. There was something deeply instinctual that told her he wasn't being deliberate. He had good reasoning but again, she didn't know the entirety of it.

"I think you need to explain to me why that would be a bad idea?" Isra proposed sternly. She didn't wholly understand, but she was also going to give him the benefit of the doubt. She knew Astrid well enough, and he was not a man to lie.

"There have been the four main families. They have been there since the beginning. The Grimsbanes. The Passes. The Somersbys. The Daughtrys. All at war. No one is exactly sure why, but it's been going on for three hundred years. Now people will get to hear you are Damien Daughtry's daughter. Well, heads are going to roll. They are all connected. All interlinked with one another, and it gets worse. Damien Daughtry, your father, well, he's pretty scrupulous, and he's had plenty of enemies. Some of those may transfer to you. I know that's unfair, but it's the way of it," Astrid disclosed to Isra softly.

"I think I understand how most work. It's not a shock to me. You know, I've only had a few days to digest this but I'd really like to meet my father. You say you know him?" Isra quizzed with a curious glance.

"I do," Astrid quipped back. "But..." he paused ever so swiftly, "I strongly advise against it." Again came the ironic pause of desolation before he continued, "Unless you want to lay eyes on Everilda again."

"Yes. I've thought over that, too. I don't care much for her. It's still a lot to take in. Me and my sister. My sister betrayed me with the same man. *Twice.* I have to admit, I don't value much there. I don't see it being a product of longevity. But that's something I believe Damien and I will see eye to eye on as I hear he's not fond of her either," Isra commented with a wistful stare.

"He cannot stand the sight of her. It's sad. She's his daughter and he wants absolutely nothing to do with her. He only acknowledges the existence of Everilda due to Rhiannon, his love. Other than that, he'd never even speak to the girl," Astrid admitted mournfully as he was hoping that Damien's response would indeed be the latter when it came to Isra.

"I want to see him," Isra pressed on.

She wasn't letting this one go. But that was her biggest weakness. Not letting things go when they needed to be, and this was something for sure she needed to let go of. Reliving her past wasn't on the highest order, especially now with Samuel wanting Isra to get the light folk off of his back.

Astrid understood, though. He knew why Isra wanted to meet Damien. Having already conversed with Damien many times regarding Isra, he knew what the warlock's response was likely to be but Astrid relented as he dropped his firm stance.

"All right. I'll take you to him. Just be warned, we can't linger in any place too long. Get yourself dressed, and we'll go as soon as you're ready."

Astrid gave Isra the nod that he was willing to cross the borders for her. It was true, Sprawnbell was also a hellish dimension and that's why Damien chose to reside there, but last time he checked, Damien was in exile so it would be tricky, to say the least. But Astrid wanted to bring Isra there so even if they ended up not being able to see Damien, Isra would have an understanding of what her father was like.

"Ha!" Isra chuckled and closed her eyes, pointing her index finger to the top of the ceiling while concentrating upon her tiny, elegant form. She slowly dropped her finger, imagining a white light covering her from top to bottom. A mass of tiny glimmery stars appeared all around Isra. Astrid could barely see her anymore until she quickly shifted into a very long, white glistening dress. It was tight-fitting on the waist and ruched around the bust. The dress also had thousands of glittering diamonds embedded in it.

"Well, if there is such a thing as angels, I'll be damned if I am killing you," Astrid uttered sweetly.

Isra laughed at this comment as she turned to him. "That's refreshing to know, dear. Shall we go?"

Isra wanted to hurry along; after all, Astrid had told her they'd have to go right away.

Astrid looked back at Isra with a very bemused and comical expression on his face. He was trying hard not to laugh at this moment as Isra stood there looking breathtaking in that pristine white gown. The whiteness was ever so prominent in the dark bedroom that was gently lit by candlelight alone. He couldn't take his eyes off her.

She was proving to be quite the distraction, much to his dismay, for he needed to focus. If they were going to get along to Sprawnbell without any issues, he needed to get his head in the right place. However, eyeing Isra up and down from her eyes to her feet while she was adorned in that mesmerising dress, all Astrid could think about was how she'd look without it.

It might glitter a little more if we dropped it onto the floor. When I am able to peel it off her beautifully cute body... but one must not tempt oneself until these necessary errands have been taken care of. I would like to latch my hands onto her waist before I reach around her back, tugging down that zipper slowly as it reveals her soft and gleaming peach skin hidden beneath that mass of fabric. Alas, I cannot engage in such frivolity right now. Pity. It's the midnight hour. Oh well, can't be too disappointed. There's always three o'clock in the morning.

Astrid chattered with himself eagerly as he thoroughly pursued the idea of talking Isra out of going over to Sprawnbell. They could have a real jolly time of it over here and snuggle up under the soft bed covers. He was so tempted to do just that, but needs must, as the old saying goes.

"You know it's not that I don't appreciate the irony, but you an angel? I might lose all concentration with you wearing that!" Astrid guffawed in Isra's direction before he quickly saved himself by saying, "But the irony is most amusing! Come on. Let's be going. Things to do. Warlocks to see. Ugly half-sisters to no doubt taunt!"

He chuckled sardonically and grabbed on to Isra's hand, closing his eyes as he pictured Sprawnbell in his mind.

Thankfully, Astrid had a photographic memory so this was no trouble for him. He concentrated deeply on the visually striking images he most remembered of Sprawnbell when he'd flown there in his feathered raven suit.

"Close your eyes," Astrid told Isra softly.

He gripped onto her hand a little tighter now as he felt the energy surge between the two of them. It wouldn't be long before they'd be at his old domicile, so Astrid prepared for lift-off.

ASTRID OPENED his eyes as he felt the air around him. He didn't feel the cold very much unlike many other souls, but in Sprawnbell, it was definitely noticeable, even for someone like him. The infamous rectangular black mansion stood out before him and Astrid proudly looked on, admiring his handiwork. Yep, he'd got them over here in one piece and they'd soon be knocking on that ever so faithful door leading them into the Daughtry home. But first, he had to introduce Isra to the place she'd never visited.

Wretchenheart was her first experience of a demonic realm but Sprawnbell was more eccentric, cut off from the rest of the world. Still, it maintained the hellish ideals, just without the grandeur of Wretchenheart. Sprawnbell had no castle to claim its name whereas Wretchenheart did. Demons and those souls that sucked dry everything but darkness could roam freely in Wretchenheart without a care but in Sprawnbell, you had to be extra careful.

"Now open them," Astrid instructed Isra.

He looked up to the cobalt-blue glimmering skies. A million tiny white stars looked extra spectacular tonight but perhaps it was simply just the weather. For an early September night, it was drawing on closer to the fall.

"Oh, wow!" Isra gushed as she looked ahead of her.

The grand jet-black mansion certainly looked prestigious enough to satisfy the demands of a warlock but that iconic sky was something to behold.

"Yeah. I worked here for many years, assisting Damien. Long before I knew of your existence, of course."

Astrid had to be careful now... he'd only recently discovered Isra was Damien's daughter, that was true, but there must have been quite the cover-up as Astrid couldn't recall a time when Damien was having it off with another. But then again, ravens seldom interfered in their master's business. It just wasn't appropriate to do something without asking.

"Anyway, let's not put off the inevitable," Astrid urged Isra.

He boldly stepped forward and rapped on the door. It was nerve-wracking for him because he hadn't even made the common courtesy to inform Damien that he and Isra were making their way over here, but desperate times called for extremely daring measures.

Surprisingly, within a few seconds, Damien popped his head around the door as it swung open. He saw Astrid and looked concerned. His dark black, combed-back hair looked somewhat unkempt. He laid his yellow eyes straight onto Isra. He had never seen a visual of his daughter before but that shimmery white-golden hair in ringlets with those lime-green piercing eyes immediately caught his attention.

"Astrid," Damien remarked gently.

The warlock carefully peered around both sides of him to ensure nobody was witnessing this that shouldn't be, for he was extremely diligent of eyes and ears being on him and his family who weren't visible to him.

"I see you brought whom I am guessing is Isra," Damien presumed as he gave Isra the once over with his yellow-tinged eyes. "Well, I see you're keeping her well. No trouble there."

"He's quite the muscle," Isra mustered.

She didn't want the first meeting with her father to be rude or inappropriate. Unlike Everilda, Isra wanted to give off an impression of decorum.

Damien giggled. "Oh, don't I know it."

Astrid resisted the urge to bite back at that commentary. He'd already seen Damien's cautious lookout and muttered hastily, "Nobody will be around in these parts, Damien."

"Yes. True. But one can never be too careful in these times, Astrid. Well, why don't you both come in?" Damien invited Astrid and Isra, closing the door behind them.

He pointed to the room just adjacent to the door, which was their living room. The large black settee sat predominantly in the centre whilst a rustic fireplace stood on the opposite side of the room. There wasn't much to say about it other than the large array of oak bookcases dominating the room. Isra sat on the edge of the black couch as she caught sight of the shoulder-length golden blonde hair bobbing up and down along with a mass of dark reddish-mahogany that was situated next to it.

Before Isra could open her mouth, Damien handed her a cup of hot raspberry leaf tea. The scent was so pungent it was imagining yourself biting into one of those tiny light pink fruits. Astrid was also given a cup of it, but he held it steady on his lap as he watched the three women with much interest.

Damien noticed Isra's eyes fixated upon the back of Everilda and so he cautioned her before anything could escalate.

"I am aware, Isra, that you already have quite the lengthy history with your sister, and I trust you won't bring that into my home. Do we understand each other?" Damien asked sternly. Of course, with someone like Damien, it wasn't a question. It was a polite command.

"I will do my best to refrain from indulging in nonsensical warfare," Isra answered with a kind voice, although Everilda spun around, glaring upon Isra before flashing Damien with an equally bemused death stare. It was clear the outlandish veteran warlock had some explaining to do.

"Ah, yes." Damien pointed to Rhiannon and Everilda, and both women stared at Isra with such intensity that you could almost hear a pin drop among the awkward, sullen silence. "This is Isra. Rhiannon, meet Isra. Everilda, this is Isra, as you know," Damien announced in a friendly manner.

Everilda wasn't greatly pleased as she retorted idly, "Yes. We have met already."

Meanwhile, Rhiannon was more concerned as to why this mysterious blonde was sitting in her home, drinking her raspberry leaf tea whilst her daughter Everilda looked incredulously angered by the event. Considering Rhiannon was a demoness, her fierce concern for her offspring grew even more as she listened keenly to Everilda's words. However, Rhiannon didn't know the scandalous details just yet.

"Yes, I know you have," Damien answered his daughter coldly.

There was no love lost between Damien and his mortal daughter. He made his feelings towards her very clear, and even Isra observed that this was an incredibly dysfunctional relationship. Part of her even felt sorry for poor Everilda. She witnessed this man she barely knew completely dismissing the words Everilda spoke. He didn't know much of the history between the two women but it was very clear that Damien had no interest in Everilda's side, and Isra couldn't help but think that was so hurtful. Like a knife placated into the gut. A dull ache you couldn't shift no matter how hard you tried to will it away.

"Who is this young woman? I don't believe I have had the pleasure." Rhiannon greeted Isra sharply but was also fiercely grilling Damien at the same time. Rhiannon was instinctively very protective towards Everilda so when she saw her darling girl react so coldly to Isra, she instantly knew something was up. A mother always knows best what her charmed offspring tries so hard to conceal.

"Isra," Damien quipped quickly. He was trying not to cause a scene but ultimately he knew he would when he uttered, "Isra is my illegitimate daughter that was conceived whilst I had an affair when having so many tribulations with Damaris," he confessed with a low brow.

Damien knew this news wouldn't be well received but he had to be honest with his partner and daughter because it was the right thing to do.

"Uh-uh," Everilda mouthed in an annoyed tone. "So you cheated on my mother, who wasn't exactly the nicest of folks. Sorry, not my real one," she quickly added, catching a bemused glare from Rhiannon.

"It's complicated, Everilda. You don't even understand half of it, so let's not go into the gory details, shall we? Now, are you going to be civil or do you need to be elsewhere for the remainder of this little visit Isra has kindly paid us? I'd like to converse with my daughter," Damien coldly snapped.

Rhiannon instantly reached over to Everilda, putting her arm around her daughter tenderly as she uttered, "Come now. Let's go upstairs. This has nothing to do with us."

"I am sorry. I didn't want this," Isra began in a sombre tone. She placed her hands on her lap as she drained the last of her raspberry leaf tea. She seemed altogether very cooperative, which baffled Everilda, as she'd seen Isra's very worst side.

"Oh, it's no trouble you being here, Isra. Everilda is just a sourpuss. Well, you know that already. I don't need to elaborate, do I?" Damien retorted, although at least with Isra, he was smiling instead of glowering at poor Everilda, who evidently got the worst reception from him.

"Why don't you stay, Everilda? Just sit. Listen to what I have to say," Isra suggested to her sister, which sounded so weird inside her head.

She hated Everilda... or at least she thought she did to a certain extent. But now that she knew they were sisters, things were considerably different. Plus, there was the whole element of danger Isra found herself in that made her view things in a much more diplomatic light. She had to admit, it was unusual for her.

"What could you possibly say to me that changes anything between us? So, we're sisters, great; but you violently detest me."

Everilda groaned with a low growl and slumped herself down in the middle of the couch right next to Isra, much to her distaste. She didn't want to be involved in any of this. It left a sour taste in Everilda's mouth. Isra was the sole reason Everilda was now mortal and had lost her powers, so suffice to say, Everilda wasn't greatly amused by Isra's presence.

"Things are incredibly different now, Evie. I know we've both done things we shouldn't, but times are changing and perhaps not for the better. I wish I could detail to you all I know, but there's a good chance if it gets bad, I won't even remember saying this to you," Isra expressed in a sober tone.

"*That* sounds ominous," Everilda remarked.

Isra softened her stance while staring directly into Everilda's eyes to show her sincerity and retorted, "Girl, you have no idea."

"Well, Isra, perhaps you can enlighten us all on why you wanted to see me. I understand you've only known the truth for a few days. It can't have been easy discovering your entire life has been a lie," Damien questioned with a wide-eyed stare.

Now that Astrid thought about it, it was strangely familiar. *Oh my, Damien has the same stare she does. My goodness. Why did I never see it before? Ha, like father, like daughter. Interesting, I must say, but time is getting away from us. I know Isra might well hate me for it, but we cannot be here for much longer. We are already too close for comfort,* Astrid thought as he watched Isra carefully; for the first time ever, she was with her family, even if she didn't fully comprehend it herself. She was home, and he'd have to drag her away as soon as humanly possible.

"I've not known for long; yes, that is indeed true. I am experiencing a perplexing time in my life, for the light-bringer, Samuel Reynaldi, has been instructed to capture me. He's wiped my memories once already. The last two years of my life have been an absolute blur apart from a few details. Namely the situation with Everilda and Jonathan. And the very moment I gave my heart up to darkness. Everything after that, I don't know what happened," Isra explained with a somewhat worried glance.

Everilda's face dropped. She suddenly realised she was not the only one who was seemingly being punished by those that dwelled in higher places.

Oh, wow. They got to her good. So much for that darkness making her completely untouchable because, boy, was she resilient when it came down to it. I never quite picked up on it before, but something has changed in her. I don't like that Astrid man. Maybe I owe him a debt because he introduced me to my mother, but I still don't like him. There's something remarkably iffy about the connection he and Isra share. I cannot put my finger on it, but it's just off. Good luck to them both anyhow, as it seems it will soon be over now, Everilda surmounted eagerly in her thoughts. She had to admit that Isra being civil with her was bewildering but it was so much more pleasant than their many standoffs.

"Oh. Samuel Reynaldi. Yes. Astrid came to me and Rhiannon for help in getting you long before any of us knew any of this. It's been quite a shocker for me, I must admit. But it's nice to finally have a daughter who has done well for herself, at least magically speaking," Damien articulated formally.

He had a feeling that Isra was an intellectual like himself—unlike Everilda, who could barely spell her own name, never mind pronouncing it.

"I'm a resourceful witch but a hot mess in the romance department," Isra admitted with a serious glance.

Damien could tell right there and then that she was being deadly serious.

"I wouldn't be so sure of that. Why, you'll never know your luck," Astrid butted in, much to Isra's shock.

She was so surprised at how he looked at her with such intrigue. Yes, it was no secret, something was developing with Isra and Astrid, but she wasn't sure of the entirety of it yet.

Astrid looked at the clock with extreme nervousness. He already felt like they had been here too long. He didn't want it to go on any longer than necessary. Astrid knew they needed to get back to

Wretchenheart. It was true, his mind had been preoccupied with getting back into Isra's bed but he also wanted to ensure she was safe, and he couldn't guarantee that whilst they were here.

"We should go," Astrid softly nudged.

He stood right by Isra as she sat on the couch. He was always near her. As close as he could be despite the bizarre circumstance he had found himself in. Discussing his potentially fraught sex life regarding Isra with her father Damien... Yeah, that was something you didn't do every day for sure.

"Yes, perhaps that would be wise," Rhiannon piped up.

Clearly, the demoness wasn't best pleased with how things had unfolded in her living room but she couldn't comment as she'd been with Damien since he was a young man in his prime. It wasn't a total blow to her that he'd had it off with someone else. She knew his marriage with Damaris was laced with deceit and unhappiness. She was just having a hard time adjusting to the fact her newly found daughter was at war with Damien's other daughter, which, by the way, Damien hadn't told her about. They'd all discovered Isra's existence in the Daughtry lineage exactly half an hour ago. So, Rhiannon wasn't handling this well and wanted her home free of Isra as soon as possible.

"Yes, Astrid, it has been a pleasure as always," Damien agreed in unison with Rhiannon. However, he was more polite about it. "Please do take care, Isra," Damien called out to her as Astrid immediately pulled her up from the couch, grabbing her hand and forcing it into his own as he began concentrating on getting back to Wretchenheart.

It was true he was practically yanking her away. Urging her to go along with him. Astrid wasn't taking any chances. He barely acknowledged Damien, other than a slight nod in Damien's direction. He focused on the energy growing around himself and Isra. The voices of Damien, Rhiannon, and Everilda became further and further away, and soon enough, the entire scene faded, and Astrid and Isra stood in the grand throne room of Wretchenheart.

16

"Well, that went on longer than I planned," Astrid abruptly announced to Isra. He still had her in his grasp. "I am sorry for my forcefulness. I'm just so concerned with your welfare. I didn't mean to snatch you away like that. But with all of this going on, well, I got ahead of myself. I'm quite the hot mess right now. Honestly," Astrid admitted softly as he reached over to place his hand on Isra's heart.

"Yet another thing we have in common." Isra chuckled as she realised Astrid was touching her just underneath her breast. His fingers moved rhythmically as though they were tracing a faint outline of her firm yet supple cleavage.

"I need to tell you something. I want to make the most of us. Here. You and I. We've slept together once already and kissed twice. But I want so much more than that, Isra."

Astrid breathed down on her as he said it. He felt hot as heat emitted from him. His body was surging as though it was on fire, just being near her. It was intoxicating.

"Uh-huh," Isra commented.

She wasn't certain about what she should say. Isra felt a strong attraction to Astrid that she couldn't deny, but she wasn't sure what their connection meant.

"What if we could be more than this? Some attraction we both feel. I want us to be united as one, Isra. I am terrified of losing you. More than I've ever felt, and it's weighing down on me heavier than before now that we know Samuel is lying in wait."

He felt incredibly emotional. He wanted to do right by her. That didn't mean he'd just be her consort. Damn, he'd be her king if she felt he was worthy enough but just for one moment, even if this all went to shit, he wanted them to be together.

"I do feel fondly for you. I won't lie," Isra confessed. "But I don't have a good track record with men. Look at me!" she exclaimed. "I'm not great in the bedroom. Well, at least in the courting area, because no doubt in a few months, you'll leave. They all do," she expressed with a sad smile. It was clear she felt as though perhaps she wasn't good enough when Astrid felt he wasn't quite worthy enough for her.

Are you kidding me? What a pair we are. I'm practically beaming at the chance to be in her bed. And she thinks I'm going to skedaddle. Oh, hell no. No, we won't have any of that, Astrid told himself gallantly.

"Bollocks!" Astrid chided. "I am not going anywhere."

Astrid reached over to Isra's lips, gently pressing his own onto hers. She touched his arm with her hand gently and whispered with intense fear, "But what about Samuel? He could come by at any moment. Should we really be doing this? Isn't it wrong?"

Astrid took her hand off of his arm and gently whispered into Isra's ear. "Let me worry about that. Just let yourself go. Let it all go. Nothing matters right now other than what you feel."

He kissed her again, only this time, he went a little slower, clinging onto her lips as he brushed against them with his succulent kiss. "The question is, what will the powerful witch do? Has she finally met her match? Are we at the point of no return?" Astrid whispered into her ear as he waited to see if Isra would give in to him as passionately as he yearned for her.

He'd waited for this moment for nearly two years. The heat between them overwhelmed Astrid. It had the pure power alone to knock him flying across the room. The immense intensity he felt for her and only her was always something he felt right at the core of him. It was unmistakable. There was nothing that it could possibly be compared to.

"I don't know what to say," Isra finally said.

She looked at him more vulnerable than she had ever been. A tiny tear dripped from her eye and it honestly made her shine like a beacon, matching the brilliance of that shimmery white dress still clinging to her feminine figure.

"Then don't say anything. Don't spoil the moment," Astrid encouraged.

Can I take this as a sign that she wants me as badly as I want her? he mulled over in thought as he placed his fingers on her breast, feeling the softness of her skin.

She didn't stop him or say that she didn't want him. He would have halted by now if she showed any signs she wasn't wholly comfortable with what he was doing. But then, out of absolutely nowhere, Isra placed her hand onto Astrid's heart and bright lime-green energy shot out of it, hitting her heart. She felt the intensity of it. Astrid softly kissed her lips again as the powerful forcefulness collided between them. He held her gently against the wall of the throne room.

"If it's too much, just say. We'll stop now. I'll go with you to your bedroom, and we'll just sit in silence. If you don't want to do this, let me know," he pressed, wanting to ensure Isra was all right with them moving forward.

"I want us to go to my room and have you kiss me, making me forget all of the others who didn't see what you do," Isra announced in a low voice.

Astrid needed nothing else. He snatched her hand into his own, taking off with her. They ran out of the throne room, heading straight for Isra's bedroom. He was going to take her right there and then on her plush velvet bed.

～

A STRID WOKE to the birds singing. Isra lay comatose on his shoulder, resting comfortably upon his body. He looked at the clock in anticipation and noted it was five o'clock in the morning. Hmm, he wouldn't have any need to wake her just yet, but Astrid was hungry.

He thought, *It will be no great loss if I run down to the kitchen and rustle myself up a snack.*

Astrid was getting used to the idea now that he no longer needed to forage in the earth for worms. He was developing a refined palette for a variety of foods, including cheese, red meats, bacon, and a vast selection of fruits and vegetables. He also enjoyed coffee as his favourite beverage. He quickly lifted himself out of bed and threw on his trousers, toddling off softly out of the bedroom so he didn't disturb Isra.

Astrid summarised that he'd wander into the kitchen, help himself to a bunch of things from the larder in his search for breakfast. Although when he opened it up, he was surprised to see two fresh peaches. He grabbed both of them and broiled them slightly under the open fire grill and watched them sizzle. He then proceeded to make himself and Isra two large coffees, which he poured into equally enormous white cups. Next, he sprinkled some cinnamon on both peaches before summoning up some vanilla ice cream from the freezer and plopped a scoop of that on each. Ha, that was breakfast taken care of. It was nice and easy. No big, elaborate fuss was required, and he traipsed back to the bedroom.

Isra was still sleeping when he got back so he gently nudged her shoulders, leaning over her as she stirred a little. He placed the two plates of peaches followed by their caffeinated beverages on the cold stone floor so they'd be good for a little while until Isra woke up.

"Mmm. Hmm," Isra moaned sleepily as Astrid gently nudged her again, only now slightly more forceful as he willed her awake.

"Morning, sleepyhead," he said softly. "Come on, sit up. I made you breakfast."

Astrid helped Isra sit up. She was still very much in a daze. He then presented her with the dish of peach and ice cream, which she ogled rather than ate.

"Eat. You should keep your strength up before I ravage you again." He chuckled as he sat his plate on his lap after he got back into Isra's bed but then he remembered the two coffees he set on the floor.

"You'll do what now, dear heart?" Isra quizzed with a wide-eyed stare.

She reluctantly took a bite of the peach and ice cream. It wasn't her usual snack. She much preferred munching on berries rather than being presented with a meal like this. She didn't have much of an appetite and often filled herself with a variety of fruity yet spicy herbal teas. Or apples. She could snack on those until the cows came home but what Astrid had served up, she'd have to eat since he was pretty insistent she followed the instructions he gave her.

"Eat. Or I'll have to keep you holed up here in bed, won't I?" he threatened with a sly chuckle to signify he was joking.

"Fine."

Isra relented and continued her task of gobbling up the food, much to Astrid's glee. He watched her with much anticipation, having already finished his meal.

Isra wolfed down her peach but left most of the ice cream as it wasn't to her liking before she then reached over and fetched the mug of coffee that Astrid placed on the floor by her bed. She just took a large gulp of it when she felt Astrid's arm around her back.

"Now just what shall we do today?" he asked as he gently nuzzled her ear.

Astrid was still very much in the sensual mood from last night but at least his sombreness had died down, which was reassuring to Isra. She felt he'd been a little bit all over the place lately.

"I was hoping I could go for a walk," Isra piped up. "I feel so cooped up within these walls. I just want to get away from here for a while."

Being kept at Wretchenheart Castle was for her own wellbeing and Astrid was far from a jailer, but Isra was a free spirit at heart.

"Hmm. I am not so sure that is wise," Astrid responded. "I can't have you wandering around aimlessly, even in these parts." His voice returned to the more deathly hoarse one again.

"I *want* to go out," Isra pressed on.

She wasn't giving up. Isra had already got her way with Astrid once by persuading him to take her to Damien but what she failed to take heed of was Astrid's determination in keeping her right where he could see her.

"I am firmly against it. We can't. Not at the moment. Just stay here," he ordered wistfully. "We can spend some time here today. There is no need for you to go walkabouts anywhere. I've spent a lot of time trying to catch up to you and now I have you…"

Astrid paused as he recalled all the times he fondly watched Isra from afar before finally introducing himself to her as he had done on the grounds of Shambre Fell before gaining her trust and then asking her to meet him in Glamvein, where they'd had that delightful picnic. It was a wild ride, but he'd chased her. Astrid broke down all of Isra's visible and not so evident walls and finally claimed her as his.

"I am not letting you go. Don't mistake this for imprisonment. I am trying to keep you safe. I need you to trust me. Can you do that?" Astrid asked gently.

He didn't want to rock the boat. For even Astrid knew that the witch he'd grown to know and love was a true rebel at heart.

"I suppose so. But I am already so irked with this place. There is nothing for me to do."

Isra groaned in an annoyed voice. Yes, she was the queen, but for a queen, she hardly ever sat upon her throne. Mind you, since Wretchenheart Castle hadn't been lucky enough to have a monarch for quite some considerable number of years, Isra was simply playing a part and throwing on some theatrics for the tourists when she first came here.

"Well, I can't promise it won't be forever. We just need to keep you out of harm's way, especially until something can be done about Samuel," Astrid said to her carefully. His face turned to sadness and his eyes seemed to have lost some of their glow, but he was trying to hold himself together for Isra's benefit.

"All right. I'll trust you," Isra agreed as she took another sip of her coffee.

Astrid clasped her onto his lap as he lay in her bed, feeling relieved that for the time being, all was well. But he needed to keep his wits about him if he was to get them through what was coming next. Little did Astrid know, his newly made enemy was seeking assistance from a nearby realm.

Samuel Reynaldi was a very preoccupied man this morning. He'd been rummaging around some of his oldest tomes to perhaps find some answers regarding just how he was going to be able to get up close and personal with Isra. Samuel knew better than anyone in Spirisity that getting himself to Wretchenheart, a demon dimension, would be a difficult feat to master. And so, he'd been digging in the archives to see if he could find something of use to him.

"Evidently, our girl has had quite the helping hand in the form of Astrid. He's done all the legwork getting her to that wasteland of a place. Not her. Isra's simply gone along with it because she knows no better. Hmmm, I wonder if I should just somehow show up, but first, we have to get Astrid out of the way," Samuel conferred to himself, completely neglecting the fact that his assistant, James, was present in the room.

They weren't in his office today. It was too cold there and since it was drawing on to autumn, Samuel decided the living room was a much better fit for the work they had on hand. Plus, all of the bookshelves were to be found there rather than in Samuel's office, which only housed a fair few of them. Notably, the prime attraction of Samuel's living room was that dynamic entity; his fond fireplace. That antique gilded gold was beaming bright with orange and yellow flame merged with the black leather four-seater couch, which sat so perfectly in the middle of the lounge. James was comfortably seated on the far end near the window whilst Samuel was closer to the fireplace, sitting in the middle.

"And have you ever considered that maybe she's going along with it because she has no memory of what she did previously?" James suggested with a low brow. He too was browsing through an epic tome, trying to find something they might be able to wield against Lady Isra of the Dark.

"Yes. Highly amusing. I already know that," Samuel snipped with a gruff tone. "Hmm, there is nothing here. Not a single word about disarming a witch in a demon dimension without becoming a fully-fledged demon, and that's not on my to-do list any time soon."

Samuel moaned with a low growl. *Eurgh, it's almost ten o'clock in the morning. We've been on this crusade for nearly five hours and we've found sod all. I don't want to become a demon. But I wonder...* Samuel pondered to himself in thought. His face lit up; he suddenly had a wave of inspiration hit him.

"I might go off for a stroll. I feel like nature might soothe my weary soul," Samuel announced. He sounded chipper, which was weird considering he was a poster child for doom and gloom five minutes ago.

"You can't go off to Wretchenheart, though. Light-bringers cannot set foot in a demon realm without being of that entity themselves," James reminded him with a sceptical look.

"Yes, I know. Anyway, shut up. Keep working while I am gone. I might be away for a while because I have a theory and it could work, but I could do with rustling some muscle behind it before I attempt such a feat," Samuel said so cryptically that James sat dumbfounded with no idea what the light-bringer was talking about.

I can remove her if I become a demon. All right, so for a loophole, it's pretty ghastly for a light-bringer to undertake, but even loopholes have some of the dirtiest tricks in order to fool the unsuspecting onlooker.

Samuel chuckled to himself in thought as he clicked his index thumb and finger together, disappearing in the blink of an eye.

17

"Ah, now that's much better," Samuel chirped in a cheery tone.

He found himself directly in front of the brilliant white Grimsbane farmhouse in Immortal Yonder. Of course, Samuel hadn't been here since he deliberately let Isra in by means of allowing her to pass the Grimsbane magical shield designed to keep everyone out.

Samuel walked right up to the door. It was shut, but he expected nothing else on a charming September morning. He boldly pounded upon the door with his fist. He needed to catch a certain Grimsbanes' attention.

It was only a few seconds before Nathaniel Grimsbane came to the door, looking bemused. He peered over at Samuel with sky-blue rectangular spectacles hanging off his nose.

"Mr Reynaldi? I didn't expect to see you in our neck of the woods. I'm a little perturbed as to why you'd come to see me after what your Isra did to my Alan."

Nathaniel scowled impetuously. He had his arms folded across his chest in a nonchalant stance as if to show he meant business. Nathaniel wasn't interested in the self-serving light-bringer or whatever he had to say.

"Yes, Nathaniel… about that. It's why I'm here. I have a way to rectify the issue for both of us," Samuel detailed to Nathaniel in a low voice. He was being a little more cautious than usual, for now all eyes and ears would be on him, especially since the Sanctification of the Unseen's ruling.

"Hmm, and may I ask, why should I listen to you?" Nathaniel probed with great scrutiny.

There was nothing on earth that could persuade him, even if he was quite the failure at a warlock, from assisting Samuel Reynaldi with anything.

"Because you help me, and in turn, I help you by allowing you to get vengeance on Lady Isra of the Dark. So, are you interested, or do I have to dig further into the Grimsbanes' unwanted unmentionables to get what I want?" Samuel eagerly threatened with a pressing glare.

Samuel could be just as cold and as treacherous as any Grimsbane. He was making himself known. Samuel had a goal, and he was determined to get it done, even if it took dismantling heaven and earth to get there.

"Fine. Come in. Coffee is in the pot," Nathaniel snapped as he turned away from the door, waiting for Samuel to enter with a rather irritated expression on his face. He asked pointedly, "Well, are you bloody coming in or not?"

"Oh, sorry. Was just admiring the view!" Samuel uttered in a sadistic tone as he pointed to Immortal Yonder's majestic sunset in shades of fuchsia, burnt orange, and yellow with gold undertones. "It really is quite something, you know! Anyhow, yes; you're right—we must press on. There is much to discuss."

Samuel nodded in agreement and walked into Nathaniel's house. Nathaniel grimly pointed at the table situated in the dining room before sitting and then slumping back in his chair. Samuel could take a hint and didn't need to be told to sit himself down, as he had a large cup of coffee placed in front of him.

"Oh, thank you. You are too kind. Now let us get onto business!" Samuel formally announced.

He proceeded to sip some of the rich black coffee, which was delicious. It must have been a special type of bean. Samuel could taste the earth when he felt it collide onto his tongue, sliding down the back of his throat so smoothly. Samuel didn't dare ask Nathaniel what this coffee was for fear he'd anger the warlock any more than he already had, so he decided to get on with it. Much to Samuel's surprise, Nathaniel was more invested in Samuel's cause than the light-bringer gave him credit for.

"So may I ask what's cooking?" Nathaniel prodded with mild interest.

You could say he was biting the hook here, but at least Samuel saw that perhaps Nathaniel might be receptive after all. He was a stubborn bugger, but then again, the man had just lost his son less than a month ago, so what did Samuel honestly expect? A cheery mood? For Nathaniel to be walking on airs, delighting in every single part of life?

No, of course not. That simply wasn't true. The poor man was indeed grieving, and while Nathaniel wasn't going to succeed in becoming father of the year, he did love his son, Alan, even if he hadn't shown it to the boy when he was alive.

"Lady Isra of the Dark. More precisely, I have been given permission to hold her accountable for her crimes, which includes the murder of your son," Samuel disclosed with a low brow.

"Ah. I must say, I didn't expect it. I mean, the way I heard it from my mother was that Isra got off scot-free, and she even supports the damn woman! The girl who killed her grandson, and she's practically celebrating her. What gives?" Nathaniel beseeched loudly.

He clearly wasn't appeased by Isra. Samuel was going to take this as a promising sign of their future collaboration.

"Zelena has no say in what commences from here on out." Samuel made it crystal clear as he said it.

"I don't quite follow you there. Can you clarify your meaning?" Nathaniel queried.

"I have been tasked to bring her to justice. The decision was made by those up 'on high.' Zelena simply was allowed to make her case, stating that she believes Isra was mentally incapable of withstanding a relationship and my involvement was lacklustre at best. 'On high' basically stated that I neglected Isra by not being around when she originally turned the tide. They implied Alan's death could have been prevented, which I don't believe to be true—you saw for yourself what a menace Isra is," Samuel clarified. It should have been clear where they stood, but he had yet to mention the best part of all.

"And why do I get the feeling you're missing a crucial part in this search and rescue mission?"

Nathaniel narrowed his eyes inquisitively at Samuel. Yes, Nathaniel couldn't believe anything coming out of Samuel's mouth, but he'd better believe something if he was going to get his revenge.

"Because I am not. You know how the lore works. Nothing is cut and dry, old son. Isra currently resides in the demonic dimension, Wretchenheart; where I cannot touch her. I can't even set foot in the place, but here's the clincher. She's with my former employee, Astrid. He used to be a raven, although you'd never believe it," Samuel blurted out, explaining what was ahead of them.

"Aha, yes, that snide loophole that was created insisting light-bringers cannot go anywhere that is a product of darkness. However, I am more interested in this Astrid. Why would he team up with Lady Isra of the Dark if he's a former servant of yours? I don't corroborate your meaning. Surely, his duty is to the light?" Nathaniel pressed.

Being a man rooted in darkness himself, he understood that while he could go to a light realm, somebody embedded in the light could not. That was simply the way of it. Some old, stubborn fool must have got sick and tired of light folk parading around locales whereby darkness was strongly prominent and so they banned it. Because the last thing you wanted to see while eating someone's entrails was a goody-two-shoes angel or blooming spirit guide. You just don't take those kinds of risks, do you? Hahaha.

"One would presume so, yes. But alas, Astrid fell head over wing for our charming Lady Isra. A spectacle of a woman that, at only age nineteen, killed a warlock and managed to outsmart us all. She's remarkable, but for all the wrong reasons," Samuel countered in a sardonic tone as he pondered just whether he'd given Nathaniel enough of the facts to encourage him to reconsider his choice of not to help in this delicate yet timely matter.

"Aha, so the real conundrum here is we have to get rid of this Astrid fellow. Did the kindly and good loving folks at 'on high' specify him at all when they handed you their ruling pertaining to Lady Isra?" Nathaniel asked with a forewarning glance.

Nathaniel seemed to be thinking about something; he had two fingers pressed diligently to his lips as if to communicate some rational thought or improvisation, but Samuel could only dare to imagine what the grieving warlock might be thinking.

"Actually, they are very keen on speaking with him. They won't even begin to go into why, but that's usual business for them." Samuel paused as he explained this important detail to Nathaniel, remembering something he had yet to divulge.

I can't say too much here, but if I want him to trust me enough to help, I have to give him something. Even if it's just a crumb. A tasty tidbit of which I might rationalise giving him the rest of the cake if he's just tempted enough to bite, Samuel thought as he pursued this idea thoroughly.

"They are called Sanctification of the Unseen. Heck, I've been referring to them as 'on high' for as long as I can recall, but no; it turns out they have a whole other name that not even I, the Lord, Light-bringer and Chief, was granted permission to know," Samuel candidly informed Nathaniel.

"Sneaky bastards." Nathaniel made the snide remark with a sly chuckle, finding the latter amusing.

To be considered divine enough for the cause, you had to be a bastard. Spiritual matters weren't of much importance in these times, but that was the rule. They made it astutely clear what their preferences were. You had to be unmarried, preferably a virgin with no ghastly past. That was what those who floated above the soft, fluffy white clouds insisted upon. Of course, Samuel was a different kettle of fish, but he rarely let that type of information slip.

Samuel was a slippery one, as we know. But when his father, Bernard Reynaldi, sadly perished, they decided it was going to be his son, Samuel, that would be given the grand role of light-bringer. Many came to question how someone with no connections to the light-bringer lineage got in there like a shot. It was a stab in the dark, placing Samuel in there, but like everything else, there was always good reasoning behind every decision they made.

"Aren't they just? My assistant, James, is somewhat of a novice. He's only been on the Lady Isra of the Dark case for two years, but Astrid was my right-hand man, and he knew the business like the back of his claw. I still remember how Astrid came into this. He was a poor, wandering soul, and I sheltered him after hearing a most endearing story. I never once suspected he'd fall for a witch on the blooming job, but I guess one can never predict these things, can they?" Samuel quizzed Nathaniel, as he was also making a profound statement.

Everyone made mistakes, even the light-bringer in charge. Nobody is perfect. That type of existence whereby every last action you undertake and every word that emits from your lips is gold dust, well, it's fictional at best and impossible for a world to be like that. There's darkness, danger, and even possibly the tiniest hint of betrayal. Lies curdling alongside the truth are what normally expose it, but nobody can detect it at that time because no one person is going to get it completely right. That's just the way the grand cosmos works. It reacts to all and sundry who inhabit it; you can't fathom whether they will be good or bad as the chemical reaction is going to occur either way.

"No, we can't. You're quite right, Samuel. Nobody can make judgments on that until it happens either," Nathaniel agreed. "Then our first priority is taking Astrid out," he stated in a stern tone. "We should place all efforts on him first. My money says if we do a search and destroy mission regarding Isra, he's going to leap to her defence since she's proved quite problematic already. And he with her."

Nathaniel made the suggestion as surely he must have considered just sending in someone who could physically get to Wretchenheart to ensnare Isra.

"Yes, but she won't falter easily. Neither will he," Samuel

admonished with a forlorn glance. "But, wait... My manservant, James, managed to get into Wretchenheart once before. He was the one who had exposed Astrid's treachery."

"Now I wonder if we could get the know-how from him," Nathaniel proposed. "It might help us gather some intelligence on what the best approach to might be move forward. Now in the meantime, I do have one idea. It won't do anything to Isra. Not right this instant, but it could weaken her defences. I believe you are blessed with light magic, isn't that right?" Nathaniel grilled with an intense stare.

"I am indeed. I am only allowed to use it for the right and just reasons, though," Samuel explained carefully.

"All right, forget that for a moment. I want you to explain to me this place Isra currently dwells in... because if we can get someone into there who can perform this magic, it might be enough to get you or someone else into the premises," Nathaniel softly cajoled, although it seemed to Samuel he knew what he was talking about.

"Wretchenheart Castle, to be precise," Samuel answered promptly with a bewildering glare.

"So we need somebody who either isn't ascended yet by choice or is angelic but yet chooses to remain earthbound; hence me saying not yet ascended to the heavenly plane," Nathaniel suggested cleverly.

"Well, my assistant, James, is angelic, and he's not quite ascended just yet. Perhaps he'd be a good fit for what we need?" Samuel queried the matter in Nathaniel's direction.

He was questioning just why Nathaniel would ask for the exact locality of the place. *Hmm, he's a dark horse, this one. He seems to want to know the exact whereabouts of Isra but why I haven't the foggiest. To be continued, as I doubt I am going to find out why,* Samuel muttered away in the back of his mind.

"Right, hmm," Nathaniel chattered to himself solemnly. "We need to get your assistant in there as soon as possible," he then said firmly to Samuel, making Samuel even more perplexed; again, he didn't comprehend why.

"I don't quite understand how that has any bearings on this," Samuel uttered in exasperation.

"I know, and don't worry. Let's just have a chat with your man, shall we?"

Nathaniel requested Samuel to do the honours as Samuel threw Nathaniel a bemused look.

"Oh! You want me to magic him over here. No problem at all. One moment," Samuel responded as he closed his eyes, getting himself into the right frame of mind.

He pictured James. No doubt the bugger was still sitting in Samuel's living room, back in Spirisity, so it wouldn't be too hard getting him here in a jiffy. Samuel concentrated hard on James's image, and he visualised the tall, mousy brown-haired young chap sitting at the opposite end of this table right now.

Nathaniel jumped out of his chair as James materialised in the middle of the room, holding a coffee cup and looking baffled as to what he was doing here.

"Erm, dare I ask? You have to be more careful, just wilfully ripping me away from places like this, Samuel," James said in a cross tone.

Nathaniel softened the blow by introducing himself. "Hello, James. My name is Nathaniel. Please sit down. We have much to discuss."

Samuel interrupted Nathaniel. He wanted to get a word in edgeways before things become too complex. "James, I appreciate you didn't like being zapped away like that, but I summoned you as you are someone who can execute a matter of great importance. Nathaniel is assisting me on that, hence why we're situated at his dominion."

"Yes," Nathaniel muttered as he presented James with a steaming mug of coffee. For if they were going to talk like proper men, they should at least do it caffeinated. That equalled an immense amount of masculine brain power... or however it went. "Anyhow, we want you to go into Wretchenheart Castle and immerse it in light magic," Nathaniel detailed to James explicitly.

"Holy shit? You're kidding. No way. I can't do that. If Astrid is as humanised as everyone tells it these days, he'll rip me to shreds within seconds of discovering me on his beloved witch's premises," James exclaimed with fear.

He wasn't impressed at what he was expected to do, but then again, who would be happy about it?

"You'll be cloaked," Samuel chimed in momentarily. "I can't get in there myself. Trust me, James, I would if I could," he insisted gravely. "Light-bringers don't have any jurisdiction in places like Wretchenheart. I didn't make up the rules."

James softened his rigid stance a little, and he eyed Samuel thoughtfully. "Yes, I know you can't, but you're asking me to go in there and do *what* exactly?" James pressed Samuel for that answer that was niggling away at him. He had a fair idea of what he'd be expected to do.

"You'll flood the place with light magic. You will perform this after four o'clock in the morning when Isra and Astrid will likely be sleeping. The energy will infiltrate every single room, nook, and cranny that Wretchenheart Castle has to offer. There will be no escape. I'm hoping that within hours, Lady Isra of the Dark will feel the effects. She'll be off her game... And then I can hopefully slip in at a moment's notice. I still have to wangle that whole 'not being dark' loophole," Samuel continued explaining to James in immense detail.

"All right. I'll do it," James agreed with a nod. "I'm not overly comfortable about it, but I shall do it. I take it the ruling dictates you have to pull out all the stops to attain access to Isra?"

It was true that James often shunned some of the darker aspects of the work he undertook with Samuel, but he had a very inquisitive mind. A yearning for knowledge, which was crucial in performing at one's best because when you are learning, you have less chance of failing at something. And even if it does commence that you do fail, you've had a lesson in the way of experience.

"Yes, in not so many words, boy," Samuel expressed in a slightly frustrated tone before emitting, "Thank you. I appreciate your ever-present loyalty to the cause. I know it's short notice, but I expect you to do this tonight, so there's only around sixteen hours to prepare yourself," Samuel went on to elaborate for James's benefit so he had all of the facts at his disposal.

Nathaniel peeked over at James from where he sat and raised his hand meekly. "I don't wish to intrude, but may I ask how James can enter and you cannot?"

The question was valid and worth asking but there was reasoning beyond the core of Nathaniel's understanding, so Samuel would have to break it down in simplified terms for the warlock.

"James is angelic. Angelic beings have certain privileges that I, as a light-bringer, do not," Samuel answered him curtly.

"Ah, most intriguing. I didn't know there was such a thing!" Nathaniel chimed in, much to Samuel's annoyance. He needed to get himself and James back to Spirisity as soon as humanly possible because there were preparations that needed to be done before the main event tonight could commence.

"Yes, I am sorry, Nathaniel, but James and I must go back to Spirisity. You are welcome to accompany us if you wish? I understand if you want to sit this part out, though," Samuel offered Nathaniel the get-out clause just in case it was needed.

"Boys, I shall come along. This woman murdered my son!" Nathaniel firmly stated.

"All right, let's be going then. Much to do!" Samuel commanded, and with a click of his index finger and thumb, all three of them dissipated in a flash.

SAMUEL OPENED HIS EYES, finding himself in his living room alongside Nathaniel and James. He keenly checked the clock in front of him that hung on the wall by the fireplace, noting that it was only just two o'clock in the afternoon. He took James by the arm and sat him on the couch, proceeding to list some very detailed instructions off the top of his head.

"Right, boy. I know this might not sound pleasing, but from now, until you enter Wretchenheart, you are on a strict purification diet. You won't be able to consume any food; just water until the main event. And you need drink this for the time being to get those juices flowing in the right direction, if you understand my meaning."

Samuel mysteriously closed his eyes and snapped his fingers. A large glass tumbler of what appeared to be some rancid yellow-coloured liquid materialised in his hand.

"What's that?"

James grimaced as he gingerly took the glass from Samuel. He smelt it with a look of disdain in his eyes, as it had a slightly citrus scent but was also aromatic as well; maybe a tiny hint of spice in there.

"Lemon water with the tiniest hint of chilli powder. No whining now. Drink it all down. What you are about to undertake is a big deal, and of course, purifying your body is a must if we are going to succeed," Samuel explained to James.

James held his nose with his thumb and finger as he took a large gulp of the liquid, feeling it surge down the back of his throat and hit his stomach, causing it to growl ferociously. It surely didn't like this mixture being thrown inside it, but Samuel threw Samuel an unsympathetic look. Behind him, James saw a ginormous green glass bottle that housed even more of this foul liquid beverage, much to his alarm.

"Yes, you'll drink all of it," Samuel asserted with a firm tone. "Oh, don't worry, you don't have to consume all two litres of it in one hit. We'll space it out between now and two o'clock. We have plenty of time," he affirmed with a low brow.

James took yet another swig of the foul-tasting liquid that wasn't as bad the second time going down his throat as it was the first. "Wish me luck!" he chortled nervously.

With just twelve hours to go until James would be emerging into Wretchenheart uninvited and then filling the place top to bottom with light magic, the heat was on. There would be no coming back from this. Samuel would hopefully have his way in, and James would be the facilitator of everything he hoped to gain.

18

The clock struck just past four, but Astrid and Isra were oblivious to this since they were getting quite cosy in Isra's bedroom. Astrid finally declared what he had truly desired from Lady Isra of the Dark and she was receptive enough to allow him to show her what she had been missing, asking him to make her forget all those that hadn't seen what he did, as Isra had fondly said to him. They had been making up for lost time, much to Astrid's delight. He had waited for this moment for almost two years. In his mind, it seemed so much longer, but none of that mattered now.

Astrid gently traced his fingers over Isra's heart as he playfully straddled her fine form while whispering sweetly in her ear, "Ha, this is real, isn't it? I never imagined in all of my wildest dreams that it could be, but it is. Now, let me pamper you like the queen I always deemed you."

"You say the most endearing things, Astrid," Isra muttered.

She felt her heart skip a beat. Her breathing intensified with every fleeting second he laid on her body. Just the pure sensation of him on top of her sent powerful tingles all over her skin.

They had been lying in bed, tangled between those soft silk sheets since midnight. Now it was drawing into the morning. The passion was not fading between them. Astrid had shown Isra just who he had wanted all this time and that he didn't care what all the other men in her life neglected to see, but Isra was preoccupied. She suddenly felt light-headed. The room around her began to spin as her eyes flickered.

Astrid caught this as quickly as it had begun, and he asked her softly, "Wait, what's wrong?" with much concern. He realised his beloved was feeling not quite herself, which was odd since she never got like this.

"I just feel a little dizzy," Isra muttered in exasperation, feeling tiny beads of sweat dripping down her forehead.

Astrid quickly leapt off the bed and grabbed a glass of water that he'd set aside on the floor before they'd got cosy. "Here, drink this. Slowly." He placed his hand gingerly over the top of her forehead. "You're sick. I don't know how. It's nearly impossible for you to get sick, but it feels magical in some form or another. Just keep sipping that," Astrid commanded.

Isra felt more out of touch with everything around her. She was losing her grip on reality. The bedroom she was in with Astrid, she could barely even feel present in it now. It was like she was somewhere else, but her body was right here.

"Rest now," Astrid whispered as he lay next to her.

Their fun escapade of earlier was over. Astrid watched over Isra as she gasped weakly. Her entire world was being torn apart and she floated in and out of consciousness. Little did Astrid or Isra know that there was a very familiar face that had invaded their fortress only a few feet away below.

James opened his eyes, finding himself outside the eccentric entity better known as Wretchenheart Castle. Funny, when he was here before, he never went near the castle, mainly due to the fact he wasn't aware of its existence. He was a novice explorer in these parts of the land, so naturally, he just wanted to get on with what he had to do and get going again.

Walking up that dynamic pathway that led to the drawbridge was momentous. It was illuminated in bright orange lights, which looked quite eerie considering it was cut off from the rest of the demonic realm. Needless to say, Wretchenheart was known for its creepy quirks, and this was no exception. James knew that in order to get into the castle, he needed to be able to lift the drawbridge down, which was impossible since the occupants from inside needed to lower it, but thankfully, James had been imbued with so much light magic, there was no need for such a thing.

"Well, I can't say they didn't try."

James chuckled and softly closed his eyes, and he focused on himself being inside that majestic castle. Sure, Astrid and Isra had done a marvellous job of keeping their unwanted out, but when you have the power of magic at your disposal, nothing is impossible. He slowed his breathing to the point he felt it rising through his chest and then waited as he imagined himself in that grand empire of what Samuel had described as an esotericist's grand hall, meaning the throne room where Isra was initially crowned queen.

It only took a few seconds, and then he was inside. James opened his eyes and noticed all the gold around him... the gold walls followed by brilliant white ceilings and then those bright silvery-white chandeliers, which ironically would be the same colour as the magic he was about to unleash all over this prestigious fortress.

James quietly walked around the grand throne room of Wretchenheart's eccentric castle. He took note of the gold and ochre tones dominating the room, while the gold gilded chair with red flush cushioning stood out amongst everything else. *Well, this is it. This is where Astrid whisked her away. I have to admit, for a demon realm to have a castle like this, well, it certainly is something special. It's a shame I have to envelope it in light magic, but here we are. I work for the cause and if 'on high' deem that Lady Isra must be stopped, whatever the cost, then that is what I must do,* James thought. He felt extremely nervous about being here like this.

He was alone without any heavenly assistance at four o'clock in the morning, about to unleash this magical enlightenment without a care into this historic monstrosity that housed the light's most reckless villain.

"She has made a name for herself. I'll give her that. At only nineteen, she's conquered a feat that many of her living immortal relatives could only dream of achieving. Still, you have to have to appreciate the irony of it all," James cajoled to himself as he prepared to get into position for what he was about to do.

Unbeknownst to him, Lady Isra was being affected by just him being in Wretchenheart Castle. He carried so much potent light magic in his possession that when it would be released, Lady Isra would feel the effect of it right away. James had not been given the exact details on how it would happen or what Lady Isra would feel, only that it was necessary and Samuel needed a way into Wretchenheart.

Being a light-bringer, he couldn't do the job himself, so he needed a second in command to get it done in his absence. Samuel had made it clear that if Isra was weakened enough by magic beyond her ghastly dark comprehension, then just maybe Samuel might be able to slip in. It was promising, but nobody had any idea if such a thing would be attainable just yet.

James began to hum himself a little tune, whistling gently as he concentrated on all of that bright, white silvery energy shooting right out of him and into every corner of every room in this magnificent castle. He continued his process and opened his eyes and watched in awe as the grand throne room was quickly covered in silvery-white mist. James now visualised it going downwards, where he figured the dungeons would be and other parts of the castle he couldn't account for as he'd never been here in person before.

He imagined the energy circulating all around the ground floor, all around the drawbridge, the moat guarding it, and any rooms down on the lower floor level that he may have not known of their existence before he quickly saw the white-silvery misty magic all around in the throne room; only now, it was climbing up to the ceiling at a rapid rate. The throne room was saturated in it.

The only thing James could do was watch as the energy ascended past the ceiling and presumably onto the second floor, where Astrid and Isra's bedrooms were located. James didn't quite have the knack to go up those stairs and be caught in person by either one of them. He knew the likely outcome if he had happened to bump into Astrid, and it wouldn't be pleasant at all. James would have to play it safe and use his magic from a well-guarded distance, and so he watched as the magic floated upstairs.

James closed his eyes once more. He pictured himself standing on the second floor, watching the magic linger all around that dingy corridor that was lit ever so perfectly with shimmering candles dotted all the way down it, lighting up in the darkness. James imagined Astrid and Isra's bedrooms and any other rooms present on that second floor. He saw the magic swiftly centred on that area, down the end of that corridor, and entering into any room near to it.

He then softly whispered, "All right now, any place we missed, please do collide with it. Surround everywhere in your forcefulness with due haste because now we are sealing our work with a kiss."

And with that, James demonstrated by blowing a kiss from his mouth in the direction of the powerful light energy to signify he was sealing it in this bountiful fortress. Trusting in the process, he indeed managed to get that stuff in absolutely every nook and cranny so that there would be no escape when Isra and Astrid finally realised something was awry.

James knew now he had done what he set out to and it was time to take his leave. He didn't want to linger in this place any longer than he had to because Astrid would definitely use James's innards for decorations if he caught him here. James looked wistfully at the time. It was almost five o'clock. With only a few minutes to spare, he'd surrounded the entire castle in pungent light energy for almost an hour. James closed his eyes and imagined himself back in Spirisity, where Samuel would be awaiting his return, wanting to hear everything, no doubt.

He stood by the wall, where he had been the whole time, only to knock a large, crystalline lion figure onto the floor. It crashed wildly as it broke into a million pieces. The floor of the throne room was covered in tiny shards of glass. James knew he needed to make his exit because he'd made such a racket that he'd surely have woken Isra and Astrid up with all of the commotion.

ISRA HAD FINALLY DOZED OFF, breathing rapidly as she flew in and out of consciousness. Astrid placed a cold compress on her forehead. The heat got to her to the point she only had a silk sheet covering her modesty. She'd sweat that much. Besides, she was already naked anyway, so there was no need to strip her clothes off. But still, this mysterious sickness had worked its way through Isra, causing her to jolt without warning until she finally succumbed to deep sleep.

Astrid was wide awake, sat up next to Isra in her bed. He stared absent-mindedly at the wall when he heard a loud crash. It sounded like something hitting the floor and then shattering. *This is odd. It's just me and Isra here,* Astrid thought as he proceeded to throw on a clean white shirt and a pair of black trousers before he left the bedroom to investigate just what had made the large clattering sound that had spiked his interest.

He quickly ran downstairs, grabbing a candle to illuminate his way as he paraded barefooted into the grand throne room, suddenly becoming aware that the room was filled with what appeared to be a white-silvery coloured mist. Astrid didn't need to do much to figure out what this was. Someone had been here, in their home. When he took his focus off it, it completely vanished as though it had never existed.

Astrid didn't waste any time running back up to the bedroom, storming through the door. He ran to Isra's bedside and shook her awake. "We need to go now. Someone has been inside the throne room. Come on, get dressed," he said to Isra softly as she gasped awake, still having issues with her rapid breathing.

She appeared to be dizzy upon waking. "We must go?" she asked weakly.

Isra sounded numb, but Astrid didn't answer her. He turned to Isra's closet, proceeding to thrust open both of its wooden doors in a frantic frenzy. Astrid reached into Isra's closet, fumbling around until he pulled something out of it without even looking or caring to see what he'd grabbed. He threw the black linen dress with long black lace sleeves onto Isra as she laid in the bed, absolutely bemused at what was occurring.

"Yes," Astrid stated, explaining just what he'd witnessed when he dashed down those stairs into the throne room. "Someone has been inside your throne room; now normally, I wouldn't give these things much credence, but I saw this mass of what I can only describe as white-silver coloured magic, and then it dissipated in a flash."

Isra got herself slowly out of bed before she pulled the long black gown over her head. "That sounds rather peculiar," Isra mustered, struggling to maintain her footing as she stood up, but at least she was dressed now.

"Yes, anyhow, Wretchenheart isn't safe now. We should go immediately before anything else happens," Astrid instructed in a formal tone. He cautiously looked at the ceiling. He was rather perplexed about the whole thing. Astrid looked worried, but he wasn't saying entirely just how flustered he was, just emitted, "There's something not right with all of this."

"You're telling me. How can I be here and feel as though I am going to collapse at any moment?" Isra asked weakly as she leaned against the wall for stability.

"Grab onto me," Astrid called to Isra. He swiftly ran over to her, thrusting her right arm around his neck. "Take my hand!" Astrid pleaded with her softly.

Isra extended her left hand to Astrid and he latched onto it as if his life solely depended on it. "Where are we going to go? Surely, we can't go to Shambre Fell?"

She felt increasingly nauseous the longer she was ranked up, waiting for Astrid to get them out of there. Having been rudely awoken and then being told they needed to disappear from the only place she'd known as a refuge was disorientating at best, but now everything just seemed to be upside down—literally, since Isra was experiencing blurred vision along with the headaches and feeling as though the entire contents of her stomach was going to erupt at any moment. She guessed she could possibly put it down to stress over finding out who she was, but Isra had taken it in her stride, so that didn't make any sense to her. It was baffling. She had no clue as to why she felt like this, but perhaps sticking by Astrid's side right now was the best course of action since he seemed to know more about this otherworldly stuff than he cared to.

Astrid concentrated heavily on that eccentric grey mansion he'd soon be whisking Isra away to. *It's only a stone's throw away, at least in the metaphysical sense,* he chided to himself.

He pictured the iconic cobalt-blue sky with all those dazzling white stars as it would be seen in the dead of night before he softly clicked his fingers, still holding onto Isra as they dissipated into the nether realm.

19

"Hmm, here we are," Astrid announced.

Isra slowly opened her eyes, stunned to see where they were. "Sprawnbell again, huh? You figured you'd take me to the nearest place whereby I am hated by at least two occupants. Interesting tactic," she said sardonically.

"Yes, well, I'll ignore that due to how weak you've been. But seriously, Damien doesn't have any issue regarding you being here. Come on. I'll prove it," Astrid crossly replied.

He proceeded to demonstrate by pounding on the door of the Daughtry mansion with a finesse that would make anyone think someone was trying to gain access to the vicinity that definitely shouldn't be. Luckily for the Daughtrys, Isra and Astrid weren't intruders.

"Astrid!" Damien retorted in a low voice as he stood by the open door. Strangely, he didn't open it or rush forward to invite Isra and Astrid in, only stood by it while holding it ajar.

"Hello, Damien. We don't wish to intrude, but there's been a development over at Wretchenheart," Astrid stated, looking around him cautiously.

He was trying to ensure nobody saw him and Isra lurking around these parts. That wouldn't be best welcomed by either Damien or Rhiannon since both of them were very happy to live a secluded existence that wasn't witnessed by anyone.

Damien had his arms down by his sides as he changed his voice to a much more serious tone before regretfully expressing what nobody expected him to say, much to Astrid's shock. He'd hoped getting Isra here would be their ticket to evading Samuel and the rest of the enlightened beings.

"It's getting bad over there, huh? Well, I am not sure what you expect from me," Damien commented.

Before he could say anything else, Astrid interrupted with panicked concern. "We've had to leave Wretchenheart. Someone—I don't know who or what, for that matter—has been trespassing over in the castle. I can't fathom how they accomplished that, but it sounds like invaders because of the bright silvery mist lingering in the throne room."

"Yes, I figured that much with you and my daughter standing here at five o'clock in the morning, but I am not going to deliver welcomed news, Astrid. You cannot stay here. Neither of you can. There is simply too much light upon the both of you. Yes, I am not surprised you've had a disturbance in Wretchenheart. It was bound to happen sooner or later," Damien said coldly.

"Neither of you will be safe here. Those wandering eyeballs of Samuel Reynaldi's flunkies will be looking for you both. This is the last place you should seek refuge. He's not stupid. They'll send someone here. I'm sorry. It's not what you want to hear, but I must ask you to proceed with caution because if they manage to get somebody to infiltrate what was seemingly a demonic dimension out of bounds, then nothing is sacred. Not anymore," Damien admonished.

Astrid turned to Isra thoughtfully and mustered, "Time to come up with a secondary plan. You need to be incognito. It wasn't my first choice, but I guess it will be good enough."

Isra and Damien looked confused. Neither one of them had any inclination what he was talking about.

"Thanks anyway, Damien. I apologise for disturbing you at this unsightly hour," Astrid responded before he turned his attention to getting back into a state whereby he could visualise the next place they'd head.

"No trouble at all, Astrid. You are always welcome. It's just in these circumstances, it's best we avoid it for obvious reasons. Good luck, old son," Damien replied before he shut the door on both of them, leaving Astrid and Isra out in the chilly September winds.

"So, what now?" Isra pressed. She hoped he had something in mind now that their first option had been wiped out of the equation.

"Don't worry," Astrid said softly. "Just stay close to me. Don't let go."

He motioned and indicated for her to keep hold of his hand. Astrid knew that by recollection alone, it would be enough to get them to where they needed to be. He had so many fond memories of Isra in this place that it was surprising he hadn't thought of taking her there sooner, but he'd been preoccupied with so much else that he simply had not given the idea consideration.

"I still don't understand. Where are we going?" Isra pressed with much inquisitiveness.

"Just trust me," Astrid answered before continuing with his task.

He needed to concentrate. Astrid knew that to harness the magic within him, he needed to focus. And it was challenging to do that with all of Isra's questions, but there he was, standing with her hand clasped in his own and with one fleeting breath and a deep visual of where they needed to be, they were soon away.

Astrid took one small step for fear he'd be over the edge if he put a foot down wrong. He realised he was back on the infamous mountain peak.

Thank fuck for that. All right, so we're here. Great, now maybe we should look beyond the mountain to see if there is any sign of life because this place can't be all there is, Astrid thought as he stood with Isra in tow. He had taken her all this way; he wasn't going to abandon her now.

"Oh, my!"

Isra gasped, putting her hand to her mouth in shock. She stood back in disbelief. The majestic mountain peak she stood upon and the entire area around it seemed like a lost wasteland. She hadn't recalled being here, which was ironic when you considered this was the very same location she turned the tide, as Samuel so often fondly put it.

"Yes. I wasn't sure where else we could escape to, what with everything going on. Glamvein is a secluded wilderness. There is no other better place I could think of with such short notice," Astrid explained cautiously.

He looked weary and anxious, but at least he had calmed down somewhat. He looked at Isra with a friendly glance. Astrid was her protector in this scenario, so while he was exhausted, he certainly wasn't being beaten that easily, much to the disappointment of their enemies.

"No. It's no quandary, honestly," Isra excused him as she turned her attention to the fact they were standing on this prestigious mountain peak with nowhere else to be seen for miles around, except that beyond the mountain there seemed to be masses of greenery, so perhaps there was some kind of civilization around there. *It's a nice spot for sure, but we should consider getting off of this monstrosity and finding some suitable shelter. Even if it's just some ransacked cottage.*

Isra pondered the idea and turned to Astrid with a bemused glare.

"Why don't we try getting down from here? Maybe there is somewhere nearby we might find that is comfortable to stay. Since we might be here for some considerable time?" Isra earnestly proposed.

Well, at least she was being practical. Being ripped away from the grand splendour of her castle certainly did a lot for her character, but Isra was most at home in the abundance of nature, so it was no surprise she was an avid explorer at heart.

"All right," Astrid agreed. "I don't really know what else there is other than this mountain, though. I've been here several times with you, but we've never gone beyond it."

He went on to explain, which puzzled Isra, but then she figured the likely reason was for that fact it was locked in her lost memories.

"I guess I just don't remember it, huh?" Isra chuckled nervously. "All right, so we'll go that way," Isra pointed to the narrower part of the mountain peak, "and maybe we will find whatever lies beneath this."

Isra led Astrid along the way as she proceeded to walk down what appeared to be a narrow path. Strangely, Astrid had never seen it before on all of his travels to Glamvein. But then Isra, who was slowly walking with Astrid down this long winding pathway, had somehow walked this thing to reveal an open, wide space of luscious green and what looked like several houses dotted in a line whilst abundant lemon and cherry trees stood out among the shrubs and plant life. Astrid looked above, and there was the mountain peak, again towering over them.

"Wow, I suppose you witches do have intuition!" Astrid marvelled as he looked back in awe at the majestic mountain peak.

"Uh-uh. Sometimes it works," Isra motioned sardonically.

She edged towards the greener area, where she noticed a cottage sitting on its own. It had a baby-pink painted colouring whilst dark chocolate planks of wood made for the door and the framing of the windows.

"How quaint," Astrid laughed as he saw Isra make a beeline for the cottage.

It was now that Isra suddenly noticed a small girl with short chestnut-brown hair that couldn't have been any older than eighteen standing aimlessly outside the cottage, tending to some plants in the adjacent garden. Some tiny light purple petunias and sunlit yellow daisies demanded the girl's immediate attention, and she watered them graciously.

Isra, who was more than happy to have found someone who lived in this bizarre new land, strode right on over to make the girl's acquaintance.

"Oh, a local citizen. Wonderful," she announced. Isra made her way towards the girl, who was incredibly nervous to see Isra for some reason that Isra had no knowledge of. "Oh, don't be afraid. I mean you no harm," Isra started as the girl dropped her watering can in a defensive manner.

"I know who you are," she said weakly.

Isra now noted that the girl's hair was cut in a bob style cut whilst her bright blue eyes wandered. She circled Isra visually with great anxiety.

"Do you?" Isra asked quietly. "Because honestly, I am having trouble remembering. I have been the victim of a great calamity of which I am not aware of the damage caused, but I am told it is exceptional."

The timid girl was growing wearier and wearier of Isra by the second. This was a bewildering notion that Isra could not comprehend, but she figured perhaps she and this young juvenile had indeed crossed paths in the past. *I don't know her but part of me may happen to—the dark, ghastly side of me of whom I cannot recall. No matter, I will have to explain myself to this tragic young woman and hope she wilfully gives me a pass.*

Isra stared at the young girl with much intrigue, wondering just why she was so frightened by her.

"Yes," the girl answered plainly. "I saw you hand over your heart to the darkness. It was a long time ago, but seeing you here makes me feel as though it was just yesterday! But I remember it well. It was a little over two years when you made that transition. I spoke to you. You were out of it but perhaps you don't have memory of such a thing." The girl explained with caution, but she was being polite towards Isra, which was a plus.

"Ah. I am afraid a great magician stole my memories, so if we have met, alas, I have no memories of it," Isra disclosed to the girl. "I am Isra. I feel so rude being familiar to you and not having your name," she said sweetly.

Friendly familiarity may have reassured the girl but despite it all, she was still standoffish. She replied dryly, "Cora."

"Cora. It is absolutely divine to know you. May I ask you something? We have travelled from a neighbouring realm and seek somewhere to stay for the night. Do you know anywhere?" Isra pointed at Astrid as she asked the question in a low voice so as not to unnerve Cora any further. But just one forewarning glance from Astrid's dark hazel eyes with that eerie golden-yellow sheen made Cora even more uncomfortable. She noticed the raven-man's glistening silvery-grey hair, which made him look even more menacing in her opinion.

I don't like that man. The way he stares at me is just awful. I don't know who he is, but I've seen this witch lady before. I witnessed her go over to the dark side. She had been crying. I could see that when I met her. Her face was ever so slightly moist at her tear ducts and she was frustrated, but then she started speaking to the sky and boom! Lightning flashed everywhere. It was bright gold and gleaming as it collided with the midnight-blue skies. You'd think this was a spectacle to behold but then there was the chaotic storm that brewed from inside her. She started shouting and then she ripped her heart out of her chest. It was unnerving to see. I thought maybe after that she was done but no, she raised her hand upwards, clutching her still-beating heart inside it, and offered it up to the powers that be.

Earlier in the day, I met her, as she was the one that awoke the forbidden magics. I remember it now; she was gleaming in that dazzling green. She was weak and forlorn, maybe a little disoriented as she woke up dazed from that mountain crevice but yes, that was our first meeting. Truthfully, though, nobody knows I caught a glimpse of her when she offered herself on a plate to the fiery night skies and goodness knows what delectable things she's done since that moment. It doesn't bear thinking about. I am a child of the light, a charming village herbalist who does nothing but help those in need. I will never be wretched or cold or as heartless as I deem this witch to be.

Cora mulled this over in her thoughts as she brought her mind back to the very first meeting, which thoroughly clarified why she was so nervous, but needless to say, despite what Isra had told Cora, she was still wary of Lady Isra of the Dark.

"I am sorry for that experience. I am not too aware of places to shelter, except there may be the old house that's only a few minutes away from here. I live with my father, who is retired, so I am afraid I cannot host anyone to stay at my home," Cora explained meekly.

"Oh, that's all right," Isra piped up. "I am sure Astrid and I will find somewhere."

Isra's wandering, piercing green eyeballs caught sight of the most extraordinary thing. In Cora's garden, if you turned a little to the left and walked about ten yards, there was a man almost completely swamped in a dark violet cloak, but that wasn't all. He was hovering in front of a dark, jet-black cauldron, whispering what sounded like a dead language into it.

Isra was fascinated, but Astrid was restless. He stood there with his hands tucked into his pockets. He seemed bored with this little charade playing out but, of course, Isra always had to give in to her curiosity.

Isra started to stride over to the old man. Cora shouted, "No. Wait!"

Evidently, she didn't want anyone to see whatever he was conducting, but Isra only found this even more intriguing. She watched as the cloaked man softly poured some luminescent green liquid into the deep, antiqued cauldron, and then a gleaming gold scroll appeared out of nowhere. From Isra's fond recollection, this could only be one thing: soul magic.

"Oh, my goodness!" Isra uttered in disbelief, but she'd seen it with her own eyeballs, so it would be impossible to discount it now.

"You've seen me?" the man cried out in horror. He immediately backed away from the cauldron as he saw Cora now heading towards him, who was also shocked.

Isra applauded him. "Please pardon my intrusion. That was most mesmerising, sir."

"You can't tell anyone what you've seen here, girl. Why, they'd throw away the bloody key," he pleaded with Isra. The man looked terrified as he tried to fight his case.

"Father!" Cora called out in an anxious tone. She sounded

increasingly worried. Isra detected the fear resounding in Cora's bright sapphire-blue eyes.

"Why can't we tell a soul?" Astrid cut in. He'd been standing there before all this chaos had erupted and now was just as invested as everyone else in this interesting development.

"He's just conducted what looks like soul magic," Isra blurted out in a melancholic voice.

She was deeply curious now. Why would some charming, sweet old man be performing some of the darkest spells known to be forbidden, hiding out in this cute gardenia of some wishy-washy cottage out in the sticks? It was most enthralling.

"Yes. I have. But it is of the greatest importance," the man explained in his defence. "I am Ailwyn. I am but a mere mortal man, but I do practise the great arts," Ailwyn said proudly as he lifted his cloak, revealing a half-bald head covered in a mass of idly growing white hairs with warm green eyes like a serpent.

"The greatest of forbidden arts," Astrid interceded. He appeared to be well aware of these things but perhaps it was because ravens had an understanding of the darkness all humans face better than mankind.

"Yes. You are correct. It is strictly prohibited, but please don't misunderstand me. I am a lonely soul with only my daughter for kinship. I am simply trying to do good," Ailwyn deflected in Astrid's direction, but the raven-man wasn't convinced in the slightest.

"Perhaps you both may want to come in for tea," Cora offered desperately.

She didn't want this young sorceress and her mysterious man running off to whoever might listen to their engaging tale if they had half the chance.

"If it's as good-natured as you proclaim, then why do you deem it necessary to take hold of some poor peasant's soul? No doubt they have some control over it. So it's highly unlikely it's the latter," Astrid mouthed in an undignified manner. He'd heard these tall tales from many peaceful village folk time and time again.

There is always a sob story. A reasoning of why they conduct these fearful acts in the name of goodliness. But the trouble is that it's never good. Not really when you peek below the surface at it. Their intentions may be, I'll hand them that, but when you look deep enough, there's always a dreadful reason for them needing that sort of dark ferocity. I've seen it all before. But I have an inkling that perhaps these two wretched souls may indeed be useful for mine and Isra's cause, Astrid conversed with himself in his thoughts.

"No, that is quite all right. I believe Astrid and I will be on our way," Isra announced plainly as she flashed Astrid a scrupulous look. An idea was brewing inside Lady Isra of the Dark's mind, and only time would tell just what wickedly delicious thought she was cooking up in there.

"I beg of you, please don't turn my father in," Cora relentlessly continued her plea.

"Oh, don't worry yourself, child. I'd be more wary of those who walk among us that tread on the light path," Isra retorted softly as she again turned her attention back to Astrid, who seemed to also be giving her an inquisitive look. Perhaps they'd just shared the same idea.

Isra turned away from Cora, much to the cottage girl's frightened delirium, and marched over to Astrid, who swiftly pulled her aside. He announced mysteriously in her ear, "I have a very bad idea. I have no comprehension whether it will work, but we might just up the ante here."

"You want to turn that old man into Samuel, don't you?" Isra gushed softly.

She looked back to see if Cora was still looking back at her and Astrid, but she had disappeared. Perhaps she had taken her father and had rushed into the house.

"Yes. Do you think any less of me for it?" Astrid questioned Isra with a wide-eyed stare. He was prepared to do whatever it took to get Isra off the hook and so it didn't surprise her too much the lengths he was willing to go to.

"No. But isn't it risky; offering up Cora and her father to him when he wants me so badly? Couldn't he just snatch me away with him if we make a request to him like that?" Isra pressed. She wasn't in fear, but she suspected it would entail more risk than Astrid was wholly prepared for.

"It might be, but at this point, we have nothing else left to lose. The question is: do you want to attempt it? We could summon him. I'll be with you, and the rest will be decided by fate. What do you say?" Astrid proposed with an eager expression.

He was accurate in that there was nothing left to be taken away. While his plan did have some minor flaws, it wasn't completely out there by suggesting they try and get Isra off the chopping block by offering up someone else. Sure, Cora was innocent and that wasn't going unnoticed, but in desperation, you'll do anything.

"All right, let's do it, but further beyond from here. Who knows whether Cora and her old man are still eyeballing us. Besides, I feel weary around these parts. Let's see if we can find somewhere quiet to muster the courage to unleash the holier-than-thou one," Isra chortled sardonically.

She wasn't kidding about feeling unsettled. There was something so creepy about Cora's home village; it made the ends of her hair twitch, and that was a very rare occurrence indeed.

"Fine. Come on. Let us take a walk," Astrid agreed as they proceeded to get the heck out of that village as quickly as they could.

Astrid led the way even though he didn't know where they were headed. He figured if they trudged enough down the well-beaten path, maybe they'd find something of relevance. Of course, they couldn't go back the other way unless they wanted to arrive back at the mountain peak, so they had to follow the path down from Cora's village and see where it would take them.

Astrid pursued this and further down they strode into what seemed like an undercover forest but a closer glimpse, it was saturated in magic. An unknown wilderness that was protected by the highest order of forcefulness. Astrid noted the glimmering lime-green gateway that stood in their way as they came to the end and could go no further. The gateway was masqueraded in the form of a door but upon closer inspection, the keyhole was also beaming brightly with ferocious green energy.

Hmm, and just how one might enter such a paradise? Astrid asked himself.

Isra was straggling behind him and had now noted the glowing doorway that beckoned in front of her.

"Guess this leads us to whatever is behind that door," Isra remarked as she stood by it with her arms dropped by her sides. She almost put her right arm out in a bid to attempt to wake it open, but Astrid stopped her.

"No. I don't know if that's the best idea."

"All right then, what do you propose?" Isra quizzed with disdain.

"Just show some patience, will you? I want to spend a little time with this thing before we go prodding around in there. It's located by Glamvein, so it might also be harmonised with those same rotten magics you awoke only two years ago. It's promising, but I just want to ensure we're doing the right thing, so trust me," Astrid instructed as he walked right up to the gleaming green door, stepping back as green sparks emitted from it, sizzling at him as he got closer.

"It responds to magic. That tells me it will unlock for either one of us," Astrid announced as he pressed his palm against the glittering lime-green keyhole before closing his eyes, willing it to unlock.

Astrid heard a click, and he opened his eyes in a flash. He saw Isra making a beeline for the door and he held her back as it flew open.

"We still need to be careful in these parts. Sometimes I have to question if you know exactly what you are doing. Wait," he commanded her.

Astrid waited a few seconds before walking through the bright, shimmering doorway before he signalled Isra to come along by waving her over with his hand.

"It looks like the coast is clear," Astrid uttered, just as he found himself face to face with an inflamed robust oak tree. The entire thing was burning impetuously in a green flame. The flames were so hot Astrid could feel the intense heat and he was only a few feet away from it.

"Or maybe not. Stand back. This tree is under a spell of some kind but now I am going to place one on you," he told Isra as she stood obediently behind him.

"Erm, you're going to do what?" Isra asked, feeling bemused. She wasn't comfortable with the idea, but she presumed Astrid had good reasoning for such a drastic measure. He always did.

"I can't have you left wide open like this. Trust me. This won't harm you in any way."

He slowly breathed in and out before closing his eyes, focusing on the energy of the fiery oak tree in front of them. He imagined Isra in all of her splendour, in that classic yet seductive black gown with the long lace sleeves. He pictured her in all her finery, even those bewitching lime-green piercing eyes and that almost white, shimmery golden hair that came down in ringlets by Isra's shoulders and back.

Before too long, a vast uprising of heat surrounded Isra. Normally, she'd be freaking out or be taken aback by such an occurrence, but it was Astrid, so she didn't even flinch. Isra took one look at herself as she felt the heat rising upwards and discovered she was engulfed in bright, neon green flames. It didn't harm her, neither did she feel it but then again, Astrid promised her that much.

Then he turned around to Isra and said, "All right, let's get down to it."

Isra wasn't sure what he was undertaking at this point, but all would soon be revealed as Astrid began chanting what seemed like ancient words that had been long lost from civilization; however, his intentions soon became known when he added in, "Samuel Reynaldi, Samuel Reynaldi!" right at the end of his little enchantment.

The air surged around them. A forceful gust of wind shook the fiery tree and the forest-green glass blades that grew below it. The fire from Isra grew in intensity. The green she wore so brilliantly glowed like a beacon as white, silvery smoke billowed around the orange and yellow flames bursting out like a sunset as a figure emerged underneath all the bluster.

20

The person dusted themselves off. They had finally emerged as the mass of white, silvery smoke dissipated and they strode forward, revealing themselves. It was the jet-black, slicked black hair that stood out but the way those sky-blue eyes glared at Isra and Astrid was enough to tell them trouble was afoot.

"Ah, it's you two. Can't say I am terribly thrilled about that!" Samuel announced in a disgruntled tone. He wasn't too happy at being summoned and he stood with his arms folded across his chest. "All right, so what do you two want? I must admit, it's been a while since someone dark demanded my presence when they are deemed to be my bounty. You have to find the irony amusing. Well, I do, anyway."

Samuel chuckled sardonically as he flicked some more of the dust from his black trouser legs, shaking it off in an annoyed manner.

"We know of someone who may be of particular interest to you." Astrid narrowed his eyes at Samuel as he divulged this intriguing notion at Samuel's disposal.

"Oh, very good," Samuel marvelled, clapping his hands proudly as he saw Isra standing in the blaze of green flames. "I like the theatricals. You ensured beyond a shadow of a doubt that I can't get to Isra. Very smart. Just a shame it won't last forever. Eventually, she'll have to come out of that. Anyway, let us continue with our current business."

He knew the Sanctification of the Unseen wanted no one else but Isra, but he thought since he'd been summoned he should at least listen to what they had to say. *You know, it's peculiar. It doesn't matter how many years I've known Astrid and Isra. They always manage to come up trumps on delivering me yet another shocker. So now they want to trade someone else to me in the hope I'll release my impending desire for Isra. All right, we might be able to work with that if I wasn't desperate to keep my role as light-bringer but hey, I am always willing to hear the kids out.*

"Maybe you'll be willing to consider a compromise? We've seen a girl and her father in the woods. Cora and Ailwyn Skevner. They would be of particular interest to you as her father has been caught practising soul magic." Astrid gave Samuel the full details so he could do with it as he saw fit.

"Hmm, soul magic, eh? That's forbidden, but surely, I would have caught that on my radar. A pity, as I seem to have missed that one, but in any case, I can look into it. I can't promise I will let Isra off the hook, as I know that's what you are seeking, however, I can be jubilant in the fact that I will give it some thought," Samuel proposed earnestly.

It was true Cora and her father didn't pose much interest for the light-bringer, but this was an attempt at stalling him. He wasn't delusional to the truth. He could see that just by looking at Astrid. The way he stared at him was so outlandishly polite that the raven-man was willing to do anything for his true love. And therein laid Samuel's biggest obstacle.

"Thank you," Astrid commented in a gracious tone.

He must have thought that Samuel was pleased in some way with what he'd presented him but Samuel couldn't care less about little Cora or her father.

"I do believe you awakened the mountain at Glamvein with very similar ferocity, Isra, did you not?" Samuel quizzed wildly, but then he dropped this line of enquiry as he haphazardly placed a hand to his lips. "Ah, but that is right. You do not remember. A tragic shame, one would say, but it is what it is."

"Alas, I do not," Isra responded plainly.

She stood behind Astrid, so Astrid was the one Samuel would be bargaining with here, which he found intriguing. Isra very often had a lot to say for herself.

He may well have coached Isra beforehand to say nothing because it is unusual for the witch to be so mute. But never mind, eh? For mishaps do occur, even in the most well-thought-out stratagems. She may slip up unknowingly and then I shall strike, but for the meantime, we will act accordingly; time is of the essence. She is but a delicate flower in which I shall tread carefully by assessing the situation before I come waltzing in. Yes, so for now, I shall simmer down, Samuel thought. He seemed to have come up with a plan that might be of use to him.

He knew it was no good playing the bad guy. *Sometimes, you have to make the decisions that everyone is going to hate you for but ultimately, in the end, people will view you as the villain anyway no matter what you do.*

"No, of course, you don't. I made sure of that. All right, kids, let's not worry about any of this for the moment. Astrid, take Isra back to Wretchenheart. I will ease off, and we will convene at some other time where perhaps we can come to some kind of arrangement. In the meantime, I will consider your very generous offer. No doubt, those 'on high' will be appreciative also. Farewell," Samuel imparted as he proceeded to click his fingers, making a very swift getaway that left Astrid both confused and stunned.

This was not what he had expected at all. But little did Astrid or Isra know that the heat was truly on now.

"So, have we got away with it?" Isra questioned with a thoughtful gaze.

She wasn't completely clear on what had just happened. She had very few encounters with Samuel Reynaldi; at least as far as she could recall, but seeing him being so pleasant was bewildering to her.

"I really could not tell you. He's being unorthodox, but if he says go back and we'll discuss things later, perhaps he is going to relent," Astrid suggested.

"Uh-huh. I guess that means we could go back to Wretchenheart and not be preoccupied with this whole thing. Just get on with our lives!" Isra implied meekly.

She had no better judgement at this moment other than maybe the light-bringer had a change of heart, which didn't seem right in the slightest, but Isra had seen for herself that his attitude had shifted. That she couldn't deny.

"I suppose going home is the best-case scenario," Astrid announced soberly. "I am a little baffled by his change of tact, though. It doesn't sound like him. Perhaps Samuel is having a mid-life crisis. Oh, to hell with it. Let's go. I am getting quite tired of Glamvein."

SAMUEL WAS BACK in his office by around five in the evening. It didn't take long at all to get back over from Glamvein. In fact, he materialised in a flash but what was staggering to him was how well Isra and Astrid had taken his admission. He'd hopelessly agreed without questioning it. He was prepared to come in now at any moment but he knew there were a few details to finalise beforehand.

"James. I am afraid the end is nigh. I need to discuss with you just how you felt during your expedition to Wretchenheart because honestly, I've just told the lie of the century," Samuel enunciated profoundly.

James looked at Samuel in a perplexed manner. He wasn't clear on what had just commenced but all that he heard was that Samuel had told a lie, and knowing Samuel, it was likely to be a whopper.

"It wasn't what I expected. It's a fucking demon realm, for fuck's sake. You had me hunting down the most notorious sorceress the light has ever known there. Was I scared? Yes. Was I petrified that something would go wrong and Astrid would come bounding down those stairs as fast as his skinny legs would carry him? Yes. Did I fear I'd be ripped to shreds? Also a strong yes. But it went all right. There was no trouble while I was there doing it. Everything is as exactly as you ordered. When they return to their domain, there will be no escape from what lies in wait for them," James exclaimed while also telling Samuel how it went down.

Truthfully, he knew Samuel needed to know all that happened, as the light-bringer was very precise. He needed that blow-for-blow account, but James was very careful not to let on that he'd smashed a statue while he was there because he didn't want to anger Samuel. Not while he was this motivated to just get on in there and full-stride ahead. So James cleverly left that part out and just moved on to questioning Samuel on what he had done that would raise eyebrows this time. Because let's face it, Samuel was a known prevaricator by now to many, even those who knew him best.

"Uh, and just what might that be then?" James pressed the issue further with a stern tone as he sat upright on Samuel's luxury four-seater leather couch.

"I've just come back from the realm of Glamvein. Of course, we know it well. It's iconic for Isra for obvious reasons but Astrid and Isra had actually summoned me... Well, it's complicated. But I just told them all right, I'll lay off for a while and for them both to relax," Samuel admitted carelessly.

"Because we do that *when* exactly?" James inquired with a sardonic tone. "No, seriously though, I can't believe you went through with that. They brought you there and you just said all right, all is well?" James continued his line of questioning with an extremely baffled glance at Samuel.

"I did exactly that. They offered me a trade. Some pathetic peasant named Cora and her magician father instead of Isra. It was admirable really, but I said I'll think it over and that they should go back to Wretchenheart," Samuel admonished with a sinister tone. He had meant it when he had told them to go home as though nothing was wrong.

"But we may be interested in these two at a later date. I am just shocked you agreed to that so willingly," James piped up awkwardly.

He hated the idea of berating Samuel, but there was incredibly good reasoning this time.

"I haven't agreed to anything," Samuel said pointedly. He sat up against the soft cushioning of the couch as he emitted carefully in a low voice, "Astrid and Isra are desperate, which means the time to go off to Wretchenheart to claim her is drawing even closer. I need to get there, boy. I have to make it happen tonight."

"All right. Short notice, but fine. We'll find a way. Just what do you suggest to get over to a demon dimension where you can't physically tread?" James implored with a sceptical tone.

"I do the unthinkable," Samuel pronounced.

"Oh, wow."

James narrowed his eyes at Samuel, circulating on Samuel in disbelief as he couldn't quite comprehend what the faithful light-bringer had just suggested. It was so diabolical that it just wasn't done. Not when you work in the light. You don't go to those lengths when you are an enlightened being.

"I know what you're thinking, boy. Trust me, I have considered it myself but it's the only way, and we need to strike. Now," Samuel declared as he sat clenching his fists before he added in, "It's now or never."

21

___

Astrid and Isra entered the solid wooden doors of Wretchenheart Castle after the drawbridge had gone back up behind them. The loud clanking sound signified all was well as they bounded into the throne room, only to be stopped in their tracks, staring aimlessly at one another. Sat on the gold-gilded throne was truly a sight to behold.

"Hello, kids!" Samuel announced with a snide grin.

He had generously positioned himself on the extravagant throne, outstretching his right leg across the seat as he sat comfortably against the plush red velvet cushioning.

"Samuel," Astrid blundered awkwardly. "I didn't expect to see you so soon after our last meeting," he stammered, seeming quite flustered with himself as the situation had totally thrown him for a loop.

"Astrid," Samuel returned at him with a slightly amused tone. You could detect the sinister glee in his voice. "Yes. About that. Well, I didn't either, but here we are."

"How did you get in here?" Isra asked Samuel.

Her face had almost completely dropped now to the point she wasn't sure what was happening. Having previously assumed she would indeed be safe in Wretchenheart, this was certainly not something Isra expected.

"Ah, yes. That. Well, let's just say I had a helping hand from a friend in very high places. But that's not what you want to ask me, Isra. Oh no, you're more curious to learn what your fate shall be, aren't you? Hmm? Well, one can only wonder at this juncture. The game's up! Isra, you'll be coming with me shortly!" Samuel commanded her with a stern glare. "For you have been quite the naughty girl. But it's no matter because in the end, fate always has its wicked way."

Isra stared Samuel dead in the eyes. It looked as if she wanted to mutilate him as she stood there next to Astrid, not quite knowing what she should do. "Uh-huh. And yet you told us you'd mull things over," she said and confronted him with a harsh glare.

"I lied," Samuel admitted with a smile. "Sorry about that. I had to convince you all was well so you'd both drop your guard and, well... it worked out smashing, don't you think?"

Isra scowled at Samuel. She wasn't amused at him being here or the fact that perhaps she could be saying goodbye to Wretchenheart sooner than she thought.

"You lied to us? Why?" Astrid probed.

He had both of his hands scrunched up into fists, preparing to let loose at any second. He was very pleased that Isra was standing next to him instead of being in close proximity to Samuel.

"I had to," Samuel expressed candidly. He pointed his index finger at Isra accusingly. "It's the way of the world. Everyone lies. Betrayal is practically an art form. It's just that some do it better than others. You should know that, Isra, by now. How many souls have sold you candy-coated misalignments only to then have them bear false witness? But, of course, you know that!" Samuel reminded Isra coarsely before he changed the subject and also lowered his tone.

"Thank you kindly for the tip regarding Ailwyn Skevner, by the way. It was very smart of you, Astrid. Ailwyn has been taken into custody by the Sanctification of the Unseen. Another dark soul holed up in purgatory. Very well done, son," Samuel emitted formally.

Astrid scoffed. "You're welcome."

He folded his arms across his chest with a blank expression aimed at the light-bringer. The nonchalant stance would perhaps be seen as being elusive. However, Astrid stood ready to unleash his frustrations upon the man who had guided him for so many moons.

"At least I have some hope that despite your transgression congregating with our queen of darkness here that perhaps, in time, you may regain your focus. It saddens me to say it, but honestly, Astrid, how far you have fallen. It truly astounds me. I knew from the start you were in far too deep but I gave you leeway more times than I cared to count. And still, you faltered. EVERY. SINGLE. TIME!" Samuel yelled obscenely. "But it is no quandary. We cannot help who we fall for. It is what it is."

"Great. I doubt it," Astrid blurted out abruptly.

"And now, Isra, it's over to you. We have two choices here. You can come along with me willingly to a place of my choosing. You will remain a witch and all will be well... or we can play it the hard way, and I'll wipe your memories of this event and we'll do the very same. What is it going to be?" Samuel asked plainly.

He was perked up on the edge of his seat as he awaited the young witch's answer, which he suspected to be a hard no.

"What makes you think I will go with you?" Isra interjected. She gave him such a frosty, iced glare that it was hard to imagine she was going to be swayed by any of this.

"You'll come with me," Samuel told her softly. "You won't like what happens if you don't," he said in a serious voice. He was likely referring to when he famously disarmed her at Nefaria Sands, but alas, she wouldn't remember that.

"And what about Astrid?" Isra piped up in an exceedingly ambitious tone.

Ah, of course, she brings that up. Why am I not surprised? All right, we shall play this little charade. I will allow her this much, Samuel conferred to himself in thought as he pondered this next issue at hand.

"Aha. I knew you were going to ask that. Why, Astrid will go back to being a raven and you, my girl, will be back where you should have been many years ago," Samuel announced so that it was astutely clear what the procedure was here.

"I don't quite follow," Isra muttered in a bemused voice. She didn't comprehend Samuel's meaning because she had no idea what he was linking that to.

"I am your legal guardian, Isra. When your father, Damien Daughtry, and your mother, Gwendolyn Passe, handed you over to me, a contract was made whereby no contact was to commence between you ever again. I was to be your guide, your strong-willed father figure, who would indeed be there to support you in years to come. Alas, this was not to be. But it's all right, we shall make up for it now. What do you say?" Samuel proposed while also disclosing this tantalising piece of information.

"How about no? I am not going anywhere Astrid cannot accompany me. And as for your threats, he was transformed into a raven by a witch so surely that person is the only one who can transfigure him. For a light-bringer, you aren't bright, are you?" Isra rebuffed him sardonically.

She had her arms pressed against her chest in a standoffish manner. Clearly, Isra had no intentions of going quietly.

"And you have nothing to say about me being your kin? Interesting. I thought your ears would have at least pricked up with that one," Samuel remarked coyly.

"She's known about her father for less than a week. How do you expect her to suddenly take this bit of information in?" Astrid beseeched Samuel in a harsh retort.

"Granted these are circumstances that cannot be helped. We all lose our sense of whimsy but even then, there must be an ounce of forgiveness. Otherwise, how can one move on?" Samuel continued in answer to Astrid's question.

"My father and I have only just met and he never once mentioned you. How peculiar," Isra snapped. "I guess it's all that love and light crap. It must be embarrassing for him to even admit to himself that he got me entangled with that, and by the way, how am I supposed to trust anything you say when I have no memory of any of this?" Isra asked in a stern voice. "Come on, I am dying to know how you think you can waltz in here with your fancy suit and well-mannered tone and expect me to fall at your feet. I mean, really!" Isra scoffed with a scowl. "I thought the bottom feeders were pathetic, but this is truly something else."

"I know you have a hard time trusting people, Isra. It's in your blood. Damien was very much the same, as was Evanora when she was your age, but it doesn't change the fact there are crimes you committed in the sanctuary of the light and those must be paid for, so here we are," Samuel elaborated broadly.

He wasn't being exactly precise right now because getting Isra to agree with him was already proving difficult without him expanding upon why she was deemed to be placed into his custody.

"Strange how I don't care for the opinions of those who are beneath me," Isra retorted in an icy voice. You could almost hear the venom that was harshly cutting off Samuel while he did his best to be endearing.

"All right. I presumed it would be this way," Samuel muttered in a formal tone. "Have it your way, kiddo. We'll play it straight and hard. Just for you." Samuel winked at Isra with a twinkle in his eye.

"And just how are you going to do anything to me, Mr Reynaldi?" Isra queried.

"Oh, just you wait and see. The most divine things happen to the wicked," Samuel remarked with a sly click of his tongue.

He found himself slinking off in his mind to a discussion he'd had earlier with James pertaining to just how he'd vanquish Lady Isra of the Dark.

22

<u>Back at Spirisity – Several Hours Earlier</u>

Samuel was becoming impatient. His nerves were getting the better of him as he eyed the large decanter of blood with anticipation. He'd been staring at it for several hours but James had said "it was the only way" and he needed to gain entry into Wretchenheart somehow. Sure, it was drastic and he'd be breaking all of the light rules ever written by doing it, but what other choice did he have?

"I feel so damn nauseous with that thing looking at me!"

Samuel groaned. He was yet again greeted by the large decanter glaring at him from where it sat on his wooden desk.

"No time like the present. To your health!" James motioned in a comical tone, although he had reserved his seriousness in the situation by expressing softly as he placed a bucket right on Samuel's desk in front of him. "Just in case you feel the urge to exterminate the entire contents of your stomach."

This only made Samuel feel even more queasy. He hastily unscrewed the lid off the glass decanter before pouring himself a large glass. The red, thick, gloopy liquid pooled into the glass so slowly it was barely a trickle.

"Oh, my goodness. This is vile," Samuel chided as he placed the glass to his lips. Not wanting to dawdle, he emitted while looking James dead in the eye, "You know that what you witness here, you cannot tell another soul? Not ever! Do you understand me? I'm breaking every single rule that was ever created in the codex. If they find out, they'll hang me to dry."

Samuel groaned as he gulped down the entire glass of blood at once. He scowled impatiently. "Oh, the things you have to do for the job!"

"Demon blood will get you there. It will get us the result we need. Isra will be rendered powerless by the time you've had this floating around in your nervous system," James explained in a smart manner.

Yes, he had to be a bloody know-it-all right now, didn't he? He couldn't have just pretended to be a bit dim, could he? Argghhhhh! Samuel wittered on in thought as he knew he'd have to force the rest of this down his neck soon enough.

"Not that bad, is it?" James chuckled. "You made me swallow that rank lemon water earlier and I managed fine," he reminded Samuel with a grin.

"Yes, but that was lemon water and not the blood of a repulsive demon. Oh, good lord, I think I am going to hurl." Samuel's stomach made a low growl as he clutched the waiting bucket close to his chest. "I don't wish this crap on anyone. Even my worst enemy. And trust me, boy, I have a few."

"At least with this, there will be no more Isra and Astrid. They will be moot. End of the line for our wicked sorceress and her doomed raven lover, who will be forced to look on from afar as she's magically castrated. Have you decided whether to house her in Spirisity?" James piped up.

He found himself very invested in whether Isra would be occupying a room in the quaint citadel that Samuel lived in since it was big enough for more than just one man. James could live here if he so desired, but he was a young man who craved his space.

"I am not going to do anything of the sort. Why, we'll go back to the original plan. Just now we have a bit of a fiery twist," Samuel pronounced.

James poured him yet another glass of demon blood and seemed to be enjoying himself a little too much.

"Don't get too excited, boy. If you ever want to ascend to light-bringer, you'll understand it's imperative no matter how gruesome the task, if it gets the job done, we win every single time," Samuel finished sharply.

~

SAMUEL WAS BACK in the room and his eyes glazed over. Isra interrupted his line of thinking, causing him to jolt abruptly.

"Oh, do they now?" Isra berated him with a sly grin. Her hand was positioned in mid-air as though she was about to launch something wonderfully grotesque out of it at any second.

"Yes. I have something super special lined up for you, my girl. It was only this evening that I was discussing it with my trusted aide. Of course, you remember James don't you, Astrid? As I recall, you two do not get on very well," Samuel admonished soberly.

He found himself pulled back to the mirage of him and James talking earlier yet again. It was such a profound moment, but yet so genius. He went back to the conversation he and James had just over four hours ago. It hadn't been a pleasant experience, drinking all that foul wretched liquid, but it did the job, didn't it? It was mission accomplished as far as Samuel was concerned but now it was time to put the final finishing touches on his grand plan.

Samuel only had to click his two fingers in place. Just once. Wretchenheart Castle began to shake violently. Isra stood in the middle of the grand throne room, taken aback at everything going on around her.

Astrid strode forward quickly, closing his eyes to concentrate as Wretchenheart Castle's throne room suddenly went up in flames. The bright yellow-orange fire collided from the ceiling before descending; heading straight for Isra as it nonchalantly skipped over Astrid. Naturally, it only wanted Isra, so going over to Astrid was pointless. These ferocious, harsh orange flames knew exactly what they were doing but nobody was betting on what Astrid would do now that he was in the clinch.

Astrid launched forward a harsh, brilliant white lightning bolt in the direction of Samuel, only for it to bounce right off of him and collide with Isra, who was penetrated by it and immediately fell to the floor. Her face filled with pain as she lay on the cold stone floor.

Samuel could only look triumphant, realising Astrid's one attempt to save his true love had brought her to her knees.

Astrid screamed out, "ISRA!" as she became engulfed in the sinister red-hot flames. There was nothing he could do but watch as his precious sorceress was saturated in it.

The bright orangey-yellow flames continued surging all around Wretchenheart's grand hall until Isra was just about visible lying comatose on the floor. Astrid couldn't see her face but her long, shimmery golden-white hair was splayed out as she haphazardly laid on her stomach.

"What have you done?" Astrid yelled at Samuel. "Look at her!"

He pointed at Isra furiously but Samuel said nothing, which only infuriated Astrid even more. Astrid made one more attempt to get back at Samuel and focused his energy, this time resulting in bright neon green flames aimed right for the light-bringer, but Samuel simply brushed them away.

"Now I shall have none of that!" Samuel warned with a low brow, mocking him with a snide grin. "Is this all you've got, Astrid? Oh, be gone. I don't have time for you, boy."

Samuel waved his hand subtly at Astrid. Astrid felt a tingling sensation at his feet. A wave of black smoke encircled him violently. He felt a deep sense of trepidation as it singed violently into his humanised body; burning him across his weary thick skin until he was reduced to watching in horror as he got smaller and smaller until he was a tiny mass of black feathers on the floor.

The entire ceiling was submerged in a furious fire. The throne room would soon be gone, but Samuel could care less what would commence now as he sat there eagerly watching everything sizzle and fray from his seat within a safe distance of the heated inferno.

Samuel finally got up from his position on the throne and walked over to Astrid, inspecting the raven with a grin. "Well, that's the end of that," he said before he turned his attention to Isra, who now laid motionless on the cold floor.

He gently lifted Isra by placing one of his hands under her chin and grabbing her by her waist, carrying the helpless witch in his arms as he proceeded to get out of there sharpish, for Wretchenheart was burning to a crisp.

"Show is over, Astrid. If I was you, I'd return to whatever existence you deem worthy for yourself," Samuel told Astrid sternly as he held Isra tightly in his arms. The unconscious witch couldn't do anything to defend herself.

Samuel waved his hand in the air, disappearing in a puff of smoke.

23

Samuel emerged with Isra in the quaint grounds of Shambre Fell, looking on at the spindling tower of that prestigious château with great enthusiasm.

He muttered, "Well, we best get you home before any more calamities can ensue."

Then he thrust open the grand, ornate wooden door of Shambre Fell, hauling himself while still carrying Isra in his arms up the long unwinding steps. Samuel didn't stop until he reached Isra's bedroom whereby he laid her on the soft, white crisp bedding mixed with blood-red velvet detailing on the cover.

"I've got you alone at last. Well, we can't have you remembering any of this, can we? Now then..." Samuel commanded his hand gingerly over Isra's forehead, right between her eyes and softly whispered, "All of what you know now and ever will about Astrid, your connection with him, and all you ever did shall remain trapped in the netherworld. You will not question or find yourself with any familiarity to him ever. Everything you've done after giving your heart up to the darkness will remain locked inside your mind. Your feud with Everilda will forever be that until a time comes whereby you both cease to exist in the same vicinity, but for now, Isra, you shall sleep because it's all forgotten. Lost in the deepest depths of your soul. Never deemed to return. And so it is."

And with that, Samuel clicked his fingers, chirping happily to himself as he slowly dissipated in a puff of silvery-white smoke.

"And that, my friends, is how you get a notorious dark witch right back on the path to greatness. In time, maybe she will see just what a force she can be, but even I know nothing is truly dead. Not now. But maybe someday this may well return to haunt me. You know, prophecies and the like. Oh, well; be that as it may," he chattered to himself as he disappeared from view.

The gentle September winds blew in from the open window that had been left ajar and the black sorrowful raven Astrid flew in, landing softly on Isra's bed. He rubbed his beak against her sleeping face.

"I don't know how I am going to find my way back to you. But be good now, trouble, because soon we'll be back and greater than you've ever imagined. I'll find my way and slip into your life, even if it takes me a hundred lifetimes," Astrid emitted as a tear dropped from his eye onto Isra's pillow.

24

1 Year Later

Lady Isra of the Dark had just come out of her tower. It was a beautiful June day, and she was pleased because the sun had finally made an appearance. She stood by her favourite oak tree, which she frequently visited deep down in the depths of the forest. Of course, this wasn't any special outing for Isra, but she did like to walk freely in nature.

Being a witch, there was a wondrous fascination she had with the natural world but she didn't dare let on that she preferred it over any kind of human company. She often desired a loving human companion many moons ago. However, that turned out to be quite the sour lemon and so she relented.

Men were far too much trouble for her anyway. She learnt that lesson with the whole kerfuffle she had with her arch-nemesis, Everilda, and all the tribulations falling for that sap, Jonathan, had brought her. It was safe to say that Isra was done with all humankind. None of them even remotely appealed to her anymore, but it didn't matter.

Isra didn't need anyone. She was perfectly happy as she was; a little sarcastic and quite abrupt with a harsh mouth to go along with it. She was a loner, a majestic queen of the night, and she needed nothing or no one to complete her.

But as Isra wandered down the soft, grassy bank she often visited to collect her thoughts, she had no idea that a jet-black raven was hovering above her. He perched very quietly just above in the secluded oak tree. On the next branch over from the raven was a neon green python coming out at just over six feet. His keen, watchful eyes were also fixated on Isra, but Astrid said nothing as he caught sight of someone else gazing upon his love.

Isra sat beneath the robust oak tree, ranting callously, much to Astrid's amusement. He could hear every decibel.

"Oh, those pathetic humans. Don't they have anything better to do than to spy on me? It's a pity really but they can't quite grasp it in their heads that I am done with their kind. Done, I tell you. Finished. My humanity was long lost many years ago and I care very little for it."

Astrid let go of a swift chuckle, emitting, "Ha, yes, you've never liked those pesky humans. But don't worry. I've been here all the time. I've witnessed all your triumphs. I've been on claws to assist you with every defeat. Trust me, fate is a fickle thing, and you may not be able to see it right now, but one day, I'll be by your side again. It will be as though I never left. Just don't go too far with that ye olde black magic now. Otherwise, I shall have to come in much sooner than I anticipated."

And we all know just how messy things can get when Lady Isra of the Dark gets a step too close to that dark magnitude.

It would really be chaotic if her raven lover had to step in but step in he would because Astrid knew the true meaning of love. And that was for better or for worse, you do whatever it takes to save the eternal soul of the one who is damned, no matter how chaotic it gets. That's the beautiful synergy of loving another.

INTRODUCING HER DARK SOUL
DARK SPELLS SERIES BOOK 5

From the beginning, there has always been magic. It can destroy us, but it can also be the best thing for us. Things are not always black and white; witches are not always bad, but they are not always good, either.

Back to a time not so long ago, there was a witch named Lady Isra, and she was incredibly powerful. She possessed many abilities and qualities: power, control, authority, and beauty. But yet she had no heart, and a witch without a heart is a wicked witch indeed because, as this story tells, she became darker as time went on.

We began in autumn when the leaves were tumbling down from the trees in bold shades of cherry, flamed orange, and burnt copper. The land was changing; the season of summer was escaping. Many men and women cared not to dwell here.

Amidst the beauty of the land, a majestic shining tower stood on a hilltop and was the centre of it all, showcasing the land's most ferocious villain. She was not at all kind, graceful, or loving. She had lost a love many years ago, and now only bitter tears flowed. Tears of what she had lost, tears of what she'd once had. Tears of fear, regret, and pain.

Life for this witch was never quite the same as it once was. She kept to herself and spoke with only the animals, having a strong connection with them. Isra admired their beauty and power. She knew many of the beings by name, and some were even guides and messengers who helped her from time to time. They were not afraid of her, despite the consuming darkness inside her soul. They saw good in all beings, a trait not very well known.

In this land, the witch was respected but also feared. It was said in many villages, "Do not cross the witch! She is villainous and doesn't take kindly to being crossed." The best advice the townspeople could give was, "Stay away from her."

The witch did not care for them or their words; she lived in seclusion and had done so for most of her life and was comfortable with it. She spent most of her time studying her craft and learning more about the world she lived in, reading up on all the secret and not so secret knowledge of the magical world that few knew of or even cared about.

Sometimes people would come to the witch because they'd heard of the things she could do. She could banish, but she could bind and return selfish and negative behaviours back to those who had originally cast them out, as well. She knew every curse and all the hexes. If someone had a problem and wasn't afraid of her, she was the one they could go to for help.

A young lady had come to the witch and asked for her help, for another woman was attempting to take her husband. The witch prepared a spell, and after doing everything that needed to be done, she sat the young woman down and told her what to do. When they were done, she thought it was the last she would hear from her.

A week later, on a full moon, the young woman contacted the witch again. She had been sitting at her table sorting herbs and putting them into their correctly labelled jars when a loud knock on the old, stiff oak door startled her. She saw it was the young woman, invited her in and made some tea.

"He's going to leave me for her!" the young woman cried.

The witch, having heard this story much too often, told the young woman to calm down. She grabbed a dagger and asked the young woman to hold out her hand. She did as the witch requested. The witch carefully slashed the dagger across the young woman's hand, making an incision just below the young woman's marriage finger. She let the thick, red blood drip onto a piece of parchment and then into a cup of water.

"Write his name on the parchment. And drink the water. This will bind him to you and only you. It has never failed me," said the witch in a soft tone.

The young woman wrote her husband's name on the parchment and gave it back to the witch, who folded it in halves a few times, then wrapped string tightly around the parcel. She handed it to the young woman.

"Now place this somewhere hidden, close to where he sleeps. Go, you must do this immediately!"

And with that, the witch never heard from the young woman again.

It was situations like these the witch was best at solving; a little magic went a long way if a person knew how to use it. Magic is not something to be misused, although as time went by, it got misused, but the witch was okay with that. She liked being powerful, dark, and hidden. She enjoyed coming out of her fortress only at night, rejoicing her hatred through the dark misty skies.

She loved opening and closing mystical doors, as well as removing things that were no longer useful. This was the life she led and her heart no longer bled, for it had been torn years previously by another's inner needs but there will be more on that later. Nevertheless, she was seen as somewhat of a dark saviour.

Autumn came and went, and the snow of winter fell.

It was time for another very dark spell.

DARK SPELLS READING ORDER

1. Her Dark Love
2. Kissing Darkness
3. Seducing Darkness
4. Queen of Darkness
5. Her Dark Soul
6. Her Dark Heart
7. Her Dark Rose
8. Darkness Reborn

ABOUT THE AUTHOR

USA Today Best Seller Isra Sravenheart resides in the UK. She is an avid reader, particularly in the fantasy and paranormal genres, and very much into all things fairytale and dark in nature. She is also a witty wordsmith.

Isra is known for being obsessed with coffee and very particular towards cats of which she owns four of the buggers.

You can follow Isra through her blog, or any of these social media platforms:

ALSO BY ISRA SRAVENHEART

The Dark Spell Series: Books 1 through 8

Heart of Oz

Tainted Siren

The Divine Spiritual Truth: A Twinflame Romance

www.ingramcontent.com/pod-product-compliance
Lightning Source LLC
Chambersburg PA
CBHW070345200726
48294CB00003B/788